FUTURES
TO LIVE BY

Polestars

FUTURES TO LIVE BY

POLESTARS 12

Ana Sun

NEWCON PRESS

NewCon Press
England

First edition, published in the UK
by NewCon Press
41 Wheatsheaf Road, Alconbury Weston, Cambs, PE28 4LF, UK

NCP351 (hardback)
NCP352 (softback)

10 9 8 7 6 5 4 3 2 1

ISBN: 978-1-917735-05-6 (hardback)
978-1-917735-06-3 (softback)

Cover design by Ian Whates,
utilising images by Enrique Meseguer and Alan Frijns
Editing and Typesetting by Ian Whates

Contents

To O., for everything, in every universe.

Writing Futures to Live By
An Introduction

There's a word I've been looking for that doesn't seem to exist yet – the antonym for 'solastalgia' – a word that could counter the meaning of distress due to environmental change in one's locale, but also an antidote to the sense of defeatism.

To look for such a word isn't a denial that these sentiments exist, but more that I believe in a genuine need to see past the challenges we are facing. Speculative fiction has had a long history of giving itself a serious task: to seed warnings through dystopian cautionary tales that show how things can go wrong. Evidently, none of that has worked – to the extent we could argue these tales have been used as blueprints by an elite few, pushing our world to spiral ever faster into a polycrisis.

Therefore, some of us have been wondering whether we need more stories of futures where we succeed at adapting to human-made climate change or find balance with Nature within which we live.

Writing climate fiction surfaces the inevitable grief, a process that sometimes takes me whole days – sometimes weeks – before I can adequately articulate words into a story. I've learned to factor in time for breaking down in tears during the worldbuilding of a solarpunk story: what are we truly going to lose in the next twenty, thirty years? Land, lives, history and heritage, flora and fauna – what else?

It's easy to give in to despair. But it's also equally tempting to take the shortcut through pollyannaism; a candy-floss veneer of green-frilled aesthetic – without questioning the systems that enable such places to exist, without the critical examination of our own belief systems and cultural biases, and the hold these have on our storytelling.

For myself, exploring solutions to the environmental challenges that form the backdrop of stories I aspire to write, I feel the need to peel back every aspect of our world, however mundane. Speculative fiction has the keys to examine how our existing economies, governance models, power dynamics and infrastructure work – or how they don't – and therefore what ensuing consequences might look like when factors change. But without articulating the kind of a world we want to live in and how we might get there, we can only rage and raise protest placards in streets littered with advertising that continue to prey on our insatiable desires, reminding us where to spend our dwindling disposable income – if we had any left.

In particular, I strive to make conscious effort to look towards scientific areas of study – and there are plenty of reasons to hope. Take for instance, 2025 data by the World Happiness Report[1] shows how humans are kinder than we think we are. Contrary to popular belief, according to Prof. Penny Spikins, there exists compelling evidence that the species we originated from were kind and compassionate[2], all the way back to the Stone Age. In his book *Humankind*, Rutger Bregman offers more recent examples, along with several explanations of why our compassionate nature can be corrupted by those in power. But one of his most compelling deep dives is the story of Kitty Genovese, whose brutal murder gave rise to the bystander effect because the press perpetuated the story that thirty-eight witnesses did nothing to help her. We learn how that single instance of unchallenged journalistic spin on human indifference – because stories of humans mistreating each other sell well – went on to bias the social narrative for five decades.

But you might be pleased to know: the bystander effect has finally been resoundingly disproved[3]. Current statistics show that if you got

---

1. *World Happiness Report 2025: People are much kinder than we expect, research shows.* (2025) World Happiness Report. Available at: https://worldhappiness.report/news/world-happiness-report-2025-people-are-much-kinder-than-we-expect-research-shows/

2. Spikins, P (2018) *How Compassion Made Us Human: The origins of tenderness, trust and morality.* Pen and Sword. Available at: https://www.researchgate.net/publication/326718360_How_Compassion_Made_Us_Human_The_origins_of_tenderness_trust_and_morality

3. Brown, G (2019) *Bystander effect: Famous psychology result could be completely wrong.*

into trouble, in 90% of the cases, someone would go out of their way to help you. It only took us fifty years to set the story straight, that we are not naturally horrible to each other – quite the opposite. The sad fact: our brains are attracted to threats and fears, and it's precisely this weakness that's exploited by unscrupulous politicians, some parts of the press, and – well, anyone else who benefits from mutual distrust.

In a similar vein, the narratives we've been fed about climate change would lead us to believe we've already sped past the point of no return, and that no one cares. And yet, 2024 global study on attitudes towards supporting climate action showed that we systematically underestimate the willingness of our fellow citizens to act[4]. Much of the "it's all too late" mindset can likely be attributed to the misunderstanding (and potential misnomer) of 'climate tipping points'. In the context of climate change, a tipping point more closely resembles a shift to a different stable state rather than a cliff-edge[5]. Few of us are probably aware that there are also nearly as many positive tipping points as there are negative ones – or that the potential collapse of the West Antarctic Ice Sheet may take several hundred years or a millennia[6].

This means we have time to act – and adapt. Everything we do today to reduce our footprint on our Earth has an impact, every effort we make to strive for sustainability matters.

Real change will take collaborative effort, and this is why I try to shift away from a classic hero's journey in my stories, and instead, focus the lens on communities working together. It is likely that we will see a multitude of technological solutions in concert rather than

New Scientist. Available at: https://www.newscientist.com/article/2207693-bystander-effect-famous-psychology-result-could-be-completely-wrong/

[4] Andre, P et. Al (2024) *Globally representative evidence on the actual and perceived support for climate action.* Nature Climate Change. Available at: https://www.nature.com/articles/s41558-024-01925-3

5. *What is a Tipping Point?* (2023) Global Tipping Points. Available at: https://report-2023.global-tipping-points.org/what-is-a-tipping-point/

6. Purcell, C & Keary, M. (2023) *West Antarctic Ice Sheet tipping point: a risk for millions in coastal regions.* German Watch. https://www.germanwatch.org/en/blog/west-antarctic-ice-sheet-tipping-point-risk-millions-coastal-regions

one silver bullet; through my own fiction, I am keen to understand how this delicate balance could hold together without resorting to techno-centrism. I prefer grounding my solarpunk stories in real places so we can imagine how an actual, physical location may one day be transformed.

Choosing hope is a difficult path, it means doing the tough, emotional work of overcoming current regressive narratives – no superhero is going to dash in to save us. If we want a better world, we're going to have to build it ourselves. There's no shortage of problems to set our imaginations alight: how might a more egalitarian economy come to pass, and what struggles would we have to overcome to get there? What would society look like, if citizens ran their own power grids? What cuisines could we rediscover, if we honour sustainable food-growing practices and have more diverse crops?

While activists fight tirelessly to expose malpractices and shift the Overton window, policymakers push for concrete changes, engineers and designers develop feasible technology, we need narratives to show us that a better world is possible, and how we might get there. Our lore has sometimes led us to believe that our lives are fated, and there are destined paths we should follow; but the truth is: a multitude of futures are possible. More than ever, we have a responsibility to forge new dreams, so that our grandchildren – and their grandchildren – can look forward to a world worth living in.

Ana Sun
East Sussex
April 2025

Shadow Among the Leaves

Some mornings, when I step out my front door, two hundred feet above the forest floor between trees shimmering with dew, that moment – so long ago now – still catches me off guard, transfixing time to stillness. That moment: when Titi climbed into a tree just like these to retrieve a wayward drone. His scrawny frame, a speck high up in the canopy, lost in a sparkling sky of deep green, his skin as brown as the belian he was scaling.

"Ti! Turun!" *Get down*, I'd yelled, my voice dampened by branches laden with lianas, buttress roots towering over my trembling eleven-year-old body, giant ferns squeezing me out. We shouldn't be here. I shouldn't have agreed to come. Heart in mouth, I watched him climb. Higher, higher. How would he ever make it down?

For a whole minute, Titi stopped moving. I couldn't see him any more. I shouted again. His impatient words crackled in my ear through our paired implants, "Don't distract me! I'm nearly there!"

That was Titi: determined, stubborn, brave – sometimes to the point of being reckless.

A cold shock stings my cheek, scattering the memory. I wipe away the splash of fallen dew from my face. On a nearby leaf, a grasshopper chirps a hesitant solo among a chorus of cicadas. A tingle crawls up my skin, the unease rattling me to my core.

Flashbacks this intense – it's been a while.

I shiver, despite the day's rising warmth, despite the microfine, temperature-control mesh that covers my entire body up to my neck, from wrist to wrist and down to my ankles, barely visible under shirt and trousers spun of bark fibres. My hand reaches for my grandmother's necklace I'd kept as a protective charm – and finds nothing. It's been lost for years, but even now there are days I wish for it.

Shouldering my pack, I lower my house to the closest levitating walkway. Like a few residences closest to the river, my house floats anchored to a host hybrid tree, running on a combination of embedded solar cells and nanoleaves higher up in the canopy. Most other buildings in town are stacked on scalable stilts, but out here on the fringes I enjoy the gift of being alone.

Pain has a way of dulling over time; like patina on silver, revealing cracks, deepening crevices.

I steal a breath, two.

Titi didn't die that day. No, that wasn't how he died.

The walkway takes my weight and counterbalances it, wobbling a fraction. To my left, the Rajang River runs the clear colour of light tea, glistening through mangroves that capture power from its flow. The Rajang of my childhood had been murky and brown, choked with silt from upriver logging. To think we used to swim in that dirt. Floods during the wet monsoon regularly swept logs and debris downriver, stifling everything to death.

It's so different now, since the logging stopped. Titi would be there in the water every day if he could.

Somewhere behind me, the deep-throated bark of a hornbill punctuates the air, followed by a flutter of wings. The next walkway hangs suspended between trees; I adjust to its slight swing, taking the turn for the town, leaving the river behind.

He'd be twenty years-old today. And I'd be teasing him: that by the Chinese way of counting, he'd be twenty-one. He'd scrunch up his face, punch my shoulder, remind me that I'd still be older by a couple of months no matter what. I'd never learned how his family – how his people – counted the years. The moment to ask had long since passed, even if we're all on friendly terms, even if they'd gone out of their way to remind me then that I wasn't to blame.

Just as well, I blame myself often enough.

Would today's Titi be stout, strong like his father? Or lean and lithe like his elder brother, James?

I pinch the back of my hand until it hurts. Fabricating things that have never happened – will never happen – won't get me anywhere. Placing one foot ahead of the other, I count time by the passing shadows of trees, a ritual to keep myself in the present.

A small child stands on the next walkway segment, reaching up and plucking what seems like leaves off a vine. I recognise her from one of my classes: the daughter of one of the medicine women.

"Good morning, Lilian," I call out.

She turns, a flash of panic fading behind her eyes, but she does not run. I smile; she struggles to do the same. Always the quiet kid, often aloof, she's the youngest of the class at five years old, but likely one of the brightest.

"Selamat pagi, Cikgu Sng," she addresses me formally. Once a teacher, always a teacher, even on a day off school.

"Collecting... leaves?" I teach music and elementary maths; recognising plants has never been my strong suit.

"Yes, for Mak," she replies, but her gaze wavers, distracted.

Strange child, perhaps just shy.

"All right, well. Say hello to your mother for me."

"Of course," she says, furrowing her brow, focusing on something behind me. The urge to glance back rises in my chest – to follow her line of sight – but I resist.

Her eyes dart to me, a mix of fire and fear. "Cikgu, who... who is that person following you?"

She points a quivering finger beyond my shoulder.

That rattling unease I'd been feeling since leaving home grips me in its ice-cold vice; again, I reach for the protective charm that's not been around my neck since childhood.

Slowly, I turn around.

Nothing.

No one.

Pak Ong's steamers expel billows of vapour, nearly as white as his hair. The kopi tiam resembles a modest house without walls, hovering close to the ground. Every morning, he lowers it while he cooks at his stall, taking advantage of the cooler air near the forest floor. High above the tiam, two smaller buildings – his residence and Madam Tan's – peek through the branches of their host trees. I spot her there at the back of the tiam, busying herself behind the counter with coffees and juices, under the watchful altar of the Kitchen God and a family shrine teeming with offerings, wisps of incense smoke curling heavenwards.

Strange how we still call places like these tiams – *shops* – a word which no longer makes sense. Not when we don't buy or sell things, not any more.

Lilian had bid a hasty goodbye, leaving me to wander into town on my own as if I harbour a curse. No one could have followed me – my house is at the end of a path. A chill ripples under my skin. I shake it off.

Madam Tan sees me first. She always seems ageless; hair dark and curled, skin pearly pale with a lively glow.

"Jiak ba boi?" she calls out to me over the din of Pak Ong's stoves, the greeting of children of immigrants, several generations of hardship stamped into our language: *have you eaten yet?*

Her niece, a lanky teenager named Grace, exits the back kitchen with two bowls of steaming noodles, one in each hand for two guests at a table. She flashes me a grin, I nod a hello, and likewise to their patrons – parents of some kids from school.

Pak Ong looks up at my greeting of *good morning, uncle* and his face, already lined with time, crinkles into a broad smile. Hands coated in rice flour, he beckons me towards his stall. "Siaw Xian! Morning! Come, I've just made a fresh batch of your favourite."

Grace hurries over to intercept, intent on leading me to a table. "Haven't seen you lately, Cikgu! Not eating here today?"

In return for teaching their children and their grandchildren, the townsfolk are more than happy to feed me whenever I can't be bothered to cook.

"Sorry..." I over-exaggerate my false regret with a shrug. "Not today because –"

Because I must head into the forest – and make it back before sundown. But I can't tell her that.

Grace scrunches her nose in disapproval. "You can have noodles here now and Pak Ong's kuihs for later?"

I laugh.

"Don't hassle." Pak Ong shoos her away. To me, he says, one adult to another. "Your usual?"

Yes, three steamed buns with marinated filling, two pieces of kuih salat – sticky cakes with a base layer of rich glutinous rice. Never acquire things in fours; no need to invite bad luck. I extract a small, insulated bag from my pack and hand it to Pak Ong.

"Oh, and five huat kuih's please." I point to the pink, fluffy cup-shaped cakes, their tops split open like geometric flowers in bloom.

Pak Ong throws me a quizzical glance. "That's not –"

"Just for a change," I cut in. "Besides, you make them so nice."

The flattery must have worked because he grabs the huat kuihs with a pair of metal tongs, then a few pieces of ang ku kuih which I didn't ask for – stuffing the lot into the bulging bag.

"Wait – Uncle, not too much!" But he's already sealed it for me to take away.

"I'm finishing up early, might as well give you extras."

Extras? Pak Ong normally makes just enough food for the day; any leftovers he'd bring to the town hall at sundown to be shared amongst those who need or want some.

He shrugs, pointing the tongs into an empty patch of air. "Meeting over at the town square – midday."

Today? Obviously, I haven't been paying attention.

Pak Ong notes my confusion. "Some people want to raise the old fort, some people don't. They're fighting it out today."

An old debate, one that comes around every few years.

Just like that, my chest clenches, my breath catches. I push the memories aside.

The last time I'd passed by the fort, it had been barely visible. Like the remains of the old town by the Rajang, most of it lies underwater. A symbol of a long-ago empire – something we'd once been proud of – left behind to fester while we'd moved the citizens further inland, rebuilding everything for resilience.

My hands close around the insulated bag, heavy with food for later, and slip it into my pack.

"If we raise it," I say, thinking aloud, "we'll have to repair it…"

Pak Ong swaps the tongs for chopsticks. "That's why I'll be arguing against it. Why waste the effort? There are other things we should be doing."

To preserve history, or to let it rest – and let the uncomfortable past slip away?

15

"Midday, right?" I ask.

"Ridiculous time. It'll be so hot."

Midday – when people from the region venture in for meals, run errands, meet friends. In a practical way, it makes sense.

Pak Ong has wound himself up into a mood, so I excuse myself, bidding a good day to Madam Tan, Grace, the patrons. But before I manage to leave, Madam Tan thrusts a large bottle of ice-cold water into my hand – *going to be a hot day lah, take this* – then waves me off.

In a town like this, one puts on a cheerful disposition regardless of how you feel inside. Everyone knows everyone, avoiding an explanation is less effort. Hiding a grimace, I turn away, stepping briskly onto the walkway that tilts upwards.

Ahead, something rustles. I stop. None of the leaves in the trees are moving – not a bird, not a creature. Maybe –

"Titi? That you?"

But I hear nothing, see nothing.

Were we friends? I'd always described Titi as a friend. But when we met, I'm not sure I had a notion of what a friend was – not at the age of five. We just liked being together.

It must have been a town family event. I'd taken my favourite toy tiger for company. Titi had been running around, expending that boyish excess of energy, but stopped when he saw me and my tiger. He said hello, reached for it – somehow tearing the whole tail off.

I'd been too shocked to cry. Titi was horrified, apologetic, promised to repair it.

I didn't believe him.

The next day, he brought the tiger back. It now wore bright red stitches on its fake yellow fur. Somehow, it felt right that it should bear the scars of its trauma.

"My father showed me how to fix it," he said, a mix of sheepishness and pride.

Awestruck, I asked, "What's your name?"

"Call me Titi." A mischievous smile played on his lips.

"That's your real name?" I'd been sure I heard an adult call him something else.

"No, but isn't that how you call 'younger brother' in your

language?"

"We're the same age –" I protested. He wouldn't hear of it.

He'd been Titi to me ever since. To others, he was Joe, or Joseph whenever his mother got cross at him. When we grew old enough to wear implants – a common compromise for kids to roam free while our parents kept busy – Titi asked to pair with mine. That way we could chat in the evenings while he remained with family in their longhouse and I stayed at home above our shophouse in town.

He had a habit of prattling endlessly about whatever fascinated him at the time. Many of our conversations started with his rhetorical questions, *Did you know –?*

Did you know our fort was the place where several tribes brokered peace?

Did you know it took them fifty years? Fifty years! Just to build the original road that reached our town?

My usual answer: "No, Titi, tell me more."

I'd mostly read books about other worlds – where dragons resembled terrifying giant birds with long necks and wide wings instead of snakes with clawed feet, or ships that travelled to other planets. Titi definitely had been more down to earth; I'd been the spaced-out, dream-weaving basket case.

But we found a common love for building things. Titi had a gift for craft, I'd always been good at math. Between the two of us, we made robots that scuttled like insects – just for fun. The mis-programmed drone that ended up in the canopy? That should've been a bird that could climb trees.

By the day that Titi so stubbornly rescued the bird-drone, our town had already begun changing. The hospital, the town hall, and the library had been moved inland onto telescopic pillars or scalable stilts to reduce disruptions if the Rajang were to flood. Next: the temple, churches and masjid, shophouses and homes. We cleaned out the old town, salvaged what we could, letting the earth – and water – reclaim the rest, giving way to the forest.

Warmth seeps from the walkway onto the soles of my feet. I hitch my pack higher onto my shoulder, feeling the weight of Pak Ong's food package, ignoring the thin layer of sweat forming on my skin – the mesh should deal with it. The birds have quieted as the day warms up; I might regret not sticking to my original plan.

It's hard to tell where the edges of the river truly are. I follow the walkways leading to the disused pier, hovering over rice-growing rafts in the shallows, shouldering thousands of tiny green spears reaching for the sky. I turn around, squinting into the rising sun. You'd have to know where the town is to see it: houses, buildings lifted up among the leaves, their roofs sometimes brushing up against branches. Walkways bridge the spaces in between, automatically sensing differences in height.

Titi would've loved how this place looks now.

Did you know our fort was the place where several tribes brokered peace?

His voice echoing in my ears, I sit cross-legged on the pier – the closest I can get to the fort without being in the water. The remains of its roof loom under the surface, an elongated pyramid. The walls still seem structurally sound. Belian – ironwood – doesn't rot.

We'd taken a swim in the fort once, when the brown river water reached only halfway up its walls. Titi had wanted to see inside.

"We'd get in so much trouble!" I'd objected. It had been drilled into us: don't swim in the river when the silt got bad – a crocodile looks exactly like a floating log.

"I brought the empurau drone, we'll be fine!" He grinned at me, pointing to the fish-shaped contraption under his arm. "Or are you just chicken, Little Fairy?"

Somehow, he'd pick up the habit of calling me by the meaning of my name whenever he thought I was being too virtuous.

We dived off the pier, swam down through the open doorway. The doors and window shutters – long missing. Nothing like cool water on hot skin. We splashed to the surface on the inside, our heads bobbing under the roof as we trod water in semi-darkness.

Light slipped in through the shutterless windows above the waterline; sad rectangles cut from empty walls. This had been once a museum, but any trace of the past had been entirely stripped away.

"There's nothing here!" I complained, my voice bouncing off the walls, the low roof. "We could have just sent a drone to scout this out."

"Yes, but now we can say we've seen it!" Titi punched a victorious fist wetly into the air, narrowly missing a wooden beam.

"No! We can't tell anyone! I'll get into so much trou –"

Something moved in the water, sliding fast from one window to the next. I gasped, pointed. Titi spun around, shining the light from our drone straight into a hideous, blinking eye.

A crocodile.

"Don't move!" Titi's voice hissed through my implant.

My heart threatened to thump out of my ribcage. My fingers closed around my grandmother's necklace, tracing the lines of flowers carved into jade. Calmly, Titi tracked the creature's drift across the surface, training the drone's powerful light, covering the length of the rough, scaly shape. It had been seen, lost the element of surprise. We might yet get lucky.

"Get out of here? Now?" Full sentences eluded me. My teeth chattered – not from the cold water.

Titi's eyes focused elsewhere. I could trust him, couldn't I? He was a child of the jungle, he'd get us out safe.

"On my mark – we make for the pier, 'kay?"

His hand gripped mine, and the rest – the mad rush through the doorway and out of the water – dissolved into a frenzied blur. We clambered onto the pier, dripping wet, panting, our breaths shallow. I touched my hand to my chest, where there ought to have been a necklace.

"It's gone!" I whispered, half hysterical.

"Yes, the croc –"

"No, my necklace!" I wailed, choking on the words. "My grandmother's necklace!"

Without warning, Titi took me into his arms, letting me sob into his damp shoulder. By then, he'd grown taller than me.

But we didn't die that day. That wasn't how Titi died.

I stare at the wavering shadow of the roof, a dark shape just under the river's gentle ripple, history lingering just out of reach. A bird tweets from the riverbank, looking for its mate.

Would Titi have wanted it raised?

"Better to leave things be," I'd have argued.

"And just let it rot?" I can picture his face, creasing into a rare scowl.

"You forgot, Ti, the walls are belian. No more crocodiles here now, people can swim to it if they want."

"That's not my point!" There, his stubborn tone, voice cracking. "It's just wasted here! We could make it ours again, turn it into something new. Embrace the past –"

I pinch the back of my hand once more. This – this used to happen all the time when Titi first died, where I'd slip into conversation with him in my head.

Today. His birthday. Maybe that's why I'm lapsing again.

The sun hangs high in the air. Nearly midday.

"Miss you, Titi," I whisper under my breath.

That rustling sound, as if a breath of wind extends a hand to ruffle the leaves of the trees around me.

Except there is no breeze.

The temperature in the town square borders on unbearable, the heat a heavy blanket.

Doubt chews at my insides. Should I have gone on into the forest instead?

Too late now.

Someone had the idea of draping strips of fabric across the square to keep the midday sun off our backs, but still, the old asphalt baked beneath our feet. Fine cracks criss-cross the uneven grey surface. Situated within an unusual clearing, this part of the town remains firmly on the ground; it might have once been a basketball court adjacent to a school. The municipal building has been lowered to one side of the square. Ascending walkways line the edges, decorated with clay urns exploding with flowers. The rest of the forest surrounds us, never far away.

Hundreds of people from the town and nearby longhouses have gathered, milling around temporary tables and chairs spirited from somewhere, greeting each other, making small talk. Pak Ong's laughter rings through the air, my granduncle's son spots me through the crowd and waves. Here and there, a few distant cousins. Most of them I recognise as parents of students.

A prickling unease creeps over the back of my neck; the distinct feeling of being watched. I search the faces of the townsfolk around me, but none pay me any heed.

"Thank you all for coming." The mayor's kindly voice comes

through a little too loud on speakers mounted on the decorated walkways. "Apologies for having this out in the heat."

"Better than rain!" someone shouts from the crowd.

"Very true." The mayor laughs. "Let's ride our luck."

I stand on tiptoes, trying to see the woman addressing the crowd from one corner of the square.

"Today we'll discuss whether we should reclaim the old fort – an important decision, I'm sure we agree on that. We'll be using our outcomes today to provide options for a vote, to capture the decisions of citizens who can't be present. I assume you're all aware that this can't be a simple 'yes' or 'no' referendum question."

Some laughter. I don't get it, but then, I don't follow the politics.

I wipe the sweat off my forehead with the back of my hand, gritting my teeth, ignoring my jangled nerves. Is it just the buzz of excitement getting to me?

A sudden, disorderly movement, bodies shuffling. The mayor has asked everyone to self-declare their initial allegiance – for, against, undecided – by standing in different areas in the square. I blend myself into the group of undecideds.

We self-organise, note our opinions, discuss, persuade each other to our points of view. Groups merge and reform, the process repeats. I bury my restlessness – trying to focus, appear engaged. The noise of conversation, like rain on a leaf. The applause as the mayor closes the meeting, a full-blown monsoon.

In the end, the townsfolk seem mostly in favour of reclaiming the fort. But next we need to decide on how.

My stomach rumbles. I should have taken Grace's offer of noodles. The sun has already begun its slow descent. I should get moving if I want to make it home before dark.

Someone is pushing through the crowds towards me. Titi's eyes, but somehow different. Titi's hair but longer. Older, taller. Knots twist in my gut as the young man, garbed in jeans and a plain t-shirt comes close.

James.

"Xian?" Like Titi's voice, but deeper, richer. "Thought it was you. Have you eaten?"

I don't know how to feel, but my lips smile of their own accord.

"No, I joined on a whim, forgot how long these things go on for." I wave vaguely at the thinning crowd. "How are you, your parents?"

His turn to smile. "We're all well. You can come visit us, you know that, right?"

Outwardly, I nod. My insides churn, apprehensive. His family had been like my own to me when Titi was alive. When I lost him, too absorbed in my grief, I'd lost them too.

James gestures towards the library. "Getting lunch before heading back to my duties. Would you like to –?" but he stops mid-sentence, as if he'd just seen how I'm attired. "You're going into the forest today?"

Shadows flit behind his eyes. Silence slides between us, a slithering snake. Pain: the numb aftermath of a scorpion's sting.

"I see," he says, without waiting for an answer. I'm grateful for not having to explain.

I force myself to meet his gaze. "Another day?"

His smile stretches into a grin, his true feelings tucked elsewhere. My heart burns; Titi's grin, but surer, more confident. "You know where to find me."

I watch him deftly hop onto a walkway, a feigned spring in his step. He turns around before the next segment, gives me a little wave.

Yes, another day. Another day when the past finally releases me from its grasp, when I can look towards tomorrow, and not drown in what might have been.

The last floating walkway towards the forest slants downwards, its last step barely visible under a clutch of fern. Humidity stifles, but the mesh I'm wearing helps me adjust – it'll keep the leeches off and mosquitoes at bay. I venture into air pungent with rot and fungi roused by the day's heat. The earth beneath my feet sinks soft under old leaves, layers of past flattened by time, breaking down into their molecular selves, back to stardust. The cicadas have begun their drone again; a bird's call warns their flock of my approach.

When had I last been here? The trees have grown, the undergrowth has thickened, but if one's heart could be a compass, then the body knows; my feet find their own way forward into our old playground.

I'd been at home, upstairs in our shophouse doing my homework, listening to a Mozart sonata I had to learn by heart for an exam. My parents had been on duty somewhere, Mum with the engineers,

Dad – probably teaching that day.

Titi said he'd come by later. He'd sounded excited for some reason. "I'll bring ais kacang, and huat kuih. And maybe a surprise."

"Ais kacang and huat kuih? They don't go together!" My protests against his zany ideas – the norm.

"So?" came his retort. "It gets eaten all the same!"

Sweet of him to bring treats on days I had to work hard.

Rain poured down suddenly, heavily, drumming loudly on our roof. Nothing to bat an eyelid at. Rain like this never lasted long.

Someone hollered in the street downstairs. I glanced up briefly from my books, hoped they found shelter from the rain. More yelling, different voices now. My attention wavered; curiosity won. I got up, opened a window onto the street, peered out. A few people rushing towards the river, their voices loud, urgent, fingers pointing, hands gesturing, getting thoroughly soaked. Something didn't look right.

Pulling on a raincoat, I hurried down and followed the crowd. The Rajang had swelled. Scores of logs swept down, screeching against the wooden sampans docked in the pier.

Someone else screamed. "In the water! He's in the water!"

There, I saw him: Titi's arms, fighting the rush, reaching for a log but unable to grab hold. Titi's hair, plastered over his face, his dark head, bobbing up for air. Something glistened in his hand before it disappeared under the deluge. How did he –? Why did –? Someone shouted his name – perhaps it was me. Shouted until my voice turned hoarse, until he disappeared under a floating log, until brown water consumed him, rippled over where his body had been. Someone found me, someone grabbed my arms, someone stopped me from jumping into the river right then. Someone took me home, gave me dry clothes.

Titi died that day. That – was how he died.

I don't remember how they found the body. I barely recall the funeral.

Sometime afterwards, James brought me a few of Titi's remaining robots. I didn't – couldn't – touch them. One day, I spotted the empurau drone entangled among other unidentifiable parts. I charged it up; it still worked.

Maybe I wanted to relive that day we swam inside the fort, maybe that was why I'd checked its visual logs. Reels of grainy images revealed the river floor as the drone circled around the fort. In the days leading up to his death, Titi had been using the fish-robot to look for my lost necklace.

A cacophony of bird calls jerks me to my senses. The forest warps time and space, and sometimes, you could end up walking into a different world.

I find the place in a small clearing between trees, the land rising to one side.

The forest grows, the forest thrives. The ferns have flourished since I'd been here last. I push back the tangle of green, and there – the small headstone, a cross carved into it. James told me that the family had given baya, buried him with his favourite books, clothes, maybe a football. Knowing that Titi had been well-prepared for that other place doesn't make it hurt less – but somehow, it helps.

I tidy a little space in front of the gravestone, light a single candle a safe distance from stray fronds.

Should I pray? I'd never learned how to pray.

"Happy birthday, Titi-ghost." My voice strange, out of place. "I brought you your favourite – well, one of them. Ais kacang wouldn't have made it in this heat, sorry."

Laying down three pink, fluffy huat kuihs in front of Titis's gravestone, I sit down on the earth and bite into the ones that I'd kept for myself. A shared meal between the living and the dead: steamed sweet-rice nothings, soft bites of pleasure. Salt from tears mingle with the sugar on my tongue.

Behind me, flickers of light mark the town some distance away, buzzing with the presence of other human beings getting on with the early evening. Beyond it, the Rajang flows – stoic, serene.

A sigh escapes me. "We're in a good place now, Titi. Wish you were here to see it."

How he'd have loved the way we're embracing the past, owning up to how history shaped us, reconciling who we have been with who we are.

A few trees away, something rustles. Fear squeezes my chest. A shadow, soft at first, materialises among the leaves, a familiar silhouette. I dare not breathe.

Happy birthday, Titi-ghost. See you next year.

Dandelion Brew

I wheel my serving cart and solar generator onto the aft deck of Lion's Tooth, careful to push straight and slow; manoeuvring anything on a vintage canal narrowboat demands more patience than brawn. Somewhere in nearby shrubs, a moorhen chirps, summoning the day to begin. The waters of the Serpentine whisper and lap at the frosty, grassy banks of Old Hyde Park; perhaps recounting stories of her past days as a lake, or exchanging gossip with the River Thames that she flows uninterrupted into – with much of London being permanently flooded now, would you blame her?

Morning mist wraps silky tendrils around the trees further along the shore, but I have a clear view of the hedgerow that hides the entrance to the docks, giving our moorings a nice bit of privacy.

A perfectly peaceful morning, just the way I like it.

I dot a couple of stools around the deck, set out the spice mill for grinding roasted dandelion roots, the key ingredient in a brew I serve my customers – the closest thing to coffee available to us now, for those old enough to remember what that is. Towards the east, Big Ben chimes a four-note melody – quarter past seven.

A low, familiar rumble stops, followed by a gentle slosh of water; Raj has pulled up his boat alongside the Lion's Tooth. Every morning I make a bet with myself: which of my old-time customers, Raj or Valentina, will show up first? Looks like Raj wins today.

"You're totally clockwork, Fleur." Raj grins at me from his deck. "How you open at the same time every day without owning a timepiece is beyond me."

"A dandelion's shadow does not lie," I quip back.

Chuckling, Raj hops over from his boat to mine, carefully sidestepping planters of dandelions dotted around the deck, avoiding collision with a red admiral fluttering in their midst.

Though *I'm* lying, of course. Who needs anything fancy when I have Big Ben's chimes? Most modern technology is nothing but a waste of nature's resources; I steer clear of that stuff where I can.

Footsteps ring on the jetty and Val makes her way down, her jet-black tied up in a bun, unlike my mousy locks which I prefer to hide under a headscarf.

"You're late, mate!" Raj calls out to her.

Val flashes a gesture. It must have been rude; he laughs.

And this is how our mornings usually begin: what better way to start the day, than a natter with friends over a cup of dandelion brew?

I turn around to prepare the infusions. Something glistens over the water. A boat I've never seen before slithers into the Serpentine. Unlike mine, its cockpit is covered, presumably connected to the main cabin. The small deck on the bow looks like an afterthought, the smooth chrome surface designed to reflect its surroundings. No windows, no running lights – surely a safety hazard if you ask me. It's ugly and fascinating the way oil slicks are.

"Seen that colossal craft parked at the mouth of the Thames?" Val asks. She makes it across the plank that bridges my boat to land.

"That one?" I point to the strange vessel.

Val squints. "Nope, much bigger. Much less shiny."

"The annual Christmas shipment?" Raj pulls out some kind of device from his pocket to check the news. "It's come early."

I steal another glance at the sleek thing in the water. It's headed our way. What is it? Who's on it?

Val settles on her favourite stool. "That ship gets bigger every year. S'pose those who need their turkeys gotta have them."

I stay out of this conversation, idly listen to them debate the day's news. Unlike Raj, I've always avoided tech to tap into newsfeeds; my customers' gossip is enough. The Christmas ship typically crawls through the Thames around the first predicted frost, which means I should begin the annual forage soon.

Scooping some dandelion root and my secret blend of spices into the mill, I press the button. Nothing happens.

"You gotta plug it in, love," says Val.

They laugh, and I let them. How I miss my old hand grinder. Things made slowly with love never fail to taste better. I pour the grounds into my brewing vessel. A drop or two of lemon oil, a slosh of boiling water.

The mystery craft has stopped a few boat-lengths away. I ignore it.

The moment I express the dark liquid into a jug, a sharp tang of citrus mingled with the rich earthiness of spices, the fragrance permeating the air. Waiting until I have Raj and Val's attention, I lift the jug high, arcing the fragrant brew into warmed cups without spilling a drop. Not just me showing off – though that helps with anticipation – the elaborate pouring ritual cools the brew to a drinkable temperature.

"So good," says Val, taking a first sip.

Pride flutters inside my chest. Moments like these? Best in the world.

After Raj waves goodbye from his cruiser and Val departs on foot, the strange boat pulls up. Its engines unbelievably silent, it cuts through water without a sound. My pulse quickens. How does it drive? Can it submerge? How do you even board the thing? Then I see the windows – small rectangles on either side of the craft fading from chrome to clear. The thinnest of lines appears around one of them before it slides outwards. Why am I holding my breath?

A clean-shaven man with pale brown hair leans out, flashing a smile with perfect teeth.

"I hear you serve a mean dandelion brew." His accent marks him out – not from these parts then.

I really shouldn't judge people by how much unnecessary tech they surround themselves with.

"Sure," I reply, trying to sound nonchalant. "Any preference?"

He shrugs. "Surprise me."

Ah, one of those. With effort, I lift the corners of my lips towards my ears, forcing a smile.

I turn towards the serving cart to prepare another round of brew. A loud thump. Old Lion's Tooth sways and I nearly lose my balance. Cursing under my breath, I spin around, meaning to tell him to tread softly on the old girl. The words stick in my throat.

"I'm Adriyel," he says. I tell him my name.

"I can see you grow your own." He gestures at the abundance of dandelion plants around the solar panels on my roof, and the ones flourishing in neat pots on the deck.

"These? They're decoration." For some reason, I laugh. "People expect to see dandelions on the boat, so here they are. What I use for brewing is seasonally foraged – tastes better."

To make a point, I retrieve my watering can and gently douse the plants with collected rainwater.

He seems genuinely interested. "Is that why your boat is called Lion's Tooth?"

Now I'm smiling. "Yes, *dent de lion*. Dandelion."

"Refers to the shape of the leaves, doesn't it?"

He must be the sort who won pub quizzes. He settles on a stool – Val's favourite. Summoning my best professional self, I hand him a steaming cup of brew. From his pocket he extracts a small object – a large insect of some kind, complete with a pair of wings, three sets of legs and antennae. Chrome, just like the boat.

My smile fades.

A blinking light on the insect's back shifts from yellow to green; its wings whirr into a blur, drumming up a buzzing noise that brought shivers down my spine.

All of a sudden it flies straight for my face, and I stumble backwards, saved from splashing into the Serpentine by my cart being in the way.

Adriyel's laughter made me squirm inside. "You needn't be afraid, it's just a data-collecting drone."

I steady myself, dread flooding my chest – the wretched thing is soaring towards my dandelions.

"What's it doing?" I demand.

"Just assessing the health of the flowers."

Assessing? That thing might as well be a flying weapon. I straighten, take a deep breath, struggle to regain composure.

"Won't they upset the real bees?"

Adriyel shakes his head. "They don't interfere, they just observe. We use a bunch of these to map the overall condition of flora in the area."

I raise an eyebrow. He taps something on his wrist, and the abomination flits back and lands precisely at his feet. He turns the drone upside down and switches it off with a double tap on its belly.

My insides tumble, I suppress the urge to retch.

"My boat is a research lab," he explains between sips of brew, without waiting for me to ask. Why do some people just assume you'd be interested in their lives? "Anyway, my team and I are conducting a study here until Christmas, so you'll see me around."

That explains the snazzy boat. This can't be good. This is precisely the time of year bees gather for overwintering. Anything that disrupts their pattern will be disastrous.

"Interesting," I say.

I know exactly what I'd do if I see one of these in the wild.

I'd quash it.

By the time I make it to Hampstead Heath, the sun already hangs high in the sky – if only it would be brave enough to poke its face through the clouds.

As a child I'd go with Mum by the overground to Gospel Oak, then we'd walk from Parliament Hill out to the Heath. Once it'd even been possible to amble from one end of London to another. But as I grew taller, the city began flooding more regularly, and waters continued to rise. My memories before moving to London were hazy; only that Mum said we'd fled from our birthplace, because the seasons had become too hot to bear.

I'd taken the easiest route: sailed eastward through the Thames then up to North London, where the river meets the expanded waters of the ancient canal in Camden Town. From there, I moored Lion's Tooth and journeyed on foot.

The good thing about dandelions? They grow everywhere. I prefer gathering ones which grow near the shade of trees, as they tend to be less bitter.

But today, a waist-height rope cordon stretches out from the old hornbeam, deep into the field and back around the far side beyond the wild cherry tree, caging in the common hawthorns, the ash, the elm, and all grassy ground in between where dandelions love to grow. Metal posts secured the ropes at intervals, each topped with some kind of indicator, all of them flashing a silent warning. Whoever installed these hadn't bothered to put up a sign that humans could read. Maybe they carry some kind of an embedded message only other devices can decipher?

Well, to hell with that.

Fortifying myself with a deep breath, I swing one leg up and over the rope, then the other.

No alarms blare.

Just normal rope with over-engineered posts. Figures. I retrieve a worn hemp bag and my trusty trowel from my rucksack and get down to work. Always easy to lose oneself in a task like this – gently loosening the long, slender roots from the ground; with each plant I take, I silently thank the earth for its abundance.

The sun has dipped significantly lower by the time I'm satisfied with the heft of roots my bag holds.

A persistent, low buzz rises from somewhere among the trees.

I freeze, squinting into the shadows.

There: a dozen, small flying drones. Just like the one Adriyel had yesterday.

I shudder, reminding myself to breathe. No need to be afraid of them, he'd said. Still, every twist in their flight makes me flinch.

The drone closest to me circles through the air and settles on a wild pansy. I inch towards it, stopping a few feet away. It doesn't react. How sensitive are these things? Slowly, I take another step, then another, fingers gripping tight around my trowel.

No matter what Adriyel says, these outlandish machines will confuse the real pollinators. No, research or not, I can't let them ruin the habitat like this. We've all suffered enough.

I lunge forward, left foot beside the flower and smash the drone ping-pong style with my trowel. It buzzes loudly, protesting in an arc across the grass but I can't see where it ended up. Did I miss?

But there it is: an unnatural, metallic dollop on damp earth.

I bend down to collect the carcass. The light on its back still blinks – yellow. Not dead, then. One of its wings seems a little loose. Other than some surface scratches dulling the once shiny chrome, it appears intact. I flip it over, double tap its belly, turning it off the way Adriyel had done, and drop it into my coat pocket.

One down. I crouch, and sidle towards another drone hovering over a fennel flower. Swinging my arm back, I swipe at it. The sound of colliding metal – oddly satisfying. The creature hits the ground, and

I crunch it with the heel of my boot. A third drone levitates nearby over some clover, but it takes flight before I can get close.

Do they know when one of their own is struck? Do they think like a hive?

A louder, higher pitched buzz rises behind the trees – and where there had been no shape, a sudden dark, heaving cloud rises.

Blood pounding in my ears, I take a step backwards. They are headed *this* way. The third drone I'd aimed for spins around, flying straight back at my head.

Oops.

Clutching the bag and trowel close to my chest, I make for the rope as fast as my legs can take me. The buzzing crescendos, but I dare not look back. Something twitches in my left leg. Pain shoots up my calf. Wrong time for a cramp. I limp-run towards the rope, a sharp zap on my shoulder makes me yell. They sting? Another drone reaches my arm. The shock bolts through to my hand and I clench my fist to not drop the trowel. The rope is not far now and I dash for it. My left foot catches on something. The sky swings around and damp grass strokes my face, something thorny grazes my cheek. My foot throbs, I ignore the jolts and bury my face in the ground, bracing for the onslaught.

Nothing comes.

Behind me, the buzz dissipates. They are leaving? Gingerly, I flex my left leg. Good, don't think I broke anything. I push myself upright, and glance over my shoulder. Seems the dreaded machines have decided to leave me alone, resuming flitting between the wildflowers. Perhaps they have been designed to withstand attack by overly curious fauna? I suppose I'd qualify.

I bunch my hands into tight fists. Next time, I'm bringing a net.

A long, exaggerated blast from a ship's horn jolts me awake. A minute or two later, a second blast tears through the air: the signal for a big ship travelling in low visibility. The Christmas boat?

Mind heavy with fog, I force my leaden limbs to move. On Lion's Tooth's deck ephemeral clouds form and dissipate in front of my face with every breath. The sun hesitates on the horizon, rendering the morning light timid and indecisive.

Come to think of it, there *is* another good dandelion patch down south in Kingston; it tends to be muddier and less pleasant, but I can cope with that. I can't afford to skip a season's forage, especially during these precious days just after the first frost.

The ship lumbers up the river, a shadowy behemoth blotting out the horizon. Stacked high with row upon row of crates, they'd had to demarcate the topmost edges with safety lights.

I track its course across the water, gauging its speed.

I sigh.

The unfathomable wisdom of the water authorities eludes me; the unstoppable colossus has obstructed the exit of the Serpentine, and would do so for the rest of the day. No one would be able to get in – or out. No way I'd be able to head south this morning. I might as well open shop – though it would be a while yet before Val or Raj would show up.

Plenty of time to stroll up to the docks before the day gets busy.

From the jetty, I glance back at the river view in the half-light.

The detailing I'd meticulously painted on Lion's Tooth gunwale earlier in the year catches the fading lamplight from the docks, glinting a glorious gentle gold. My heart swells: my boat, my home.

The entrance to the docks is a well-kept secret: a hidden gap within a hedgerow, one that only the locals know. I open the gate, and stop. A cordon stretches right across the opening, spanning so far from either side – I can't see where it stops. Unlike the flimsy rope affair I'd encountered on the Heath, several rungs of wires had been strung from pole to pole.

Something prickles on the back of my hand. I jump back, trying to dislodge the thing, but it's only a peacock butterfly – we'd surprised each other. It flits in a confused spin, then lands on one of the wires. A sudden sizzle cracks through the air, the butterfly tumbles onto the grass, twitching once, twice. It stiffens, going completely still.

Horror squeezes a strangled gasp from my throat.

Electric fences? Why?

Beyond the boundary, the now-familiar buzz of drones rattles the peace – Adriyel's drones. My stomach churns. There, through the grass, they hover, harassing the last of the season's wildflowers.

Anger rears inside my body like fire, my shoulders tense.

This cannot stand.

The poles have been impaled into the soft earth, but whoever installed them hadn't bothered to dig proper holes; the grass around the fence – a mess. Even badgers would've done a better job. But that gives me an idea.

I hurry down to Lion's Tooth and fetch my trowel from my rucksack, grabbing a pot of dandelions on my way out. Working fast, I dig my flowers in so they brush the bottom rungs of the fence.

Would one pot be enough?

I raced back to the boat, and do the same with a second lot of dandelions.

On my third run I brought my watering can. Still some rainwater left.

Water touches the wire, a soft hiss rises.

The result is unexpectedly pretty. The wet weeds should disable the fence – or render it less powerful. I scan for the drones. I'd assumed the fence somehow controls the drones; in truth, I don't know how any of this works.

I spot a drone not far away: it pauses mid-hover on a hawkbit, the light on its back blinking yellow. Another slightly further away seems stuck in a circular flying pattern. Maybe they will just stay that way until their batteries run out.

Either way, it would take whoever is responsible quite some time to find the cause of the short.

Take *that*, is all I care to say.

I returned to Lion's Tooth and set up shop for the morning. None of the regulars know anything about the cordoning. After I return from Kingston tomorrow, I'll file a complaint at City Hall. This can't go on.

Late morning comes around too quickly, and I clear away the morning's cups, mugs, and wipe down the serving cart. The day remains cloudy, shrouded by fog.

"Hello again," a voice calls over my shoulder.

I yelp. It's Adriyel.

"Sorry!" He smiles, but I'm not feeling charitable.

"Would you like me to surprise you again?" I twitched an eyebrow.

"Oh, sure." Behind me, he settles on a stool.

I turn my back to him to prepare his brew, dragging out the silence, filling it with my simmering wrath.

"You don't open in the afternoons?" Adriyel asks.

"What?"

"I said, 'you don't open in the afternoons?'" A breeze stirs, messing with his pale brown hair.

"I'm no robot." I scoff.

He says nothing after that.

The question burns my tongue: surely he would know about the areas that had been roped off, and what for?

After a time, I can't hold it in any longer. "So what's with these cordons then?"

"Cordons?"

Irritation creeps into my voice. "I ran into one in North London yesterday while foraging, and now there's one here." I point towards the hedgerow.

"Ah!" He creases his brow. "These may have been set up by others in my team. I only build the drones."

"Have they taken over all common land in London?"

"I highly doubt it. It's a short-term study –"

"Well, they'd blocked our exit." No use hiding my annoyance now.

The corners of Adriyel's lips flicker up briefly, as if he's deciding what to say. "Maybe they didn't see the hidden entr–"

"Well, I'm filing a complaint tomorrow," I cut him off. "You'll be in a whole lot of trouble, disrupting our normal lives here like th–"

"What?" His eyes widen. "Why?"

Shock? Surprise? Or is he just good at pretending?

"How do you think I'm supposed to serve brew to people if –" I'm shouting now; I can't help myself.

"Fleur!" His voice is raised too. "Don't you get the news? We've told the authorities about this months ago. It's been approved! We're just doing our job like we said we would"

That shuts me up. Is this all my own fault? Did no one think to mention this to me? No one remembers that dandelion brew doesn't manifest out of thin air. I could have contested this… months ago?

Adriyel's lips form a thin, thoughtful line. "I've lost a couple of drones since yesterday. You wouldn't happen to know about them?"

My cheeks flush.

His gaze bores through mine like a diamond drill. "You were *foraging*, you said?"

My patience evaporates, my voice rises. "Do you even understand what you're doing? There's no such thing as 'observing' nature without disrupting it!"

He leans back, his face unreadable.

I can't seem to stop. "I'm sick of the likes of you... you arrogant good-for-nothings who think you are *independent* of the world we live in. It's this kind of outlook that got us into this climate mess in the first place..."

I catch myself – where has all this anger come from?

Adriyel throws both his arms up in the air. "This is nonsensical, we're on the same side. We just approach things differently—"

"Nature is *not* your playground!" My shout rings out across the docks.

He waves one hand at me, as if dismissing a fly. Then he's back in his boat, pulling away fast, even before that strange, not-quite door shuts properly behind him.

My body shivers, my hands shake. What am I thinking? Yelling at a customer isn't the done thing.

His boat slides into the centre of the Thames, where the morning fog swallows it whole with him inside.

I bury my hands in the pockets of my coat. My fingers bump against something hard: the broken drone. I hold the offending object up to my eye. Better not turn it on, or Adriyel might get an alert on whatever he wears on his wrist.

I straighten its lopsided wing; it clicks back into place.

If only relationships could be mended so easily.

Third time lucky, I tell myself. In the early hours, total darkness reigns, the air heavy and oppressive. Hard to tell if the fog lengthened the night, or if the night harboured the fog. But I know Lion's Tooth so well I don't need any light to find my way around.

I push my boat away from the mooring. Despite her age, the engine hums – the upgrade I did several years ago had been worth it; we cut through the water with quiet confidence. My plan: beeline across the Thames in time to get to Kingston just after sunrise. Water splashes gently against the boats in the docks; most of them keep their generators off at this hour.

About halfway across the river a shape lurks. Another boat? I pull back on Lion's Tooth's throttle, in case I must steer clear. I pick up the radio and try the open channel.

"This is Lion's Tooth on 16 calling unidentified craft. Are you in distress? Over."

No response. I let a minute pass and repeat my message.

A crackle, then –

"Fleur?"

Adriyel? What's he doing out here?

"Lion's Tooth? This is Silver Bullet." Through the tinny transmission, he takes a deep breath. "I'm fine, my engine stalled and won't restart. Request assistance. Switch over to 68 to coordinate? Over."

My heart sinks. He's the last person I'd want to run into right now, but if he's in trouble, I can't leave him here.

I flip our comms channel. "Lion's Tooth – switching to 68."

A loud horn blasts. It's close – too close.

"Shit." Adriyel's voice croaks over channel 68.

I scan towards the west. The Christmas ship bears down upon the Thames, probably on its return journey, a mountainous shadow, its true shape blurred by fog. It won't have time or space to turn. But I can't speed up, not when I don't know exactly where Adriyel is. Are they completely out of power?

I call into the radio. "Can you see me?"

"Yes! I'm about thirty degrees to your starboard…"

Narrowboats have never been designed to be fast. Lion's Tooth steers well, but I won't have a lot of room for error. I swing the tiller and pray that I won't actually hit his craft or miss it by half a mile. This would be hard enough during daylight – but in the dark?

I switch back to the open channel and hail the commercial ship. They respond immediately.

"Leviathan to Lion's Tooth. We see you and we're slowing down. Can you move out of the way? Over."

"There's another vessel in distress – I'm picking up the crew first!"

"Another…?" The captain of the ship sounds confused. "I don't see…"

Then I hear him swear. You're really supposed to keep obscene language from channel 16.

"Lion's Tooth, we'll veer port side. Please move as fast as you can!"

Two short blasts from the ship's horn confirm it's changing course to avoid us. The light from the Leviathan reflects off the water at the wrong angle. Where the heck is Adriyel?

"Silver Bullet, can you turn your lights on? Over!" Estimating his location, I adjust the tiller.

"Negative!" he calls back. "Battery fault! Over!"

The thought hits me like a sackful of sand. I forget all protocol. "I have one of your drones!"

"You what?"

Surely the device Adriyel wears on his wrist still works?

"One of your drones, I have it! Can you set up a homing signal?"

I fish the fake bug from my pocket, switch it on with a double tap. Its wings whirr, and it hovers out of my hand, green light blinking bright in the dark. Let's hope this thing has enough battery left in its frightful body.

"I've got it!" says Adriyel.

The little drone flies forward – fast.

The Leviathan sounds another horn blast, so loud that I'm sure the entire continent could hear it. My ears hurt. The ship is so close now, the lights of its topmost containers look like stars in the night sky.

There – the light from my boat finding Silver Bullet's stern.

"Get ready to jump!" I yell into the radio.

Then the horizon tips to one side and back again; my boat, our boats swaying madly now. Leviathan's wash, a rising wall of water, heads straight for us.

Why isn't Adriyel moving?

"Adriyel! Jump! Or we won't outrun the ship!"

"But my research –"

"Won't be any good if you're dead!"

The captain of the Leviathan hails me. "Lion's Tooth, we no longer have visual on you. We've turned, but... "

I ignore him, searching for any signs of Adriyel – a moving silhouette, a glint of drone – anything.

He's balancing on the skinny deck of Silver Bullet, hanging tight onto its side. I stabilise Lion's Tooth against the tide and counter-crash of Leviathan's wash. Somehow, I manage to get my topside alongside his. He hesitates, gauging for the right moment to jump.

"Now, Adriyel," I mutter through gritted teeth.

The sides of our boats swing up and down; the waves have got bigger.

His foot slips, and his body slides down – no! But the next moment, his hand grabs the gunwale of my boat. Shoulders heaving, he steadies himself.

"Now, Adriyel!" I shout over the radio and into the air.

A thunderous thump; a human body landing awkwardly on a wooden deck. Lion's Tooth rocks wildly – but she holds.

A sudden unnatural brightness floods my vision: the lights from the ship, showering down upon us like an explosion of a final dawn.

The captain hails me on the emergency channel.

Whatever, I'm busy right now.

"Hang on!" I push the throttle forward, holding firmly onto the tiller.

Adriyel, flat on his back on my deck, gapes up at the Leviathan. "We won't make it!"

"Shut up!"

Lion's Tooth and I, we'll get out of here alive.

The ship looms close. Can it make a clean turn, or will it hit us before it does? I accelerate, but it's not fast enough to fight the angle of the waves.

"Trim her up!" Adriyel shouts at me suddenly.

"What?"

"Trim her up!"

I freeze, but only for half a second. Lion's Tooth has a vintage chassis, but she has a capable engine – but I've never tried to – how does one do this again? My sweaty fingers find the lock on the shifter and I push the throttle as far as it goes. Somewhere in the engine room below deck, something clanks.

We shoot forwards with a fresh burst of speed – too fast – bouncing upon the water like a skimming stone.

"Go! Go!" Adriyel cries.

My heart thumps, I can't hear myself think. If we get too close to the ship, the wake could be enough to flip us over.

A spine-chilling creak rips the air. Adriyel's boat scrapes along the side of the Leviathan, the wail of metal being crumpled then crushed. Angry waves guzzle Silver Bullet in one gulp. The side of the giant ship, a whisker away –

"Faster!" shouts Adriyel.

"She doesn't go any faster!" I yell back.

But Lion's Tooth has a lion's courage, or a cat's nine lives. The

Leviathan passes behind us, a monstrous shadow at our backs.

Adriyel stumbles over and finds me at the controls. Dark circles ring under his eyes, his hair a wet, ruffled mess.

"I…" he starts to say. He slides back down onto his haunches.

Why is the tiller wobbling? I look down; no, my hands are shaking. It takes a bit more effort than usual to throttle down.

Further down the river, the ship sails onwards; on the Lion's Tooth, we bob in its wake. The captain emits a quick horn blast. A salute, of a kind, perhaps.

"Thank you," Adriyel finally manages to say, his smile sheepish, forced. "Let's not do that again."

"No, let's not."

I don't know why, but I start smiling too.

Maybe because it feels good – just to be alive.

This morning, Lion's Tooth and I are moored once again at our usual spot. I wheel my serving cart onto the deck and I set out the implements, the grinder, the stools, and wait to see if Raj or Val makes it first today. In the distance, Big Ben chimes a four-note melody.

"Good morning!" It's a voice I don't know.

A sizeable boat has pulled up alongside mine. On its deck, a petite woman with a warm smile waves at me. Beside her, stands a slight young man, barely out of his teens. Then, there's Adriyel.

After our ordeal the other morning, I'd made us some brew; he couldn't stomach breakfast. When I told him I'd been planning to head to Kingston, he asked if he could come.

"Sure," I'd said, certain that he'd be bored. But after watching me forage awhile, he wanted to help.

"Interesting, really," he'd said afterwards. "How being in contact with the earth this way teaches one to read the signals nature gives you. I'd never realised it's not about taking everything you can."

I'd shrugged. "Foraging is about respecting the balance."

When I dropped him off near City Hall (I did file that complaint), I thought that'd be the last I'd see of him.

So what is he doing here? Now?

"Hello, I'm Mae," the woman says. "I lead the research team that Adriyel's part of."

I try to smile; my face aches. What do they want?

"Firstly, thank you for bringing him back." She gestures at Adriyel, who appears to be scrutinising his feet.

"I'm sorry about the loss of your research," I say, and I mean it.

They hover expectantly, so I motion them over to my deck. The lean fellow seems the most enthusiastic. While they settle, I prepare some brew.

"We have an idea," Mae finally says.

What now?

"Our data is all drone-gathered, and given your foraging expertise, we'd like your help to interpret the data."

I almost drop the measure of brew in my hand. Me? Expertise?

"I've seen you work," Adriyel pipes up. "If you can help us understand trends from the data we have, we won't need to send out as many drones. And we'd be able to tell which patches might be healthier from year to year, especially given the unpredictability of the weather."

I don't know what to say.

"You don't have to decide now." Mae is winning me over with her smile.

"No – I mean yes," I say, tripping over my own words. I inhale deeply. "I'll think about it."

Footsteps ringing along the jetty sounds like Val's. She'll be surprised when she finds out she isn't the first customer today.

But what better way to start the day, than a chat with strangers over a cup of dandelion brew?

The Perpetual Metamorphosis of Primrose Close

When the last petrol-powered car drove out of our London street for the final time, we cobbled a party together for the occasion. It might have been Skinny Harper's idea, though given the unrestrained outbreak of home-made bunting strung from tree to tree, compostable confetti on the tired asphalt, and solar barbecues in the communal garden outside of Middle Block – maybe it didn't matter who thought of it first.

Standing side by side on our doorstep at No. 9, Juniper and I had the whole view of Primrose Close except the bit directly behind Middle Block. Dotty – our black cat – poked her curious face from between my ankles and sniffed the air with educated disdain.

Leaning into my shoulder, Juniper's tawny paint-stained fingers squeezed my good hand, her dark eyes a little glassy. "Can't believe we've finally done it!"

"Yeah," I said, grimacing, failing to sever a loose thread from my plain brown dress with prosthetic fingers. "The confetti, though…"

Juniper straightened, pushed aside a stray lock of my greying hair and kissed my cheek. A smile stole across her lips. "Just let people have their fun for one day, Celeste my love."

"I'll be good," I said, smiling back. "Promise."

All that unnecessary waste should disintegrate by tomorrow, but why didn't we make confetti that could feed the birds and insects? There: a good provocation for my geography students in our next remote study class.

The dang thread wouldn't break; I released a tiny pair of cutters from my forearm and snipped it off.

An overnight drizzle had fizzled out, leaving behind a warm spring

41

Sunday morning. The oak tree in front of Middle Block burst with new leaves, flanked by cherry trees exploding with pink blooms, their nocturnal bioluminescence short-lived this time of year. Fragrant smoke curled up from the solar barbecues on the patchy lawn, promising charred vegetables and grilled lab-grown meat, complimented with sides of hopefully uncharred salads.

Mr. Atkinson, from the luxury apartments at No. 25, showed up in a classic hemp-weave suit under his exoskeleton; his carer droid accompanied him in a sunny yellow blazer and polka-dot bowtie. Eddy-42's boxy, metal chassis stood taller than everyone, his face a square screen with luminous lines curving into a smiling face.

Temporary tables of sandwiches and cakes stood to one side, already collecting a growing crowd of residents. Lucia and the under-thirties crew from House 39 came cosplayed as vintage dieselpunks – ironically, I assumed. Children of scurrying age continually begged Eddy-42 for a ride upon his broad shoulders.

Chaos, in other words – the kind where a butterfly flapping its wings might be left confused as to which universe it caused a storm in.

The car in question had festered at the abandoned site at the end of our street for several years, deteriorating from a rich boy's toy to an eyesore we could no longer ignore.

João from No. 27, the most tech-knowledgeable of us, had been the first to ask around the neighbourhood. "Anyone know how to start this thing?"

No one seemed to know.

Eventually, we borrowed a spark from Eddy-42, siphoned some petrol from an old generator, and managed to resurrect the rust-ridden wreck.

João had volunteered to drive the spluttering once-silver vehicle to the borough's recycling centre. He took his sweet time pushing the car along in low gear, waving to loud cheers and raised glasses of tipple, a broad grin plastered across his tanned face, long hair pulled back in a black ponytail. Multi-coloured bunting and ribbon trailed limply from the boot. Mostly, I wanted to know how he managed to stuff his colossal muscular body into that tiny car.

"Some kind of luxury sedan, isn't it, Ms. Celeste?" asked Mrs. Lim from the vicinity of my elbow; a petite, slightly plump lady from No. 53, her shimmering pink tracksuit perpetuated an effect of a blossoming peach. "Why did they make cars that seat only two people?"

"Or fits only one João," I said.

We waved at the small car filled with João as it rolled by.

Mrs. Lim swung an arm at the length of the street. "So, what do we do with all this road now?"

I'd always thought our street aspired to be a spiral – but didn't know how. Primrose Close wormed its narrow way through boundaries of ancient estates, coiling around a mish-mash of nineteenth century conversions and post-Green New Deal renovations, before slinking into an unnamed footpath next to the empty site where the car had been dumped. In the old days, if you'd parked a car on one side another would struggle to drive around it. A camera drone flying overhead might surmise that the street resembled an angular question mark with four awkward corners instead of smooth curves, hooking around the Middle Block of flats and its deadened turf – currently being smothered by barbecue smoke. Townhouses lined most of the straight outer edges; non-uniform blocks of flats squatted at the corners. The house numbering scheme tended to be guesswork on a good day, a lottery on any other.

"Maybe we could create a playground for the kids." Juniper's eyes sparkled, in the way that I'd always loved. "On that unused site, for instance."

"Skateboard park!" A shrill voice shrieked at waist-height. It belonged to Roger, Bertha's kid from No. 33, his small right hand throttling the life out of a rigid T-rex figurine.

Juniper crouched down, ruffled his mouse-brown curls. "I didn't know you skated!"

I hid a smile at Juniper's feigned ignorance. *All* of us had been suffering the roar of Roger's skateboard on the street since Christmas.

"I'll skate to the moon when I grow up!" He zoomed away, lifting the reluctant dinosaur above his head as if it were an ascending rocket.

"Maybe we could make a spaceship-playground, for our would-be astronauts," I said.

Perhaps an antidote to Roger's skating habits.

"Love it!" exclaimed Charu, the physicist from No. 37, bouncing up alongside Mrs. Lim. The electric-blue sequins on their spacefarer outfit probably blinded all the stars in the multiverse. "We'd still have a clear path for the bicycles, right? Though the delivery and waste management drones –"

"They'd fit on the pavement if they need to land," interrupted Mrs. Lim, clasping her hands together. "We could have proper picnic tables! More flowers, herbs – ooh, we could grow some of our own food."

The few enthusiastic cries of "yeah!" piping up nearby bewildered me. Our idle chatter had drawn company.

"Sounds fabulous," said Mr. Atkinson, one hand on Eddy's arm for stability.

I leaned down to scritch Dotty between her ears with my good hand. "We'd have to weatherproof everything, though. Remember last year's storms?"

The sudden silence descended faster than an avalanche. Thoughts shifted: the cost of replacing roof tiles, the power outages, the fallen branches and how long it took to clear the debris afterwards. How our street had almost flooded.

Trust me to ruin the mood.

I inhaled a long, greedy breath, forced a cheery smile. "So, um, how about a street meeting next week – let's get some ideas down together?"

"Yes!" The chorus of agreement around me chimed a loud, hearty affirmative.

And just like that, I was made responsible.

Should've kept my big mouth shut.

The first challenge – though I didn't know it at the time – came in the form of Glen Harvard from No. 49.

He showed up on our doorstep two mornings later with a small witch in tow. The giant rim of her black pointy hat hid most of her face, golden curls covered her shoulders like a silken cape. I stared at the tiny spinning broomstick-shaped drone floating above her head, transfixed.

"Say hello to Ms. Arsenault, Esme," said Glen, pushing his black-rimmed spectacles up the smooth ridge of his nose. Other than the shock of his yellow hair, he was entirely monochrome: a light grey jacket over a creaseless white shirt tucked into black trousers.

In a high little voice, Esme said, "Hello, Miss Arse…Miss Arse-no —"

"Morning, Esme," I interrupted swiftly, and knelt down so I could address her properly. "Unfortunately, I don't have any treats today, Halloween is still months away."

Esme tipped her head up and shot me a poisoned glare.

"I could hex you, you know," she hissed. Her face twisted into a scowled attempt to look fierce, an impossible feat for her angelic face. I suppressed the urge to laugh.

Glen's face clouded over. "Sorry, Celeste —"

I waved him off. "No need to apologise for a girl with powers. Isn't that right, Esme?"

Esme's glower morphed into a wide grin, nodding conspiratorially. Glen shifted, discomfort manifesting shiny beads of sweat on his forehead.

"Now, Esme, can I talk to your Dad first before you hex me?"

"Okay," Esme giggled. "I like your arm, Miss Arse-no, can you do magic with it?"

"Not exactly, but *sometimes* it can seem magical —"

Glen cleared his throat. Clearly, this conversation wasn't going the way he'd planned.

"Celeste," he interjected, his voice firm. "We're meant to be at school shortly. Harper told me that you're the coordinator for this changing-the-street thing." He stabbed an unsteady finger at the drab grey asphalt behind him. A nervous chuckle escaped his throat. "I happen to be an architect – I'm qualified to help."

"Sure!" I said, a little too brightly. Anything other than shouldering the burden by myself. "Street meeting this Saturday afternoon. Are you free?"

Glen responded with a quick sequence of thumbs up, a wave and a hasty "See you then!" and dragged Esme back into the street before I could say anything else.

I let my gaze linger on father and daughter, her tiny hand in his, her skipping entirely out of time with his walking pace. A formless worry nagged at my insides.

"They're adorable," said Juniper, appearing behind me. In a house as compact as ours, she'd heard everything from the next room.

"That was fine, right?"

"How could it not have been?" Her lovely forehead furrowed, puzzled.

I shrugged. "Just a feeling."

Collaboration, co-leadership – how it was supposed to be done. Right?

The natural place to hold an assembly seemed to be on the third bend of the street, roughly a midpoint between both ends, just outside Charu's front door. Earlier on, shuffles and thuds punctuated the humdrum of small talk as the residents brought out folding chairs, office chairs with wheels, office chairs without wheels, dining chairs and stools. Everyone seemed to have lugged extra seats in case someone else needed one, so in the end, a cluster of spare furniture stood forlornly to one side. Eddy's oversized, robotic body gleamed from a bar stool, acting as a comms conduit for Mr. Atkinson who, it seemed, was not well enough to join us.

João, six-pack rippling under a t-shirt, found us a flipchart. Mrs. Lim fluttered around, fussing over a stack of pens, paper and assorted stationery on a folding picnic table. Charu, pragmatic in a grey playsuit, carried out a hot water urn for those who might want tea. Lucia passed around some biscuits that smelled suspiciously grassy but tasted sufficiently innocent.

At around two o'clock, with an encouraging nudge from Juniper, I made my way to the front, waited for the crowd to settle, and tried to ignore the itch under my prosthetic forearm. I summoned my old classroom teacher persona, the one who could remember every name in case I needed to call out a misbehaving student. A skill not needed today, of course.

"Good afternoon, residents of Primrose Close," I began. "Today, we're going to decide how we might make better use of our street – now that there's not a single car left."

A cascade of cheers erupted.

"I'm just your facilitator –"

"Not just!" a voice interrupted. Probably Harper, still in his nurse's uniform, fiery red hair neatly combed down. He grinned at me from the back row.

A scrabbling noise to my left turned a few heads.

"Excuse me, Celeste." Glen had scrambled hurriedly onto his feet, narrowly missing the broomstick drone over Esme's head. "Mind if I share some thoughts to get us started?"

His glasses perched precariously, threatening to plunge off the tip of his nose, his yellow hair unkempt in that annoyingly stylish way. I stalled. We'd talked over the agenda yesterday – that we'd invite a discussion on the criteria that mattered to everyone, collect their ideas, then vote on the best ones. What now?

Glen coughed for attention. "Today, no doubt you'll be bringing your thoughts, but we should have to consider that it all must look harmonious at the end. Like, if too many ideas aren't compatible, we might have to –"

A hand shot up from the crowd.

"Yes, Mrs. Lim?"

"Mr. Glen, what do you mean by 'harmonious'?"

Glen barely paused for breath. "I'm sure you all know about golden proportions, yes?" Then he launched into a tirade of multi-syllabic words, and sentences that ran on and on. Among the seated crowd, Mrs. Lim's face contorted into confusion, Charu fidgeted. Esme began kicking at the seat in front of her. Roger tugged at his mother's sleeve, whispering a shade too loud, "Can we go home now?"

The skin under my prosthetic prickled, but removing it now would be as tactful as disrobing in public.

"Glen…" I tried to cut in. Words continued to tumble from his mouth, his hands motoring in grandiose gestures. Eventually, I reached over and tapped him on the shoulder.

He stopped and stared at me, eyes dazed, arms held frozen in mid-explanation.

"Glen, everything you're saying is valid." I might have lied a little bit. "But shouldn't we discuss what we'd all like to do first?"

Frustration flared behind his blue eyes. "But what if it looks crap!"

The words echoed down the narrow street, bouncing off the doors and windows, pinging off the bricks of façades.

A sharp, collective gasp.

I stole a gaze at Juniper's still figure in the front row, her dark eyes brimming with worry. But she'd taught me how to deal with these situations from her past days as a counsellor: acknowledge the emotion first, deal with the rest later.

Some days, I wished I had a god to call upon. "Absolutely, you're right, Glen, the aesthetics will be important – or we'll all die from daily doses of ugliness."

Nervous laughter scattered through the crowd.

"That's why we need your expertise," I continued smoothly. "But maybe we can start with what's important to everyone?"

He stood quiet then, hands balled into fists, chest rising and falling. At length, he nodded.

I exhaled, relieved.

Sensing an opportunity, Charu bolted upright from their seat. "Right, everyone. Day's getting on. Celeste, how would you like us to do this?"

Quite simply, I let them talk, making sure even the quietest voices were heard.

After the first half an hour of open discussion, themes emerged: those who didn't have their own garden dreamed of quiet corners where they could sit outside in peace, others wished to openly socialise, and everyone wanted a safe space for the kids to play. More plants, more flowers. By the second hour, a long wish list had been scrawled onto the flipchart. Paper sketches – where people had tried to explain their ideas – had been passed around.

"What do we do with all these?" breathed Bertha, who got to participate fully because Eddy allowed Roger to use his metal bulk as an imaginary alien landscape for the boy's adventurous T-rex.

"Way ahead of you," João's gruff voice boomed from the back row. He'd been tapping away on his tablet for the last half hour. Just then, Harper moved up next to him for a closer look, a skinny pale imp against João's dark, mountainous stature.

"Right." João stood up to address the assembly, though no one could have ignored his presence. "I'm broadcasting a link – from that you can use your device and vote on as many ideas as you like."

I didn't know we could do that. Much better than counting raised hands.

"*And* we should be able to continue using this app to chat about things going forward," he added with a teeth-gleaming grin, clearly pleased with himself.

An indistinct murmur suffused the air. People pulled out their devices, fumbled, tapped, mumbled to themselves.

Esme tugged at my arm. "Do kids get a vote?"

"Absolutely!" I replied, before anyone could object.

Overhearing us, Harper beckoned. "Come on, Esme, you can use my phone." She bounded towards him, hat rim flopping, broomstick drone above her head whirling.

Then Mr. Atkinson's raspy voice emanated from Eddy's built-in speakers. "Celeste, Glen – is there a way we could test our ideas as we build them? In case things don't quite work out the way we presumed?"

"There's a good thought," I said.

Glen stroked his chin, pondering. Thankfully, he seemed to have calmed down. "Certainly. First, we'd need some sketches – which I can get started on. But we could model in real life too."

Chairs were being folded up, rolled or carried back to where they came from. Snippets of conversation, the occasional burst of laughter.

"That went fine, Celeste," Juniper said, patting my hand, without me asking.

"Mmm," I said.

If I could convince Glen to share his sketches as he went along, we'd probably do all right. The last thing we needed: a hero who thinks he can save the world all by himself. Even if the whole world was just our street.

Over the next few days, the chat platform João set up bubbled with constant chatter. Questions gushed as residents obsessed over details. "Would we get in trouble with the city council?", or "How might we finance this?", or "Where can we get material from?"

Glen had been sure that we'd have no trouble with the council if we didn't make any fixtures permanent, which was the plan anyway while we "build prototypes" – whatever he'd meant by that.

The original idea of a garden patch evolved into multiple islands of raised beds, so that people who suddenly found themselves needing a sprig of rosemary while rustling up a meal wouldn't have to go on an expedition though the whole street to find some. A group of keen gardeners formed around Mrs. Lim; turned out she was a retired horticulturalist. Who'd have thought?

To my amazement, finance became a non-issue; people were happy to chip in what they could. Harper seemed to know a number of sources for reclaimed materials. All the while, Glen happily shared his sketches and cheerfully took on any feedback.

Perhaps I needn't have worried.

One evening, a week or so after the street meeting, I'd just finished marking a stack of assignments and happened to gaze out from our upstairs window. Dotty slept stretched across my desk, a possessive paw on my prosthetic arm that I'd left to one side. Having been born without my right forearm, most of the time I got along just fine without it when alone.

Down in the street, João, Mrs. Lim, Pedro from No. 55, his teenage daughter and a few others of the newly styled Garden Club members gathered around a loose pile of reclaimed wood. In his hands, João held a small chest the size of a shoebox. He opened it, and a fleet of small bots floated upwards, darted around the planks and offcuts as if taking stock, then began cutting through the wood. The Garden Club clapped and whooped. João handed the small controller to Mrs. Lim, encouraging her to try it.

"Are those safe?" said Juniper, joining me by the window. Still wearing her artist's pinafore, she set own a fresh cup of dandelion brew on my desk, her own mug in her other hand.

As if to demonstrate, João picked up a cutting bot mid-flight. Its laser automatically shut off.

"Seems so," I said. "Rather clever things."

Loud steps to the right of the street made everyone turn their heads. Eddy-42 lumbered out from Mr. Atkinson's building – to more cheers. He waved awkwardly on approach, his face-screen radiating a signature happy smile. They set to work: Eddy lifting and moving the heaviest of materials, the residents and bots assembling the new garden boxes.

"Nice of Mr. Atkinson to loan us Eddy." I sipped my brew. It tasted divine.

"He must be particularly good at holding heavy material at precise heights," said Juniper.

Of course, Eddy had been specially engineered to lift patients with care.

A part of me wanted to run downstairs and join the fun.

Instead, I stood and wrapped my pale good arm around Juniper's shoulders. Her brown hand slipped around my waist, and we simply basked in the joy that spread down the street and into our home.

Two days later, Mrs. Lim knocked on our door around midday.

"He won't let us put the plants in!" she exclaimed, half-hysterical, the moment I swung the door open.

No customary greeting, oh dear. Very unlike Mrs. Lim to forget courtesies.

"What?" I asked, confused. "Who?"

A sudden furriness around my ankles meant even Dotty had been roused.

"Mr. Glen!" Her hands clasped and unclasped repeatedly, her brow lined heavy with words she seemed unable to express. "Please talk to him, Ms. Celeste. He's driving us up the wall!"

I peered over her shoulder. The day had been uncharacteristically hot. The clouds had been burned off by mid-morning, heat radiated off the street surface. An impressive number of plant boxes clustered together on the first bend of the street, ready to be filled with plants.

I wiped the sweat off my brow. Did I *really* want to confront Glen?

"Leave it with me, Mrs. Lim, I'll find him later," I said, swallowing a sigh. Collecting Dotty into my arms, we retreated inside.

The day wore on until I eventually saw Glen hurrying past, his hand holding Esme's, her hand hanging onto her flapping hat.

I rushed downstairs, flung open our door.

"Glen! Um, question." Conflict resolution? I'd already failed.

To Esme, I simply said, "Hi!" and took her mumble for a greeting. Perhaps the weather bearing down of us meant hexing me wasn't at the top of her priorities.

Dark circles rimmed Glen's eyes, as if he'd been battling with sleep and lost. I should have simply asked if he was okay, but Glen had a way of beating me to speaking first. "Is this about the plants?"

I nodded, not trusting myself to say the right words.

To Esme, he said, wearily. "Run along home where it's cooler, darling, I won't be long." Esme threw us both a dirty, tired look but didn't protest.

"Thought so," said Glen, fingers running through his already dishevelled hair. "I couldn't make them understand that once we put the plants in, we won't be able to move those plant boxes easily."

I blinked. Surely this was a solvable problem. "The boxes don't have wheels?"

"Wheels?" Glen stared me, confounded. Then he smacked his forehead with an open palm. "None of us thought of that. *I* didn't think of that." He glanced towards the collection of neat, wooden boxes on the street corner.

"I wanted us to take the time to imagine what it'd be like if we were to *use* them. Like, would we have to adjust the heights of the boxes so everyone would reach the plants? The kids would need it lowered, but Mr. Atkinson might not be able to bend down."

A mere misunderstanding then.

"Shall I talk to them?" I offered.

"No, I'll do it," he said, steel in his voice.

"Okay," I said, and tried to ignore the nervousness pooling at the pit of my stomach.

"Thanks, Celeste," he said, in his signature sequence of thumbs up, a wave and a hasty retreat into the street.

The peace – if we could call it that – lasted an entire two hours.

I'd been about to stir spring greens into a pot when shouts flared from the centre of the street. Juniper, who'd just put down her paint brushes, darted through the front door. I switched off the stove and followed suit.

"What are we going to do with all these plants in this heat? Let them die?" someone shouted.

Mrs. Lim cowered behind Pedro. Nearby, hovered a worried-looking João, the Garden Club teenagers, and a few other residents from up and down the street. Mr. Atkinson sat resigned on a crate with Eddy beside him, his digital lips a sober thin line.

Trolleys of unplanted seedlings lurked next to the garden boxes – a lavish, sumptuous sight of green compared to the deadened grass around Middle Block, despite the oak tree's best efforts with its lengthening shadow.

"Do whatever the hell you want!" Glen yelled back, storming away. "If you don't want my help, I have plenty of other things to do!"

Mrs. Lim burst into tears. Juniper rushed forward and enveloped her tiny form in a big hug.

"He's too intense," muttered Pedro, shaking his head.

I drew a deep, ragged breath. These were just plant boxes – the very first project – how would we survive changing the rest of the street?

"He'll come around," I said, more to reassure myself than anyone else.

"What should we do?" Mrs. Lim wailed.

Juniper held her hand. "Do what you do best, Mrs. Lim, you're the expert here."

"Glen is really all right, he just needs to chill," said Pedro, sighing. Then he turned to me. "I like the idea of wheels, though. Then we can push the boxes wherever they need to go."

"Or maybe," said João suddenly, pulling out his tablet. "We can find a way for the plants to move *themselves* around."

All of us stared at him, as if he'd just turned reality inside out.

"I'd have thought watering systems were more urgent," one of the teenagers said.

"We'll find a way to do both," João said, a broad grin spreading across his face that said *you'll see* – a look I'd come to recognise.

Once again, I'd have to be the one to talk to Glen.

As if talking would solve anything at all.

Later that evening, Glen unexpectedly showed up on our doorstep, this time without Esme. I opened the door, apron still over my dress, a stirring spoon in hand – damp from stirring the bean stew that had been bubbling on the stove for the last hour.

"Can I come in?" The dark circles under his eyes hadn't gone away. If anything, he seemed more exhausted.

From within our living room, Juniper glanced up from her book. She glided next to me, slipped the spoon from my hand and whispered, "I'll take over." Her eyes said, *be gentle with him*.

To Glen, she asked, "Something to drink?"

He raised a palm, declined. "I'll try to be brief, thanks. Need to make sure Esme hasn't got herself into any trouble."

"How is she today?"

"Fine," he replied. "Settling down with homework now, I'd just made dinner."

It occurred to me then that Glen might be a single parent; I'd never seen a partner.

I lifted a protesting Dotty from the other armchair and gestured for him to take a seat. Then I perched myself on the chair Juniper had just vacated, letting Dotty settle in my lap.

Glen rubbed his face with both hands. "My wife, before she died, said that –"

I swallowed, a bitter pill stuck in my throat. "I'm sorry –"

"Don't worry, it's no secret, I just don't talk about it much. Esme gets upset if I dwell on it. And no, I'm the one who should be sorry." His words spilled out in a rush.

I wrestled with a few polite responses in my head, but none of them sounded right. In my lap, Dotty purred black hair all over my apron.

"It's hard to lose the perfectionist streak, y'know?" Glen continued, his voice strangled. "All my life, my work has won me awards. Sometimes, I forget that not everything has to be work."

Suddenly, his face crumpled, a single tear triggered a torrent streaming down his cheeks. I glanced up at a slight shuffling noise, caught Juniper's eye when she emerged from the kitchen. Despite Glen's protests, she'd brought a cup of tea.

"Milk, no sugar, right?" she said, her voice soft.

Glen wrapped his fingers around the cup. "Th-thank you."

Juniper's fingertips brushed my shoulder on her way back to the kitchen, I flashed her a small, grateful smile, and waited for Glen to regain composure.

Time was a gift I could give.

"Everyone understood you were just trying to do your best," I said, when he quietened. "Like all of us."

"You think so?"

I genuinely did, and said as such.

He wiped his eyes with the back of his hand. "In that case, promise to give me a kick in the shins next time I overdo it. Please?"

His timid smile spread into a grin.

I chuckled. "All right."

When Glen got up to leave, Juniper stepped up to the door and laid a gentle hand on his arm. "Don't hesitate to ask if you need help with Esme, okay? We are here – if you need a break."

Glen's eyes widened. He nodded curtly, holding back tears that threatened again, so I waved him out into the street.

Then I turned around and folded Juniper into my arms before she could make for the kitchen.

"The stew!" she protested.

I didn't care. My heart – a supernova of emotions. I'd married the kindest, most loving woman in the world.

Around the same time the Garden Club planted the first plant boxes, the first version of the vert-ramp went up. Charu had taken my throwaway suggestion to heart, and enlisted the under-thirties from House 39 to build a half-pipe and a rocket-shaped playhouse atop a ladder – big enough to fit several children, two adults, and perhaps one João. Someone had painted a permanent hopscotch. A few standard picnic tables manifested up and down the street, as did an old Victorian telephone box in the corner where we'd had our first street meeting.

"What's this for?" I asked Charu, when I found them painting the insides.

"A mini library," they said, grinning.

"For a moment I thought you'd got us a time machine."

"Hah!" Their eyes gleamed. "Well, a library *is* a kind of time machine…"

The vert-ramp, however, dominated the ongoing conversation. It'd been installed on the stretch between the second and third corners of the street, presumably so that everyone could keep an eye on the kids at play. Unfortunately, this also meant everyone could *hear* the kids at play – the thunderous din anytime anyone skated.

"Could we *please* do something about the noise?" went the general gist of complaints.

The crew from House 39 said they could move it in front of theirs, but other residents pointed out that this wouldn't actually change anything.

Mr. Atkinson had the better idea. "Had we thought about soundproofing?"

So, we dismantled the first vert-ramp – Roger had complained it was too steep anyway. Work promptly began on the assembly of the second. Some of us spent hours lining it with soundproofing foam, old blankets, egg cartons. When that was done, the kids painted cheerful murals on every side. Then, we coaxed a few plant boxes around it. The noise didn't entirely go away; but it became more bearable, or perhaps, we simply got used to it.

Glen seemed to have made amends with the Garden Club.

"Fascinating," I said to Juniper one evening. Sitting on our doorstep, we watched the kids skate.

"What is?"

"How it's easier to expect the worst of someone."

"Truth is," she said, "the kinds of stories we grew up with make us forget that people are generally kind."

Sage as always, my Juniper.

If you'd told me that one day this chaos would coalesce into this vibrant, living miracle on my street – I wouldn't have just laughed at you. I'd have accused you of coming from a different planet.

Things were going surprisingly well.

Until they didn't.

One evening some weeks afterwards, Lucia, one of the youths from House 39, banged on our door. Summer had nudged spring aside, but the sun fled behind a cloud, rendering a chilly end to a warm day.

Her dark hair was wrapped in a severe upknot, a pale blue blouse tucked into a black skirt. Perhaps she'd just finished a shift somewhere.

About half a metre behind her head, a rocket-shaped drone hovered, lights blinking.

"You hadn't read your messages?" Lucia said, her sonorous voice somewhere between frustration and fatigue.

I hadn't. Esme had been staying with us while Glen worked out of town, and I'd been trying to make sure she didn't hex – or vex – the cat.

"What's that?" I pointed at the drone with my prosthetic arm.

It did a backwards flip. A familiar voice grated through its speakers. "It's me, Charu. I'm flying this from the rocket ship just up the street."

Blimey. I shook my head. I couldn't keep up. "What's going on?"

"Someone has been stealing our veg," said Charu-via-the-drone.

I pulled out my phone from my pocket. Stacks of notifications filled the screen. Sighing, I put it away.

Why have they decided I was the one to call whenever something went awry?

"Let's get everyone out there," I said. "Fifteen minutes?"

Lucia nodded a curt acknowledgement and began typing a message to everyone while sauntering back into the street. How she could walk straight without looking, I'd never know.

By the time I joined them with Esme beside me (much to Dotty's relief), the assembled neighbours wore expressions anywhere from concern to confusion. All the usual suspects were present, with even Mr. Atkinson making an appearance.

"Look at those salad leaves!" Mrs. Lim pointed at sad patches of green stubble on the nearest plant box. "Who harvests like that?"

I must have looked sufficiently blank.

"Everyone had been briefed," Lucia explained, for my benefit. "You should harvest the outer leaves first, never the whole plant."

"Who would do such a thing?" Mrs. Lim continued, wringing her hands.

Mr. Atkinson moved towards the nearest picnic table, his exoskeleton hissing as he sat down. "I don't want to say it, but could thieves have been coming from other streets?"

"I can cast a spell – to poison them," said Esme, helpfully.

"On the plants? No, my dear," Charu said, lips pursed. "You wouldn't want to hurt one of us, would you?"

Esme considered this.

"Besides, spells aren't normally for hurting people," I said.

Esme spun and stared at me. "What do *you* know about –"

I contemplated a snarky reply – it had been *that* kind of day – but then Harper's soft voice cut through, "Do we *really* mind though?"

As one, we gaped at him.

He shifted his weight from one foot to the other, uncomfortable with the sudden attention. "Listen, if they've bothered to steal our food, maybe they really needed it."

We considered this.

Harper exhaled. "I mean, I live here now." He waved a hand towards Middle Block, the dull, cuboid building that the street clumsily curved around.

"But…" Harper paused. "I haven't always had a roof over my head."

In that moment, we saw Skinny Harper in an entirely new light – how one of the most gentle and helpful of our community might have had a rough journey to get here.

Harper looked down at his feet. Esme went up and flung her little arms around him.

"Wouldn't it be nice if they could meet us?" Charu wondered aloud. "Or join us for dinner?"

Eddy's tinny voice said, "I can teach them how to harvest properly."

Mrs. Lim nodded. "Maybe they could help us with the gardening."

I hadn't expected *that.*

Later on, Esme and the other kids drew up some invitations and stuck them among the plants. Those of us who stayed up late that night might have seen several shadows flickering under the bioluminescent trees, picking up the cards. A shrill, ridiculous happy tune suddenly sliced through the silent street; Esme had thought to insert a card with music in it.

A hearty laugh. A sob, or two.

We left them be – no need for confrontation, nor to embarrass them. They'd come when they were ready.

And that was how we met Milo, Khan and Quentin. Just one or two blocks away, they had been barely scraping by to make ends meet.

Primrose Close welcomed them with open arms.

The first off-season storm tore across the country from west to east. Usually by the time it reached us, it'd burned itself out lashing at the Welsh coast and settled for a solid drenching of the southeast. This time, the wind hadn't slowed. Rain bucketed down, the dark skies menacing even if we were only at the end of August. The electricity grid to our homes faltered, but the bioluminescent trees in the street continue to glow. In nervous apprehension, all of us watched how our street furniture might survive.

While we kept dry indoors, the background chatter continued.

"Would be good to withdraw all the plant boxes to a windproof place on command."

"Can the electronics withstand this much rain?"

"Crap – did anyone bring the books in?"

Somehow, perhaps because the plant boxes helped to hold water, our street never threatened to flood.

It had been a third day of rain when our doorbell rang. I'd been absorbed in lesson plans, Juniper had her hands covered in paint, so neither of us got up the first time because – who'd ring a doorbell in the rain?

By the time I got to the door and opened it, the huge figure of João had been soaked through, despite wearing what must have been an expensive rainproof coat. What was so important that he couldn't send a message?

A small puddle formed around João's feet as he stepped inside. Juniper rushed over to take his soggy coat.

"Brew?" I asked, ushering João into our tiny kitchen, his long ponytail dripping a trail of water that Dotty found fascinating.

"Please," said João.

His inability to be forthcoming with whatever bothered him made the skin under my prosthetic sting with trepidation. The kettle boiled. Juniper joined us. I ground down some dandelion roots, stuck on a brew. Dotty curled around my legs, then tried in vain to wrap around both of Joao's ankles at the same time. He leaned against the kitchen bench, shoulders stooping. I handed him a steaming mug.

Finally, brew in hand, João sighed.

"Eddy's gone."

Silence, while those two words sank in.

My voice came out choked. "What do you mean, 'gone'?"

"Hasn't been seen in the last two days. I haven't broadcast it to the group because I didn't want anyone to panic."

"Is Mr. Atkinson okay?" I blurted out.

Everyone liked Eddy – the kids, especially. The adults had come to appreciate the gentle, metal giant. He'd been endlessly helpful with construction of various things in the street. But Mr. Atkinson relied on Eddy for his medication, daily exercise, connection to the outside world, and goodness knows what else.

"He's devastated. I was walking past and saw he hasn't collected his mail – I'd assumed Eddy did that kind of thing, even in this weather. They looked like medical supplies, so I thought I'd better check, in case."

My breath pinched, wondering how close we'd been to disaster. "Can Harper help with reviewing his meds?"

"Yeah, I've texted him," said João. "He'll drop by after his shift at the hospital."

João stuck both hands through his hair. "Celeste, what would possess a droid to just leave without warning?"

I stared at him. João, our resident techie, asking me a question like that.

"Don't call me daft," I said. "Eddy wasn't sentient, right?"

"Not that we know of."

But how *could* we know?

"Eddy has a base station, obviously, like all droids," said João. "I hacked into the logs. They simply stopped at 3:42pm two days ago, then nada."

That would be the first and last time João admitted to me that he knew how to hack a system.

"I've at least deciphered the medical schedule, but I think we might need some people to give Mr. Atkinson a hand."

"We can ask for volunteers. Harper can guide us."

If there's anything this whole street project had taught me, I had no doubt we'd pull together for one of our own.

That night, after the rain finally stopped, everyone spontaneously gathered in the street, checking for damage. A fallen branch had cracked a picnic table, but most of the furniture remained unscathed. The majority of the plant boxes, however, were found bunched up against the eastern wall of Middle Block, presumably to avoid the worst of the winds. It took more than a few of us to reallocate them all around the street. The oak and the cherry trees began to glow as dusk settled in.

News of Eddy's disappearance spread.

"Could he have malfunctioned?" someone asked, probably Milo, who perched at a corner of a picnic table. The folks from the other street had emerged too.

"A hardware upgrade maybe?" suggested Glen. Beside him, Esme remained unusually quiet, staring down at her feet. Her broomstick drone whirred above her head, if at a slightly lopsided angle. I'd always thought her drone was linked to her hat, but it continued to spin lazily, a handspan or two above her blond head.

Roger, on the other hand, bawled uncontrollably into Bertha's skirts.

"You'd think the manufacturers would communicate better about maintenance schedules, if it were that," said Charu.

A slight slosh of water dampened the conversation. Harper had brought Mr. Atkinson out to join us, his wheelchair catching the edge of a puddle. Mr. Atkinson, who'd always looked chirpy, seemed worn, a little self-conscious. Perhaps without Eddy, getting into his exoskeleton had become a challenge.

To everyone's credit, we greeted Mr. Atkinson as always – with respect and a bit of reverence.

"I don't know what happened," said Mr. Atkinson. "He just walked out without a word."

"How long have you had Eddy?" asked Harper.

"Four years, thereabouts. And it was such a tedious process to lease an Eddy-42 for a long period of time –"

"You had a lease?" João suddenly perked up. Worry crept into João's voice. "When was the last time you renewed the contract?"

"I–I don't remember." Mr Atkinson glanced down at his shiny, leather shoes. "I don't want to give anyone any trouble."

"It's no trouble, Mr. Atkinson," I said, knowing that I could speak for everyone on this point. "We can figure out a schedule among ourselves, if you'll have us. We want to see you well."

Mr. Atkinson's eyes reddened. "Harper has convinced me that it's best I'm not left alone, so thank you. I wouldn't know how to repay –"

"There's no need, Mr. Atkinson," said Bertha. "We do what we can for each other."

Harper's lips drew into a grim, straight line. "We'd better find out if our Eddy had been decommissioned."

As usual, João tapped away at a tablet while we'd been conversing. "Seems like some kind of merger has taken place," he said, without looking up. "The company that manufactured Eddy units has shut down. Let's hope they open-sourced their code."

"This isn't right, they can't take the units back like that," Charu said. "We should be able to upgrade our own droids."

"My grand-aunt had a droid," added Milo. "Those companies are awful. They make it easy for you to sign up for one, but never plan for what happens when they close down – or if you want to leave."

In silence, we ruminated on this point.

Someone had set up a fully equipped kitchen on the fourth corner, in front of Mrs. Lim's house. While we talked, Quentin prepared an enormous salad. Khan stood in front of a grill, turning over innumerable vegetable skewers. It looked like they were planning to feed all of us.

"Did we get council permission to set up a kitchen?" I asked, mortified.

"Don't worry, hun'," said Charu, patting my good hand. "We didn't dig up anything, we could disconnect the water from the hose anytime."

Really, this street kept changing on its own.

"So," I switched back to the topic at hand. "Do we search, or do we hope?"

"He should have already run out of battery if he hadn't gone back to a base," João said, putting his tablet aside.

"Doesn't he charge with solar?" Glen asked.

João shrugged. No one knew. It was unbelievable how little we knew about Eddy.

"I could fly a drone and search for him," said Roger, a bit sniffily.

"I could manifest," said Esme, "but I don't know if Eddy would be able to listen."

"We don't know, love," Juniper said, giving the little girl a sideways hug.

"Listen!" João exclaimed suddenly. "He *could* listen, if we –"

He looked at Harper, who seemed to understand immediately.

"Pings, on the right frequency," elaborated Harper.

Those two had got close of late. Who could've guessed?

I rubbed my eyes. "Someone explain that to me?"

"In theory," Harper began, "if there are many Eddy's, each of them need to be able to identify their own base station – and that's done through a unique signal."

"We can safely assume it's a challenge-response type mechanism," said João. He caught my puzzled glance. "As in, the base station isn't shouting all the time – it calls Eddy at specific moments, or if Eddy asks for it. Kind of like a phone call, see?"

Phone calls! What are even those any more? But I clocked the concept.

"We should be able to figure out – from the base station – how we might be able to reach our specific Eddy," Harper explained.

They really did seem to be finishing each other's thoughts.

"Right, so we won't get a whole fleet of lost Eddy's suddenly showing up." I said.

"Exactly."

Juniper had run off to help Esme draw a chalk circle around pentagram next to the hopscotch.

Charu, who'd been sitting quietly all this time, brightened up. "We could use the rocket drone."

Two weeks later – still no sign of Eddy.

Had someone stolen him? Dismantled him for parts? We'd probably never know.

Mr. Atkinson struggled at first, especially with getting help from all of us, but gradually he became less shy about letting one of us assist him into his exoskeleton every morning. Harper recommended that we didn't automate his medication – partly to distract him from thoughts of Eddy, but also to build new habits. For small tasks around the house, João assembled a small robot with a hand – not unlike my prosthetic – that could carry things around for him on command.

Twice a day, Roger got into the rocket playhouse and flew its drone around the neighbourhood, sending out Eddy's signature ping, just as Charu had taught him.

Days passed without fuss, but also without Eddy. Nights lengthened.

Someone had made a new type of picnic table – more compact, more movable – with modular stools that stored underneath when not in use. No more struggles to climb over the sides to a table that could only sit four people, and uncomfortably so. Milo, Quentin and Harper had begun constructing a gazebo in front of Middle Block, some distance from the oak tree.

The telephone box library brimmed with books for the children on its lowest shelves, then anything from romance to crime, to cookbooks, with a few gaps here and there like missing teeth. Algae curtains criss-crossed above us, fluttering in the breeze – a new food source; at night, they added to the glow of the trees.

We got used to not having Eddy around, spoke about him less.

The children, though? They hadn't forgotten.

One afternoon, while gathering some parsley and carrots for dinner, I found Roger curled up inside the playhouse with a large glass of orange juice, his T-rex figurine on the wooden dashboard. He had been fighting to stay awake while methodically flying the drone over the neighbourhood.

Milo and Quentin settled nearby on a smaller table with a chessboard set into it – another new thing.

Esme sat cross-legged by herself inside a freshly redrawn pentagram next to the hopscotch, the broomstick drone zipping above her head like a frantic, trapped fly. In front of her knees a large rectangular box sat in the middle, making a soft *ping ping* noise at regular intervals.

"What's that, Esme?"

She looked up sharply, flicking the broomstick drone backwards. It dropped slightly to one side but recovered itself. "João gave it to me, something that tells Eddy to come home."

Could trackers be heard through the multiverse? Or maybe a little witch's means of reaching out through the ether – with intention and heart – could be just as effective?

The *ping ping ping* from the box might just have been a lonely bird, calling for its mate.

When the rains began in earnest in October, the winds picked up again. This time we'd built a shelter for the plant boxes to hide under. The new picnic tables fared better; everything tucked securely under the tabletops which we rolled into less exposed spots.

The algae curtains, however, were in tatters.

"Can't win all the time," said João.

The power cut out for the whole street after an electrical storm.

The chatter on our app, however, didn't stop.

"This building has a backup power supply," said Mr. Atkinson, from his luxury penthouse at No. 25. "Come anytime, for anything."

"I have spare storm batteries here if you need to charge your devices," posted Pedro.

The power came back later the same day, but occasional brownouts persisted.

"How about some kind of communal power scheme next, folks?" asked Charu.

Then when the rain finally stopped, the winds continued to howl.

I was reviewing a new syllabus by candlelight when something slammed hard, then banged back and forth outside. I squinted out the window.

The door of the phone booth had blown open, its glass panes shattered.

"The books!" I swore aloud.

By the time I'd pulled my shoes on, Juniper was already halfway down the street, her usually neat hair swept in every direction by the persistent gust. Charu stood frozen in front of the telephone box, one hand holding the broken door.

Water dripped off the books. The spines sagged, the pages crumpled.

The wind whipped around our faces, whistled through the trees, whooshed through the thin gaps between buildings. Charu said something, but it was impossible to hear.

Shaking my head, I started back towards home for something to clean up the glass.

A long, drawn-out creak stopped me in my tracks.

I turned around, looked up.

A fissure split open across the heaviest branch from the oak tree. It began to fall – slowly at first, then quickly – a giant's outstretched arm slamming down.

"Look out!" I yelled, but the gale stole my words.

The tree limb hammered the top of the rocket playhouse – cracking it in two – its sharpest branches crashing towards the phone booth. Towards Charu, Juniper.

Juniper!

My body dived forward, willing my prosthetic arm to extend.

"Got you!"

I pulled her down, dragging Charu with us. The branches brushed over our heads, splintering, crashing in front of our feet.

My heartbeat pounded in my ears, my breath shallow.

Broken glass, torn leaves, split wood – everywhere.

"Don't touch the ground!" I shouted urgently.

Lifting my prosthetic arm, I shielded us, cleared a path through the shattered branches. Our breaths heavy, bodies like lead, we dragged ourselves into the open air.

No cuts, a few scratches. The bruises would come later.

I drew Juniper into a tight embrace and inhaled the sweetness of her hair. She brought Charu's shaking body into our arms. And we stood like that awhile, holding each other upright against the wind.

The others had begun running towards us.

"I'll bring the books into my living room for winter," Charu croaked between sobs.

For some reason I couldn't fathom, laughter bubbled up at the back of my throat, and I couldn't hold it down. In my arms, Juniper giggled.

"Anyone hurt?" Harper called out.

I was too busy laughing to answer.

October gave way to November, November ceded to December. The rains faded in frequency, the winds dulled.

Two weeks before Christmas, I had been turning dough for fresh bread while Juniper worked in her studio. Suddenly, my phone nearly leapt off the kitchen bench with incessant buzzing, flooding with notifications. I cleaned my hand and picked it up.

"Incoming councilman!" Lucia said on the chat. "Celeste? Glen? Where are you?"

No time to put on my prosthetic arm, I tugged down my long sleeve and bolted into the street.

Quentin from the next block sat on a stool, reading to the children. Esme's broomstick drone levitated above her curls but stopped its usual whizzing; she must be thoroughly captivated. Something spicy wafted from the direction of the street kitchen, where Milo rustled up some lunch. Mr. Atkinson sat across from Khan, deep in a game of chess.

Glen was weaving his way around the plant boxes, the chess players and the sprawl of children in front of the phone library.

Mrs. Lim suddenly manifested from behind a tall plant box just across from our front door. "I'll go. He wouldn't be unkind to a little old lady."

"I'll come with you."

The councilman had arrived bundled in a warm coat, his grey hair tucked under a hat.

"Councillor Willis." He shook both our hands. "Nice to finally get to see your street."

Mrs. Lim and I avoided looking at each other. We introduced ourselves.

"My apologies," said Councillor Willis. "I'd have come sooner but we've had storms all about the place which required my attention, as I'm sure you well know."

Glen caught up with us then, slightly out of breath, his yellow hair, for once, combed into a passable neat parting.

"Hello, Councillor," said Glen, extending a hand. "I'm Glen, consider me the architect in charge."

I swallowed. Glen had just made himself liable, offered to take one for the team.

But the councilman did not seem perturbed in the slightest. He squinted past our shoulder. "You seem to be doing well for yourselves here. Don't suppose you got permission for any of this?"

"We wrote, but we didn't get a reply," said Glen, confidently.

I had to say something now. "Everything is designed to be movable, so if access is required, we can –"

The councilman laughed. "If only every street thought of doing things this way, we'd have fewer problems. What is a street if people didn't live in it? Care for it, eh?"

Glen and I exchanged a glance. Had we just got away with it?

Then Councilman Willis looked straight up at our trees. "Seems the council can at least help with your oak tree, though. Let us know."

As usual, Mrs. Lim had the most politesse of us all. "Mr. Councilman Willis, join us for some lunch? Milo over there cooks a mean veggie grill."

Genuine surprise crossed the councilman's face. "Well, that's very kind of you…"

"Then let us show you around," I said, smiling at Glen, who wore the largest grin I'd ever seen on him.

Just like that, we got our unofficial thumbs up.

A few days before Christmas, standing inside the newly completed gazebo lined with solar lights, the House 39 Choir suddenly stopped singing halfway through a jazzy rendition of "Silent Night".

"Well, that didn't quite work!" complained Lucia. "Again! From the top of bar seventeen. One-two-three and –"

They took a collective breath and launched into a verse. To my uneducated ears, they sounded fine. I'd been sitting at a picnic table, an unread book open before me, my fingers curled around a warm cup of brew. In front of the telephone library with new glass panes in its door, Juniper read one of her own stories to the kids. Nearby, Harper and João leaned into each other on a bench, short red hair against a black ponytail. Mrs. Lim held Mr. Atkinson by the arm, accompanying him for his daily walk up and down the street – though his exoskeleton probably held him up just fine. Charu, head-to-toe in a silver tracksuit, seemed deep in conversation with Khan, a chess game abandoned.

The Choir had nearly finished the chorus when a tall, angular shadow approached us from the southern entrance of the street.

Roger was the first to bolt upright from the children's corner.

"Eddy!"

He started running.

"It's Eddy!"

We all heard the swish-click of Mr. Atkinson's exoskeleton as he came to a sudden stop. Harper rushed to his side. Then, one by one, we got up, walked towards Eddy's lumbering figure – not quite believing our eyes – and met him in the middle of the street.

"Eddy!" cried Roger, throwing himself around the angular metal legs.

"Hello, Roger," said Eddy, who reached down and ruffled his hair.

"Where have you been!" demanded Esme, her broomstick drone spinning out of control above her hat.

Eddy gently peeled Roger away from his legs, but held the boy's hand as he took several steps, until he stood in front of Mr. Atkinson.

"I'm so sorry to have left, Mr. Atkinson. I didn't have the code to fight the manual recall, not then."

Wordlessly, Mr. Atkinson moved forward and they embraced, standing very still for a long time.

Mrs. Lim sniffled. Juniper's hand found mine.

When they separated, Mr. Atkinson gratefully took a handkerchief from Mrs. Lim.

Eddy knelt down and curled each arm around Roger and Esme. "Thank you for keeping the tracker on, I would've had a harder time finding my way back home otherwise."

João's brow creased. "Have they done anything to you?"

Eddy shook his head. "They were about to send us to the recycling centre. All of us."

"How did you escape?"

"I overrode some of my own code," said Eddy. "After all, I'm open source now."

Just then, the little one-handed robot came to retrieve Mr. Atkinson's mail. It paused, arm in mid-air, as it clocked the presence of another robot.

"Hello, friend," Eddy said. "Nice to meet you."

Days seem to pass in one of two ways: quiet days, where everyone goes about their business, or days where sudden explosions of messages mean something, or someone needs attention. Most of the time, a neighbour steps up to help.

Sometimes, that neighbour is me. Occasionally, the thought would catch me off guard: had I really minded, not so long ago?

Juniper has spent most of today in her studio. I stand in our doorway for fresh air, having just completed planning for the new term. Dotty had wound around my ankles once, poked her nose out, and fled back to the warmth inside.

The Garden Club have decided against a vertical farm, but already construction has begun on a greenhouse with storm sensors at the unused site. It should be ready in time for spring. Algae tubes traverse the gazebo; the curtains were too fragile.

A month ago, someone found the car and brought it back, hooting and honking as far as they could drive up the street. The chassis was given a fresh coat of paint. The boot became a bar fridge, the engine replaced by a DJ set-up. The insides? A cosy lounge that could fit several children, two adults or one João.

That's how we changed our street: one prototype at a time, fumbling our way through possibilities.

Chaos, in other words – the kind where a butterfly flapping its wings might be left confused as to which universe it caused a storm in, where there's not a dull moment between one wingbeat and another.

Chaos – the good kind.

La bibliotheque d'objets quotidiens

Is there a moment that you would miss most, across any given lifetime?

Sitting here in this hidden street in Montmartre – or at least the memory of it – might well be the moment I'd cling to at my final point of death. That first time, two hundred and eighty-nine Earth-years ago, we'd sat at the top of these stairs in Passage de l'Élysée des Beaux Arts, watching the mettlesome morning light bathe the Parisian rooftops, waiting for the first traders to open. No rattling of horse carriages yet, too early for the clattering of electric trams.

The view had lacked the usual elegance of a Paris street: four narrow flights of stairs spilled downwards, flanked on either side by buildings that were three, four stories high, until an ugly fence broke the pattern on the left, caging in the neighbouring Église de Saint-Jean as if it had committed a crime. No view on the Eiffel Tower either – a disappointment.

The garçon from the corner café had thrown me a dirty look while I sipped my coffee on the stairs instead of at a table. I hadn't cared. My black dust jacket draped down to my tawny ankles, I wore my hat plain. An anonymous librarian; travel-practical. Satchel, who then manifested as a brown and weathered leather handbag, nestled next to me out of sight – more importantly, out of the sun. No one would have known how far across time and space we'd come, how many multiverses we'd traversed.

I'd leaned back against the railing. "Can't believe we missed the final ever showing at the Théâtre Libre by a mere fifteen Earth-years." I lamented out loud, an attempt to distract Satchel from his pain.

Despite the scattering of scorch marks staining his skin, his spirits did appear to lift a little. He'd made a shuffling sound, his equivalent of a shrug.

"I *could* take you back fifteen years to the day, if you want –" He'd stopped mid-sentence when he pre-empted my response. Going back with such deliberate precision would likely land us in an alternate time-stream, and the Théâtre Libre, the first free theatre in Paris, might have put on an entirely different closing show. Possible, but not desirable. Nothing ever happened the same way twice.

Besides, he'd been hurt. Hurtling through time might not be the wisest idea.

"Modigliani still lives here." Satchel sent a blinking indicator to my retinal display, pointing at number thirty-nine on the street. "If you wanted to meet him before he deteriorates completely to drugs and drink, now's your chance."

I'd frowned. "He's still in his sculpture phase."

"Aren't you so arty-farty?" Satchel executed sarcasm like no one else. "Well, Picasso has just got into cubism –"

Boring.

That time, we'd warped into Paris by accident after having escaped a revolution in an outpost beyond Sirius B – surviving catastrophe by a mere whisker. I couldn't shake the guilt of having left in such a hurry when people there needed me, but when we finally managed to beam out just nano-seconds before a thermonuclear explosion, Satchel's leather skin had already begun to fray, barely holding together. My eyes still saw flares at certain angles. We didn't know if he could survive another warp in a compromised state. I wasn't about to test the hypothesis; I couldn't afford to lose him.

"How about the existentialists?" I said, downing the last drop of coffee. "They're still kids, right? We could drop a thought or two to kick things off?"

"Better plan." Satchel's approval had registered like a warm ray of sun. If he had physical hands, he'd have rubbed them together in glee, albeit ironically. "Simone, or Sartre?"

First, I had to find someone who would be willing to patch Satchel up without asking too many questions. I'd forgotten, however: in Paris, unless you were a café or a boulangerie selling bread, nothing opened early.

After that first time, we'd returned to this passage nearly every day – until another calamity dragged us towards Betelgeuse. The garçon from the café next door began to mind us less, even handed me the occasional free coffee with a rare smile. And why wouldn't he? A reliable, early customer, just with the odd preference of perching on the stairs several feet from an actual table.

Looking back now, Paris gave us much-needed respite. Sometimes, we'd laugh at lovers in the windows. Or we'd ridicule Earthlings' obsession with love – such a silly, ephemeral thing.

Made for great art, though.

Memories formed you, not the other way round. Memories forged from moments that might have seemed unimportant – mould you into who you would become. Memories fabricated by a time, a place, with someone you couldn't imagine living without.

How things changed.

This time, I materialised into Paris just after nightfall. Again, another accident. Again, Montmartre. Chance? Circumstance? My skin still burned from the warp, nerves jangling from the hurried multiverse flip, my vision blurred by the paralysing light of an event horizon about to devour me to my forever death.

I patted down my body, verifying that I'd made the jump intact. Whether by Satchel's doing or by some random combination of multiversal quirk, I resembled a complete and functioning Earthling – pale olive skin, dressed in something suitably discreet. The clothing style did little to tell me which century I'd landed in, but the material felt soft, natural, unlike anything I'd seen before. I rearranged the folds of my dress, but my hand found nothing where there ought to have been a weathered shoulder bag.

No Satchel.

I hesitated, swallowing panic. Could he have been transported elsewhere? We had never done a jump against such a vortical force before.

Memories formed you, taunted you for what you might have lost.

The chastening air blew colder. Winter. No snow to dampen my footsteps. I searched the empty streets in the half-formed darkness, silent for its lack of souls, lost between bioluminescent trees, shouting noiselessly across all our known comms channels.

No reply came. No link, no signal.

No Satchel. Not here.

I was on my own.

Must not let dismay drown me. Must keep moving.

When dawn broke, those same familiar stairs emerged into view, next to a newer incarnation of that café. Somehow, I'd found our old haunt, but my feet wouldn't step any closer. My heart rate had been too high for too long, sweat coated my palms. My head throbbed. The thought ambushed me: if I went back there, would I corrupt those old, cherished memories?

Nothing ever happened the same way twice; I didn't want to forget.

On the other side of the street, the buildings looked nothing like the beige Paris I remembered. Façades thrived with vertical foliage, next to glass panes containing something glowing green in the morning dim. Photobioreactors. Maybe Earth finally got its renewable energy act together.

A hand-scrawled notice hung in the window of a building I swore had once been a bank: *Nous recherchons: Bibliothécaire.* They needed a librarian. Coincidence?

The window promised books. I walked up to it, cupped my hands around my eyes to look inside, my breath misting the glass. Over the door, a wrought iron sign declared: *La bibliothèque d'objets quotidiens.* The library of everyday things.

I cast a lone shadow, dull in the half-light. My insides still screamed; my existence raw, freshly, savagely ripped in half. This must be what being lost felt like.

For the first time across all my lives, I was utterly untethered.

I couldn't just stay here. I needed to find him.

That moment, my hands sank into my pockets. The fingers of my left hand clasped around something cold and rigid.

A crystal nestled in my palm, glinting under the fading tree-light and the rising sun. An irregular double-terminated quartz, covered in miniscule notches. An Andromedan data crystal. Been a while since I'd seen one of these.

Did Satchel –? How did he…?

My knees buckled, the ground rose up to meet my face, but I fended off gravity with my free hand, holding the stone tight in the other. Pain shot from palm to shoulder as I landed – no real damage. Catching my breath, I rotated the crystal until I found something that I knew would be there: a small trapezoid. Touching a finger to the shape, a tingle raced up my wrist. A message flashed on my retina, the crystal identifying itself and what it contained. It scrolled through hundreds, thousands of categories. A catalogue for a library of things. *This* library of things.

Oh, Satchel. You impish brute.

Did he expend all his remaining energy to get me here to a place we love? It'd be just like him to give me exactly what he thought I needed: something to keep me busy, somewhere where I could help others, somewhere where I could heal – just as he had.

That I found myself in Montmartre had been no accident.

Damn you, Satchel. You never understood that you were more important to me above all else.

Human eyes were skilled at crying; I wasn't.

Or I thought I wasn't, until one hot tear slid off my cheek and onto the crystal.

It gleamed a little more.

My eyes flicked open. Day one hundred and fifty-seven without Satchel. My recurring dreams had become tiresome: me, alone, walking in circles trapped in a stifling dark room, calling out his name – receiving no reply.

Something had woken me before dawn. Birds, I heard birds. Were they a new species? Without Satchel's predictive knowledge base, I had little chance of identifying them, even with access to the library records. I never remembered Paris having any more than pigeons.

I'd found some reasonable quarters in a kind of community housing. They wouldn't let me pay for anything, yet allowed me to stay as long as I wanted. I'd begun to think that Satchel's feat had somehow landed me in a completely different causality branch. Some days, I worried that I might never find out.

My room didn't contain much beyond the basics; it served as a place to sleep, no more.

Before heading out, I wore the crystal in its vine-macramé pouch around my neck – I'd learned how to knot and weave. I pulled on my jacket – technically a *veste* – that I'd grown myself from a clutch of oats, whose roots formed around a mould I'd printed at the library. Satchel would have been amused by the numerous conflicting meanings for the word *veste*, an argument that would have lasted us weeks. The thought tugged my lips into a smile.

Knowledge doesn't just live in the dusty pages of books; true wisdom arises from the physical act of practising craft. Discuss.

So many conversations we'd never get to have.

The spring morning still carried a chill, but a mild winter meant the flora flourished. The Parisian rooftops housed stretches of food forests – something I hadn't noticed when I landed that first night. Everywhere, flowers had begun to bloom, scenting the air to sweetness.

Most days, I beelined for the library. People normally came in for all manner of things until late into the evening, though few ever showed up this early. I sought to link with every Earthling who carried a bag. A futile, exhausting habit. But so far, nothing. No reply, no signal.

Today my feet led me across the street, and before I grasped what I'd done, my bamboo-silk bifurcated skirt folded over the top step of those same stairs; I sat down, leaning back against the familiar reassuring metal of the railing.

The passage had changed name: it had become Rue André Antoine. What used to be dirty slabs of stone had been tiled over with a pale-coloured ceramic that kept the city warm in winter – and presumably cool in summer. The familiar four flights of stairs led downwards, but they too had been tiled with the same material, cut to follow the shape of the steps. Where the fence had been, morning glory surged upwards in vivid green punctuated with violet, waving in the breeze, welcoming the day. Birds chattered to each other, having long, drawn-out debates.

Two faces leaned out of a window, then kissed, longer than was necessary.

I looked away. Better not think about what you couldn't have.

Across the brightening skies, I tracked the stars, more by sense than by sight. Ophiuchus, Hercules, Draco, Ursa Minor. Pollux had begun to dip below the northern horizon, Castor following closely behind.

Memories formed you, robbed you of destiny.

If only I could have shared my immortality the way Pollux had.

That moment, though months ago now, still made my heart beat too fast and shortened my breath into gasps. My mind would replay the sequence of events over and over: when did he drop the crystal into my pocket? How did I not see that he didn't follow me through? Could he have survived that warp intact –?

"Excusez-moi, la bibliothèque, elle est ouverte?" A rich bass voice with a polite enquiry.

A specimen of an older Earthling stood a few paces away, pale and shrouded in a comfortable grey coat, gesturing at the library.

"Yes, of course," I replied in French. Deep breath. Tuck the torment away.

Most of the frequent library users knew me well. I'd never met this man before, so I introduced myself.

"Paul," he said, extending his hand. "My friends told me about you, how you are always so willing to assist everyone."

I had to smile. It wouldn't be the worst reputation to have. The more they knew about me and the library, the more people I could help.

He turned towards the building, I got up to follow him to the front door – and stopped. On his shoulder hung a brown, weathered leather bag. Not identical, but the colour and texture –

Satchel? That you?

No signal, no link. Probably not even wired.

I stopped my shoulders from slumping forward and led Paul through the entrance, unlocking the doors with my palm on the authenticator.

Spanning five stories, the library held so much more than books. The community could borrow just about any type of tool, reserve any of the machines, use any of the materials or fabricate their own. It housed the usual range from information science to histories of extra-terrestrial worlds, but also an extensive archive of manuals and patterns for one-off manufacture. Here, you could learn anything, make anything, repair anything.

The resident catalogue had been far from complete when I arrived. Without the time to train someone else, I chipped away at it little by little. The end game: to leave behind a reliable system that the community could continue to use without me.

At the front desk, Paul frowned, the grey-white of his eyebrows threatened to convene on his forehead. "I'd like to make my partner something. A surprise."

"What do they like?"

"A dress?" He looked at me expectantly, though quickly noted my attire tended neither masculine nor feminine. "Or a coat. More practical." The eyebrows knitted together once more.

"Well," I said, brightly. "I can show you some patterns – perhaps we should start there?"

I led him to one of the reading rooms. Removing the crystal from its pouch, I rested my finger on the trapezoid and noted the series of references that appeared on my retina. One immediately stood out as more promising than the others; I projected it into the air so Paul could see.

He stared at the image, then at me, aghast. "How did you know this is the style they like?"

Smiling, I kept my ruefulness in check. "I'm the Librarian."

I'm the Librarian, without my Satchel.

Gesturing to the front desk, I said, "Come get me when you're ready, I can show you how to grow fabric."

But before I managed to get there, the bell rang.

No one appeared to be at the desk, but experience prompted me to walk around the cumbersome furniture. A young Earthling on the cusp of adulthood sat waiting in a wheelchair, her hair a purple cascade framing the warm taupe complexion of her face.

"Bonjour," she said, a voice of honey and sunshine.

She had a small embroidered purse slung over one side. No signal. No link.

I knelt in front of her, so our eyes level. "How may I help you?"

"I was hoping to repair my sleeve."

I'd assumed she meant to mend a shirt, but then she rolled up her right sleeve, revealing a black sheath wrapping around the forearm which ended in a rounded stump where a hand might have been.

An electromyographic sleeve, very well made, likely by herself.

"What do you need?" I asked, not wanting to assume.

She grinned a little sheepishly. "Just something to fix the hardware, I accidentally overloaded it yesterday. I can re-program the controller later."

I scanned the sleeve and noted the fissure. A query to the quartz and I led her to the room with the correct equipment.

The bell rang again before I made it back to the front desk a third time.

What this library needed: a sentient intelligence capable of anticipating everyone's needs at the same time while I attended to those who required a bit of extra-terrestrial guidance.

But I'd lost my Castor, my Ashvin twin – on the far side of the universe.

No time to ruminate on remorse.

By day's end, I'd given up counting how many people had come through the library. The majority were searching for books or references, a small number needed help with machines. Intergalactic queries numbered mercifully rare.

Human bodies didn't hold up well for long days of physical toil. After the last person left, I closed up and headed across the road. A token to exchange for a dandelion brew at the café, a quiet moment to watch the sun set over the skyline.

I lowered myself down onto the topmost step, warming my fingers on the porcelain mug, the railing cold on my back. The birds had gone silent. The trees began their evening glow.

And there, the Gemini twins, bright in the falling dusk, bound by the Charioteer, the Hunter, the Unicorn – all rushing headlong somewhere else. The twins seemed happy in each other's company, exactly where they were.

"Excuse me."

I turned to face the source of the greeting.

A resonant baritone belonging to a tall, trim man. His umber skin glowing with an equine quality, like a horse ready to bolt, a sharp contrast to the faded brown of his messenger pouch worn over a long black jacket.

No link, no signal. No luck.

"Can I help you?" I asked, despite the fatigue weighing me down like a rain-drenched dress.

The sun had quit for the day, the stranger's face stayed in the shadow. I couldn't make out his features.

"I doubt it," he said, chuckling.

To my surprise, he sat down next to me.

His accent didn't sound local, but then, neither did mine.

We let silence creep between us; it didn't feel uncomfortable.

Then he pointed a finger at something down the street. "Did you know, a long time ago…?"

He paused. I could sense his eyes on me, so instead, I focused my gaze on the graceful, well-preserved arch over a very old door, where the *Théâtre Libre* used to be.

"Yes…?" I said, when he didn't continue.

"Did you know a vagabond artist who wanted to create a Temple of Beauty lived here? Exactly two hundred and eighty-nine Earth-years ago, in fact, he was going through a phase –"

Something prickled at the back of my neck. A memory, fabricated by a time, a place and…

I turned towards him. Definitely a face I hadn't met before. I didn't need Satchel to tell me that.

"I don't believe I know your name."

A smile lit up his eyes. "Don't worry, I know yours."

He extended a handshake.

The moment our skins touched, my sight faded – a split second. A pulse zapped through my body, an unquenchable fire, a familiar awakening. Explosion and implosion in simultaneity. A signal in high amplitude; finally, a link.

I felt his voice rather than heard it, in our private space where no matter existed.

I was afraid you'd already left, that I'd come too late.

The hundred-and-fifty-seven-day-old question tumbled out. *What happened to you?*

"We'll have plenty of time to talk about that," he said out loud. For a moment, he looked like he might cry.

Exhale.

I clasped his hand tighter, changed the subject. "Weird version of Paris you dropped me into."

Satchel raised an eyebrow. "Best version I found in a hurry, okay? Would you have preferred something worse?"

"No!" I mock-protested. "The library is perfect, just –"

"Next time, a ditch on Pluto."

"I'd have found the ice formation interesting!"

"Even with the methane?"

Here, I laughed.

Nothing ever happened the same way twice, perhaps this shear in our shared existence must happen once. Hopefully, only once.

His eyes searched mine. "Are we sticking around?"

I couldn't look away. "We could stay awhile. You could help me train a new catalogue that the library desperately needs."

"Lucky me," he said, exuding snark the only way he knew how. "Looks like I just got a new job."

Elsewhere down the street, a pair of lovers kissed, two shadows blending into one.

Yes. We could stay awhile.

In a time, a place, with someone you couldn't imagine living without.

The City Walks Through Me

At the corner of The Causeway and Little Collins Street, she bent down and picked up a piece of broken heart that had fallen out of my pocket. The night breeze fluttered its frayed edges, the fragment trapped between her slender fingers – a lost butterfly. Her long hair left unwisely loose, chestnut strands billowed around her body, a soft veil threatening to tangle, never succeeding.

Further down the empty street a cleaning bot hummed, indifferent. She turned her head this way then that, eyes searching. Shadows seeped from cracks in the sidewalk, pooling dark patches where light from the bio-lamps couldn't reach, places where ghosts of former passersby left faded footprints behind.

On the northeast corner tendrils of plants, dark green and fragrant, embraced an imposing façade rising eight storeys high into the star-studded night, its ground floor home to a French café – their cakes still better than their coffee, even after a century. Directly across the street, Yule House stood stoic in its streamlined silence, an impartial witness.

She flattened the battered shape into her palm, tugged its sides as if she might pull petals off a flower – he loves me, she loves me not.

We might meet again. We might not.

My knees hissing, I leaned back into the darkness, not wanting to ruin the moment.

But then, she walked on. Where, I didn't know.

The city loves, the city leaves behind, scattering wayward souls like mindless dust.

10:49 p.m. Veer left from Little Collins, creep through The Causeway. I'm never afraid to walk alone in this city, but still I can't resist throwing a backwards glance over my shoulder in case someone chases after me – after their broken heart, snug between my fingers deep in my coat pocket. I think I spot movement in the shadows, but no, no one. Not even a ghost's footstep.

The narrowness of the lane squeezes the air out of my lungs; I pull my coat tighter around my body, despite the warm night. The hotel, various cafés and community hubs have all closed some hours ago. Through the other side, the sudden brightness of Bourke Street slams against my senses at the same moment the music does. A fusion beat – somewhere between salsa and disco – thumps under the murmur of people dancing, chatting, having a good time. Occasional laughter.

I blink, my eyes adjust. Actual trees grow here, so this street is better lit than most. Between the bioluminescence and the coloured lights dangling in lazy zigzags from roof to roof, you'd think we're in the middle of the day, not one hour to midnight.

Someone once told me this whole street used to be a shopping district. People live in these buildings now; trading halls, communal canteens, and classrooms take up most of the ground floors. Admittedly, the residents of Bourke Street are a bit special. Every Saturday night they transform their patch into one long street party, unhindered except by the occasional shout of "Tram!" cascading through the crowd whenever the 86 or 96 show up a few blocks away.

Tonight, stalls run by locals line the streets. One could trade tokens for heaps of things: handmade scarves, home-baked cakes, bites of anything spicy-crunchy-fragrant to savoury-sweet.

Someone shoves a drink at me, a smooth concoction of fig and lemon myrtle. A little sweet but nice. Someone else thrusts a turmeric cookie into my hand. Tokens or not, seems just walking through Bourke Street on a Saturday night is enough to get you fed.

Myles had wanted to meet at Robot Bar – that quirky spot with good Japanese beers at the end of Bligh Place. I didn't; made some poor excuse about how Lin and I had plans elsewhere, muttered something about cocktails, which I know he doesn't care for. Lately, Myles has fallen into the habit of using my presence to sponge up his existential doubts – his worries about wrong life choices, the might-have-beens.

Me? I just want to live in the here and now. Regrets are for wusses.

My fingers trace the shape of the strange find in my pocket. What does one do with a broken heart? I could tuck it back into one of the public message boxes on any street corner, maybe with some kind of a note: "Hi! Did you lose your heart?" But that feels much too cold, too impersonal.

Lin hasn't responded to my messages, so I walk on.

Where? No bloody idea.

The city shakes its head at the fickleness of friends – if one could even call them that.

The gelato place on Degraves Street rolled down its shutters, while the last of its patrons stumbled off, slurping cold, creamy goodness from their sugar cones, laughing in triumph with every lick that didn't descend into a mess.

Nothing quite demonstrates the true nature of entropy as the melting of ice cream on a warm autumn night.

I tightened the small powerpack on my back and adjusted the straps of my exoskeleton – stiff fabric bellows supporting my knees, fastened to a laddered structure reaching down to my ankles. I'd finally got used to how they hissed or whispered whenever I moved, as if they alternated between disapproval and complicity. Walking stopped being difficult a while ago, but the pain – having seeped down into my bones – never fully went away. I tucked my telescopic walking stick into the pack's side pocket. In case, for later on. A small jam-jar of wheatpaste stayed hooked onto my belt, slapping slightly against my hip with each step.

Maybe because Degraves Street remained sandwiched between the Victorian sliver of Flinders Street Station visible at the southern end and the lavish neo-Romanesque Majorca Building to the north, a melange of former worlds always lived here. Not that north meant north in this city; when it was laid out, the Hoddle Grid had to be tipped slightly to account for the flow of the Birrarung.

I crossed into Centre Place, where ironwork vines grew out of the walls, clutching onto old-style lamps which could have been the eyeballs of something extra-terrestrial.

Jeanette Winterson wrote: "Star-dust that we are, will death lose its sting? Theoretically there will be no death, only an exchange of energy into what is likely to be another dimension."

So why did it feel like I'd already died a thousand deaths? That exchange of energy: transmuted from those who died to those who lived; our Earth consumed by fire, drowned by water, torn up by violent storms of air – needless wars we waged against ourselves.

But we survived, this city survived. I lived to walk, walked to live.

The public message box on Manchester Lane recognised me. I didn't know why we called them boxes, when they were, in fact, pillars. I'd always thought they'd been rendered yellow for unnecessary cheerfulness. Nothing personal for me, however. No surprise, I had no one left who'd care.

Perhaps I should channel Dickens: adopt the calm disposition of a classical *flâneur*, him strolling through his sprawling streets of London, me here in my tipped city grid. But what privilege, to observe one's surroundings at a distance! My world had been built brick by broken brick from the bottom up – I preferred to engage.

In another universe I might have slashed at the message box with a machete, drawn red blood from its yellow form, torn wires out of its gut, snapped its wafer chips across my already busted knee.

In this one, I slapped a broken heart onto the pillar with several coats of wheatpaste, careful to leave an opening. In a few days, after the next sprinkle of rain, the seed it contained would begin to sprout a green shoot, breaking the heart further apart.

Pain begets pain – that's the true exchange of energy.

The city smirked, tolerating its delinquents, secretly mourning those who had been lost.

12:01 a.m. That midnight hour, when dreams evaporate. One moment a carriage, next a pumpkin. I weave my way through pulsating dancers, undulating circles of conversation, drowning myself in the vibe. Not alone, though if I were to admit it: perhaps lonely.

Why can't I remember falling in love for the first time? Just the sharp stabs of the first heartbreak: that girl from school, her phoenix gaze sizzling my soul, black hair always in a perfect braid tumbling down her back – a silken rope. How I dreamed of unravelling that braid, to run my fingers through her starless waterfall.

Myles can fool himself all he wants. Maybe I'm the one who made the wrong choice.

Happy, vibrant faces. Smiling, laughing faces. Swaying bodies, shadows bopping to the beats, the party spilling out into several side streets. No ghosts here, only in my head.

At the corner of Bourke Street and Hardware Lane, a circle of lights blinks around the top of a public message box – a stout, cheery yellow pillar. I come closer, giving it permission to tell me what it has. Nothing interesting: a notice for residents, some uncollected private mail. No bright blue light to signify an artist has left a new song, a latest creation – or sometimes, an invitation to an event. That's the thing about Myles, I could never get him to come with me to anything I like. Nothing from Lin either.

I hesitate, the broken heart nestling in my palm. I'd assumed that it'd fallen off some kind of art installation, but now I'm not so sure. Perhaps the one who dropped it is still wandering these streets, pining for what they'd lost. Would I recognise them if I saw them? They could be tall, broody, self-immersed. Or nothing like that at all. Maybe there would be some tell-tale, forlorn look in their eyes, a disappointed droop to their chin. I'd go up to them and say, "Hello, did you drop this?" And we would talk, walk somewhere. Get away from here.

I should've just left the pieces back there on Little Collins, in case they came back. Could've waited for them. Too late now.

The city whispers, teasing me with its secrets. Or maybe all I'm hearing are rustling leaves that haven't yet fallen off the trees.

A scientist named Anil Seth once explained that we experience free will when we become aware we've made a choice, or when we know we might have chosen to do the same thing differently.

Somewhere between Flinders and Lonsdale Streets, I ducked through the lanes and alleyways, ignoring the twinge in my left calf. Something liberating about walking in a city grid: it's so easy to wholly lose yourself in the act of wandering. Should the need arise, the process to un-lose oneself is simple: find the nearest corner, look up at the street signs.

These days, Howey Place housed an L-shaped urban farm. In Victorian times, a utopian fellow by the name of Edward William Cole built an arcade here crammed full of books, furnished it with signs declaring *Read for as Long as You Like – Nobody Asked to Buy*. Rainbow

Alley sidled up against the bio-mimicking CH2 building, hiding an archway covered in murals. Bullens Lane, likely named after the clothiers who originally operated here, hosted an algae wall on the sunny side. The other wall ached for art; I gave it some.

I couldn't say if my feet just knew where to go – whether these were true choices I'd made – or if my senses conspired to deceive me, fooling me into believing I had conscious control over my direction. Perhaps predators feel just like this – riding on micro-decisions, treading on instincts. Only difference, perhaps: I preyed on blank walls and message pillars.

Somewhere near the edge of Bourke Street, I smelled it before I saw it. The still-warm biomass-powered stove, the type used by street traders to roast chestnuts. The stench of smoke, the stink of everything burning: trees, houses, animals. The sky – orange; the city – sheathed in sheets of flames. Searing heat, suffocating. Sweat soaked my shirt. The world swirled and something gripped my gut, intent on squeezing life from my body. Couldn't breathe. I leaned against something cold – a wall – tugged hard at the straps of my exoskeleton. No, no, stupid. Don't do that. My right hand found the walking stick, the trigger button.

Breathe. Again.

The air, normal. Fresh. No flames. It was fine. I'd be fine – later.

The city shivered, its existence an illusion, perhaps only a perceived mess in my head.

1:32a.m. Turn left into Swanston, and the music follows me, the buzz of the party fading with reluctance. I'd been whittling away time, dipping into side streets, checking out more stalls but never committing. Not entirely sure where to go, what to do, bouncing between two threads of thought: (1) Would Myles forgive me? (2) Why do I care? Not like he really does.

Unlike the boisterous crowd of Bourke Street, Swanston Street residents seem to have chosen quiet, their street-space home to bicycles, tables and chairs laid out for communal meals, planters of flowers and herbs dividing kerb from tram track. Everything waits patiently on the pavements, ready to receive tomorrow's bodies.

In my hand, the broken heart feels silky, yet there's a stiffness to it. Brittle, but soft. Fragile. Someone who couldn't hide their pain. This fragment could have been in any shape, any substance – it'd still feel broken.

Our elders say we should think of objects as living things, that when we make something with our hands we create a continuation of the spirits living within us. To make art is to transfer energy from one form into another. To pen words is to distil the essence of one's soul.

My last argument with Myles manifests as a knot in my chest. Or rather, his argument with himself; I'd just been the unwilling participant. I shake my head. Need to let it go – untaint myself.

I pass another message box. Nothing. Maybe Lin has stood me up. Serves me right.

A fine drizzle falls, a feathering rain, compelling the night to glitter under tree-light. Across the tram tracks, rooftop gardens fill first-floor terraces lit by glowing windows of those not yet asleep – end-of-summer tomatoes, beans, varieties of green leaves that are hard to spot from the ground.

My body jolts to a halt. Further down the street: a lone silhouette hobbles down the south side of Lonsdale, heading for the corner where it meets Swanston. I squint. Legs wrapped in an exoskeleton, hand on a walking stick. They look up; I'd been seen. They pause, a skipped heartbeat. But then they turn and cross the junction, heading back the way they came.

Them – the broken heart, theirs. Must be. I don't know why I'm so sure.

A greeting blooms on my tongue, I swallow it. My voice would never carry.

My fingers close around the broken heart. I remember to breathe.

The city shrugs, moves on. I suppose nothing surprises it any more.

A philosopher by the name of Robert M. Pirsig once concluded that what we experience through our senses of the external world could only be something we imagined. Everything happens entirely within our own minds.

At Lonsdale Street where it met Swanston – I thought I saw her again, a solitary figure standing still on the opposite corner. Could that be the same billowing hair? The night had deepened significantly, and while the trees glowed their brightest at this hour, my head still throbbed, my body damp from drizzle. So I limped across the other side of Lonsdale, headed back eastwards. Either way, it'd save us both an embarrassment. I trusted my feet more than my eyes, but her gaze weighed on me like regret upon my shoulders.

Walking equals surviving. You walk because you need to get somewhere, to escape from the here and now. You walk to stretch time thin in those half-baked seconds between footsteps, to search for the beacon of another soul, to scour for revelations in places where hours no longer have meaning, where pasts collide with presents into possibilities of futures.

The city beckoned, calling my name. Or so I told myself. Entirely possible that it existed all within my own mind.

3:42 a.m. Hover at the corner of Swanston and La Trobe Streets, where the State Library has been closed for several hours. Warm, pale light illuminates its Corinthian columns from the inside, a pearly glow stealing across the forecourt, stopping at my feet where shadows lie fallow. I settle on the bench just before the stairs. It grants a sideways view of Sir Redmond Barry, immortalised in bronze. Something rustles in a nearby tree, probably a possum.

The broken heart in my hand flutters in a sudden breeze. It speaks in a language I don't fully understand.

Could words express the hauntology of a choice not made, a path not taken? A multitude of possible universes – but I may choose only one.

I see now, where Myles gets stuck. A *saudade* for the might-have-been.

From my pocket, I extract my notebook and a pencil, bid their souls hello. I twirl the pencil in a sharpener until its point could cause damage. Craft requires sharp tools.

Across the other side of the street the Night Library extends a tempting invitation, but the tip of my pencil begins to scratch on a blank page.

Under a tree, a cloud of fireflies gathers, their glow pulsing on and off, transmitting signals to each other encrypted in a cipher I can't decode.

The city inhales. I pull words down from the air it breathes, marking paper with graphite.

I can't recall where or when, but at some point I walked past a pillar blinking blue. An unusual occurrence, considering the dead hours of the morning. Another artist beset by insomnia? For a moment, I didn't feel so alone.

It must have been after I'd dropped by the late-night shelter at the corner of Little Lonsdale and Exhibition Streets – the single-storey brick building which had originally been a synagogue and Hebrew school, then a free labour bureau, a men's industrial home, a women's shelter, a free kindergarten for children of poor parents. Sometime in the twentieth century, it became a Chinese steamboat-hotpot restaurant, then an unlikely mix of a Mediterranean bistro and an American diner in the twenty-first. I, for one, was glad the building got its soul back.

There, I grabbed a coffee, a quick bite, exchanged pleasantries with Lucio who'd been on the graveyard shift. I hadn't bothered to track my route when I left, so I'm no longer sure how many public message boxes I passed before I found the poem.

Daniel Kahneman once said that our memories tell us stories, and that's what we get to keep; what we actually experience moment to moment gets tossed away, rendered null into a synaptical void.

Too bad my memory was already so shot.

But I recognised the poetic form: a tanka – used by lovers for a hasty message the morning after, so the myth goes. Or was it the night before?

The signature showed it'd been posted in front of the State Library, just before four in the morning. There had been no name, but if that had been her whom I ran into at Lonsdale and Swanston, the timing would've been about right; I'd encountered no one else.

To not choose is to risk regret.

By the time I made it to Flinders Street Station, I'd already stopped at several message boxes along the way, reading it over and over, striving to commit the words to memory.

Over the main entrance, nine clocks showed the departure times of trains that lead away from the city, just as they'd faithfully done for hundreds of years.

The city ponders: to choose its fate, or succumb to destiny?

fireflies flicker
the way rain glitters under
time's spellbound shadows;
but do they have will to choose —
to sigh, surrender, like I?

4:11 a.m. What was I thinking? Should've just kept the words to myself, and no one need to have known. Totally foolish, self-indulgent to have wrapped it in a broadcast message, posted it as art. Luckily, I hadn't thought to sign it off.

But the deed is done; these words now belong to the city – they are no longer mine.

Stumbling into Franklin Street this time of night, its tall buildings seem hushed in their slumber, concocting benevolent dreams. The residents had turned it into an endless playground: swings, obstacle courses, climbing frames. Picnic tables linger in nooks here and there, presumably for socialising parents.

At the edge of the North Melbourne Market the high rises suddenly shrink down to ancient, single-storey buildings, a flourishing food forest tucked between architecture old and new.

Dawn soon. It'll be hours before the cafés here open; I'd have better luck back towards the train station. The smart thing to do would be to wait for a tram, but instead I walk to the end of the street, take a right turn. Knowing me, it's probably the wrong turn, and I won't find out until much later.

The public message box on the corner of A'Beckett and Anthony blinks a purple pattern. Messages. Finally.

Lin, about half an hour ago: "So sorry! Lost track of time. Raincheck?"

Myles: "Babe – can we talk? I'm wil be at Jose's tomoz rehearsal but can meet after."

Sent just fifteen minutes ago. He'd probably found someone else to get drunk with.

Too late. For this. For everything.

At each junction I pick a street I haven't already taken, stubbornly escaping from my past self.

The city sighs, gives up any notion of pretence.

There exists no clear equivalent for the Spanish word *madrugada* in English. Usual translations include: 'dawn', 'daybreak', 'early morning' or 'the wee hours', the last of which is perhaps the most accurate. But 'dawn' refers to when the sun begins to rise, whereas *madrugada* could mean any time between midnight and six o'clock in the morning. Maybe we dare not name these witching hours for fear it may make them real, when they ought to be prisoners of dreams. Yet we have three words to define the types of twilight: civil, nautical, and astronomical – the last of these being the darkest.

It must have been astronomical dawn, around twenty past five – when the shadows receded and trees began to dim – that she showed up at Flinders Street Station, her long hair flowing behind her, coat clutched tight around her body. I'd been sitting for a while on the stairs under the clocks: time's spellbound shadows.

The moment she saw me, she started, then hurried across the road, treading her way over the tramlines. My exoskeleton whispered. I stood up to move towards her, but being fleeter of foot she made it to my step before I could ready my walking stick.

For a moment that stretched too long, we merely studied each other, breathing the same air, needless words unspoken. Then she reached out, a broken heart in her hand.

Mine. Her words scribbled across it.

The city creates entrances and exits, permeable boundaries stirring time and place.

Did she have a train to catch? She shook her head no.

Would she like to go somewhere, perhaps, where we could talk? She nodded yes.

So, we walked on. Where, we didn't know.

The city smiled, surrendered to destiny, having found what it didn't know it had lost.

*

This story has been set on a location in the lands of the Wurundjeri people, and we wish to acknowledge them as Traditional Owners and Custodians.

We pay our respects to their Elders, past and present.

Soul Noodles

The shadows on the faded wall danced silently to a rhythm that I could never put my finger on. Every time I stayed late to finish the day's tasks, these silhouettes hypnotised me with their slither, lulling me into the sedate sleep-spell of a daydream.

I pinched myself awake.

Yes, just the fish in their glass tanks, assembled edge-to-edge across this open floor, eight levels up in a twenty-two-storey building belonging to the food-makers' co-op – one of the many abandoned shopping malls we'd reclaimed.

Late afternoon light refracted through windows then water, colouring the white-tiled floor with a green-blue hue. Machines hummed a low, unwavering note. The fish native to our waters – loaches, prawns, tilapia, koi – didn't seem to mind. On top of the aquaria, ten thousand tiny spears of young rice plants stood solemn in their sobriety, a field of unfettered green.

At the end of the cycle, I'd have my own quota of rice. Some of which I might mill into flour, some of which I'd trade for extra wheat to make noodles by hand – to reproduce a humble noodle dish that Ah Gung, my grandpa, had talked so much about. A near-impossible task now.

"Can't make proper kolo mee any more with no pork," Grandpa would sometimes say, usually out of the blue, often after a meal of something completely different. I'd never tasted true kolo mee; my generation never had the opportunity to sample these traditional dishes. When many key ingredients stopped being readily available – climate havoc, collapsing trade, disease, you name it – our food had to adapt. Little by little, some of us began the work to recreate the lost cuisine. Making these noodles the way Grandpa remembered them had become as much mission as obsession now – for his sake, as well as mine.

On my data display, charts scrolled – slow, languid – mapping humidity, yield and various nutrient levels. It took a certain dog-headed persistence or dutiful diligence to make sure things ran well – or both.

A soft *ding* drew my eyes to the top right corner of the display. A notification from the greenhouse on the roof: an incoming storm.

Well, that explained the day's heat. When I arrived in the morning the air had sunk heavy onto my skin; around midday it became unpleasant to breathe. But the physical discomfort was bearable. I didn't have to toil the fields under the sun the way my ancestors had.

I should go home to make dinner, but an advanced storm warning meant a rare chance to evaluate the calibration on the greenhouse. Once upon a time I might have gone out with friends after the day's duties. But Ah Gung could no longer cook; his taste buds were already fading. Being his assigned grandson, he was the only family I'd ever known, and now he had only me.

I sighed, though there wasn't anyone else around to witness my chagrin.

Check the greenhouse, go home, make dinner – in that order.

Move.

I picked up the lone mug resting next to my console, long since empty of local liberica grown and roasted down the street, and dropped it by the kitchenette on my way to the lift.

There used to be a kind of superstition: eating certain noodle dishes would grant a long life. Now that wheat was hard to come by, eating any kind of noodles had taken on this symbolism.

According to Grandpa, there was once a shop in this building that sold tie ban mian – noodles on sizzling hot plates. Sliced chicken steaming atop crispy noodles, doused in thick, savoury gravy spitting wildly while being served up, only you'd be told *Don't touch the plate, it's hot* while you salivated. If Grandpa could still recall how it tasted now that he'd turned a hundred and eighty-eight years old, it must have been exceedingly good.

But still, he craved kolo mee even more. Apparently, it had its origins in this city, a common breakfast fare. Everyone ate it, sometimes several times a week. His fixation became mine: as if a single strand of noodle could traverse the thread of history, connecting our souls across time's jagged ravines. Maybe that was what 'a blessing for longevity' really meant?

Few people remembered that old noodle shop downstairs, possibly because a place like that would be a luxury now. The lower seven floors of this building flooded whenever the rains got heavy. We forgot about a past we could no longer imagine.

Some days, our work resembled a never-ending task of mending holes in linen washed too often – a futile attempt to stitch the past into the present in a continuous line.

The lift doors opened onto the roof with a gentle swish. Heat burst upon my face, but the sweet metallic smell of approaching rain hit me harder. I squinted into the fading light, made hazy by humidity. Here, the future could be predicted by the near-black clouds on the horizon. Best not to be caught up here when the rains fall.

I paused by the safety railing lining the edge of the roof. The sun had just begun to dip below the horizon. The call to evening prayer rang across the city, riding on the cooling breeze. Snatches of conversations and whirring of bicycles filtered upwards. Sampans, amphibious vehicles and a network of elevated streets had largely replaced the tattered car-centric roads that had been ruined by rain. The end of the school day: children of all ages made their way home. Some toddled with their assigned guardians, older ones sauntered on their own, or weaved on bikes between market stalls on both sides of the street several storeys above ground.

The air inside the greenhouse blew cool on my skin; the humidity control had been working well. One year after having been allocated this building as caretaker, I'd constructed this: a self-regulating greenhouse that took up half the roof. Being at such height, it had to be storm-proof without any intervention.

Wind whistled through horizontal photovoltaic panes, modelled after our traditional louvre windows. Normally they'd swing open for airflow, but now, they had begun to lower on their own – the correct response given the environmental reading. I scrutinised the speed of their movement: too slow, given the velocity of the incoming storm. Easy enough to fix.

A single computer console squatted on top of a crate beyond the patch of young wheat and a smaller allotment of experimental cruciferous varieties. I loved this greenhouse; it felt like a living thing. A part of me wanted to believe that the plants were happier being in symbiosis with –

Something rustled at the far end. I froze.

"Hello?"

Lily, the new bioengineer, emerged from behind the wheat stalks, coloured streaks in her hair glinting purple in the descending dusk.

"Hey, it's Jin, right? You eaten yet?" Her voice rang deep, which surprised me because she stood barely five feet tall. A yellow messenger bag dangled off one shoulder, her movements efficient, even graceful. "Thought you might have already left."

I kept forgetting that the co-op had transferred her here to this building – after I'd reported that there would be space for another member. It had been what, two weeks? Four? Once, she'd asked me for samples of my rice, but otherwise, we rarely crossed paths.

I smiled, shrugged. "Just checking the greenhouse first."

Saying it out loud made me feel somehow more responsible. Not that there was much to do – the point of automating it all.

"And you? What are you doing here?" I asked. A forthright question, but curiosity got the better of me. Technically, though, the building belonged to the co-op, she had every right to be here.

"Collecting samples for developing aromatics." She grinned. "You'll have to come to my lab on the eighteenth to see. You like cooking, right? I think you'll be –"

Lightning reflected off the glass all around us, blazing a bright white before vanishing. A loud *boom* exploded above us, and it stretched on and on, thunder resonating deep into the building's foundations in a slow rumble. Lily pushed her black-rimmed glasses back onto her nose, her brows knitting in sudden worry. "I should get home."

. All the windowpanes on the greenhouse immediately swivelled shut.

"Let's go," I said.

We rushed across to the lift but not before the skies opened. Sheets of rain splattered down. The plants stayed dry; we weren't so lucky.

Side by side, we pressed our faces against the windows on the tenth-floor, trying to get a clearer view of the outside world. The growl of the storm drowned out the drone of the machines. Strange how the fish seemed unperturbed. The tattered roads at ground level had disappeared under water at alarming speed. Strict monsoon seasons had faded into history, but king tides still operated like clockwork.

Lights flickered. A low purr came from the ceiling – the rainpower generator had kicked in.

"I told my auntie I'd be home for dinner," Lily said, sighing. "She promised midin with belachan."

She'd taken the spare chair I offered her. Far too big for her small frame, it left her feet dangling. Never mind that water dripped off her hair and clothes; neither of us were dry, but at least we weren't cold. I'd thought she was older, but now I saw that we were probably close in age. Young enough to hope, old enough to know things don't last forever.

I pried my eyes away from her soft shoes. "I need to get home, too. I'm cooking."

So as not to gawk at her, I pretended to tidy my workstation, and hoped she didn't notice I was just straightening a couple of stray cables that weren't connected to anything.

"You live with…?" A smudge of mauve sparkled on her eyelids, set off by her flawless, bronze skin.

I wasn't any good at this – this making conversation.

"A grandfather," I said, my voice rusty from having lost the habit of speaking much. I reached behind the workstation, grabbed my raincoat and pulled it on. "I'll take the sampan home. We have one in the building. Will you come?"

She studied my face but didn't move, and I wondered if I'd somehow been callous.

"I've never used it before," she admitted.

"It's safe. I can show you how it works, in case I'm not here next time you need it."

Lily gathered her bag and hopped off the chair. "Yeah, all right."

She didn't have a raincoat, so I retrieved my backup from my locker near the lift. Uncertainty seized me. Should I help her into it? Would that be weird?

In the end, she spared me the dilemma by taking the item from my hand. She held it up, laughed. Made to accommodate a male physique, it ballooned several sizes too big.

"Better than nothing," she said, wrapping the blue cellophane material around her shoulders and knotting the too-long sleeves loosely at the front of her neck. The colour clashed with her bag and her hair, but she didn't seem fussed.

A lump formed in my throat, a cascade of part-embarrassment, part-shyness, part-something I didn't quite understand, so I wordlessly indicated with an awkward wave that she should just follow me.

By the time we got there, the floating jetty had come through the vertical shaft and attached itself to the landing. Seeing it invoked a golden feeling, a warmth to the chest; the prediction algorithm wasn't trivial and I'd had to install a whole bunch of sensors throughout the building for this to work.

"This used to be the carpark, right?" Lily asked.

"There might have been a bus station downstairs as well."

Our sampan bobbed in the water as if excited to see us. I reached out to help Lily aboard, but she grabbed the railing and hoisted herself onto the craft. The sampan swayed a little. I waited for it to settle and lowered myself slowly into the middle.

"Which way?" I asked, leaning over the boat's console.

She told me; opposite direction of where I needed to go, but it shouldn't be more than a twenty-minute round trip.

"That part is on the hill, I can walk the rest of the way."

"You sure? Rain's heavy. I could probably get you closer." The thought of her tiny figure under this giant rain seemed so very wrong.

"It'll be fine," she said, smiling. "I got your raincoat, we'll hit the edge of the water before we get there anyhow."

A transparent shield rose from its gunwale before we cleared the building, sheltering us from the downpour. Once upon a time I'd also be worried about crocodiles, but the city authorities had put in deterrent fences in the last few years.

Murky water stretched out in every direction. The rain rattled, rendering it impossible to carry a conversation. I would have to do something about that, maybe install some kind of noise cancellation.

We sailed past the top of an old traffic light. A construction sign floated by. Broken branches scratched the side of the boat. I should probably update the sampan's detection system to better recognise unorthodox shapes in the water.

"Oh, I forgot!" Lily suddenly shouted over the din.

"W-what?" I wasn't banking on having to head back.

"For you." From her bag, she took out a clear glass container. I could see a layer of milky-white dumplings packed neatly inside. Wontons? My mouth watered. I hadn't seen these in a while.

"My auntie had been trying her hand at Chinese fare, and made far too many," Lily continued. "Anyway, maybe this will save you from having to cook tonight."

I opened then closed my mouth, like a tilapia.

"Thank you, and to your auntie," I said, barely able to hear myself. "She's very skilled."

A blank expression washed across Lily's face. She leaned closer. A faint sweet-earth scent of moth-orchid and patchouli trapped me like a wild animal. My hand fumbled, my fingers found a passenger handle. Perhaps she couldn't hear me? I repeated my words.

"You're welcome!" Lily beamed. "Auntie is ninety-eight. She's had time to practice, I suppose."

Ninety-eight? Not a biological aunt, in all likelihood. "You were assigned?"

"Yes, she brought me up since I was a toddler, within our longhouse community." Lily looked away, across the turbid water towards something I couldn't see. "Soon it'll be my turn to look after her."

So Lily never knew her own parents either. My grandpa was already advanced in age when I was assigned to him. When we'd first suffered population loss to disease and rising water levels, an algorithm was set in place to automatically assign families – but the system struggled to understand holistic human needs. People rebelled; citizens unanimously voted to have a rotating committee selected by sortition instead.

I had a good childhood, but always a shadow lingered over us, that gaping emptiness with neither shape nor name, the sense that something was missing. The arrangements hadn't been perfect by any means, but at least we paid attention to each other's welfare now, rather than treating it as just another problem.

We reached the water's edge where the sampan couldn't go any further. I steadied the boat for Lily. She clambered over and waded across to dry land.

"See you tomorrow?"

Her wave was cheerful. Making sure to smile, I waved back.

Shrouded in my blue raincoat, her lithe body darted under the unforgiving torrent, a small misshapen dot under grey rain, until finally, she turned the corner – and disappeared.

Grandpa's wheelchair jammed up against the dining table, its cushioned arms tucked underneath. The chopsticks in his hand quivered, but he managed to fish out a wonton from a steaming bowl of clear broth in front of him. Hot filling threatened to spill out of the semi-translucent skin.

Rain syncopated heavily onto our roof and into the water collector along one wall. The banana tree outside waved violently in the wind, its broad leaves catching the splattering rain. Cool air slipped between the solar panes of the windows, not bothering to seek permission to enter. Like all the other houses, ours was raised on stilts with a spot for a sampan underneath at water level. Grandpa's seniority and years of civil service granted us comfortable lodgings with a balcony and elevated garden.

He trimmed off a wobbling mouthful of wonton. I waited. He'd been complaining lately that food tasted paper-bland, but today, he hummed a little while he ate. It took several tries before I succeeded in clamping my chopsticks around a slippery dumpling from my own bowl. Soy-soaked mushrooms, green chives tangled with salty traces of once-dried prawns; a just reward drenching my tongue. An unexplained, crumbled filling delivered an unexpected savoury-sweetness in the mouth. Not water chestnuts, definitely not tofu – none of the usual ingredients.

"Pork?" Grandpa postulated.

I turned the trapped morsel between my chopsticks, marvelling at how the filling glistened with a fine film of something gossamer-like. No, much too fragrant to be a pure plant-based oil, each bite inducing a taste explosion like... like what? I struggled to think of an equivalent. I'd never tasted anything quite like this before.

The likelihood of it being pork was close to nil; there had been no pigs for decades. Artificial meat, grown from fungi? That'd only account for the texture, not the taste.

"Could it be... lard, Ah Gung?"

Grandpa chewed, mulling over each mouthful. "*Tastes* like lard..."

Strange how one ingredient could make all the others sing.

I savoured another mouthful. How did they get lard without pork?

When nothing remained on his plate, Grandpa placed his chopsticks down, lining them neatly side-by-side. He sat back, the wheelchair creaked.

"You see, lard was always more important than the pork." He pushed his empty teacup towards me for a refill. "You could throw in anything for texture, but you wouldn't get the flavour without the lard."

The same reason why it had been impossible to make an authentic kolo mee. I rolled the sweet, earthy aftertaste around my tongue. Where did Lily's auntie get hold of this magical substance?

I re-filled Grandpa's teacup and got up to clear the dishes. The wind had changed direction; the rain pattered in an uneven rhythm against the windowpanes like a broken metronome.

A snort came from over my shoulder. Grandpa had fallen asleep in the wheelchair, his hands around the steaming cup of tea.

"It's not pork, silly," Lily said, half-laughing, when I asked her the next morning. Somewhere deep in my gut, something shrivelled up and I wanted to disappear.

"Let me just finish this task and I'll show you."

She had turned the long, narrow room on the eighteenth floor – probably a former broom closet – into a kind of lab. It smelled citrus clean, even if it didn't look like it should. Compact steel vats lined one wall, small taps jutting out in a neat row, their labels precisely aligned, names printed black in Lily's pristine cursive. The waist-height bench top along the other wall seemed to suffocate under an ageing computer, a CRISPR set-up, and so much clutter that my eyes blurred when I tried to focus on anything. Lily's waif-like body stood camouflaged among the chaos as her fingers hesitated over the computer keyboard – I kept losing sight of her.

At the far end, a rectangular window framed the persistent storm outside, resembling an old-fashioned screensaver, the heavy rain drowning everything in wet white noise.

Would it be too improper to step inside her office? Lab? Whatever this was. I'd be blocking her exit; I didn't want to be disrespectful.

Stacks of books lurked on a shelf above the bench, flanking a purple piggy bank in the middle. It wore a fake orange flower on one ear, its stare scrutinising me: *What are you really doing here?*

I hung by the door, bottling up my self-consciousness, burying it deep. When Lily finally looked up and smiled at me, it took all of my willpower to not dissolve on the spot.

The piggy bank's black-dot eyes bored straight through me. *You're ridiculous.*

I know, I telegraphed back.

"So, you wanted to know what the substance is?" Lily reached towards a vat and poured a tiny amount of a viscous liquid into a small pan. Then, she moved it onto a heating plate. "Watch this."

Over the heat, the substance shifted from milky white to clear, simultaneously releasing a smoky, salty-yet-sweet scent, almost... animalic. My nostrils flared. This. *This!* Could this be the missing ingredient? How did she –?

I stared at the vats. Realisation slammed like a sack of rice. "F-fermentation?"

Lily's smile summoned sunshine from nowhere. I melted a little from the heat on my cheeks, feeling a little less solid, a little more liquid. "Heh, yes, same way you'd make wine or beer."

Grandpa's meticulously kept archives contained a wealth of recipes that had been irreproducible; lard was such a big part of our traditional cuisine. When pigs became rarer, lard became expensive, inaccessible. So many of our people had never experienced how these foods were supposed to taste. And now? We could change all that.

I wanted to wrap my arms around her, whoop for joy, do a stupid little dance of triumph – though I did none of these things. I must have been grinning, though, because the purple piggy bank threw me a look of disapproval, and Lily stared at me as if I'd just landed from Mars.

"Can I have some?" My voice croaked a little.

She raised her eyebrows. "What do you want it for?"

I explained, haltingly, words constantly getting stuck somewhere between throat and teeth.

"Only if you'd let me taste it." Did she just giggle?

Our gazes met. I took a sharp breath. My palms felt suddenly damp. Did she mean anything by this? I searched those dark brown eyes behind black-rimmed glasses, the smile tugging the edge of those lips.

But it was as if Lily saw through me. In a quiet voice, she said, "Before you get any ideas, I prefer women, okay?"

My breathing seized, my feet became leaden.

Rain splashed against the window. On the shelf, the purple piggy bank smirked.

Forcing a smile like pulling teeth. "N-not presuming anything. Shall I come back later when you're less busy?"

Without waiting for an answer, I retreated, stopping only to retrieve the shattered shards of my heart off the floor.

Wheat noodles sloshed as I scooped them up with a steel colander from the boiling pot into a vat of cold water, all in one smooth motion. Outside the kitchen window, rainwater gushed with gusto. Sundown must have happened, but the sky only shifted between shades of grey; it'd been impossible to tell. Most of the city had been underwater since yesterday, but, from what I could tell, there had been no incidents. Sampan routes remained in service; crocodile fences held.

Straining the noodles dry, I dipped the colander back into the hot liquid for half a minute. Recipes had been recorded, but interpretations of techniques were just that: suppositions. This was the method Grandpa remembered for preparing these noodles: hot, cold, hot. Boiling water for cooking, cold water for rinsing off the excess starch, then a quick douse back in the steaming liquid to get the noodles hot enough to melt the fat. I'd be willing to wager, too, that the sequence did something to the texture and mouthfeel.

I'd made this batch by hand, and they looked good; a test strand broke off with a squeeze of chopsticks; I'd timed it perfectly. The seasoning sat ready in a large bowl: fish sauce, soy sauce, peanut oil that I'd flavoured with garlic and shallot. The fish sauce I'd made from my own fish, the garlic and shallots from crops within the building, the soy sauce and peanut oil I'd traded for. A few shakes of white pepper, a touch of rice vinegar. Then, finally, I picked up the small glass vial that Lily had given me.

"Use sparingly, it's more potent than you think," she'd warned me, when I finally plucked up enough courage to head back to her lab late afternoon.

The milky white goop seemed wholly solid.

"How much is 'sparingly'?" I'd asked.

"Like this, no more than a third of a teaspoon." She'd pinched her thumb and forefinger together, leaving a tiny gap in between where I could see right through to her eyes. My heart thudded hard, threatening to escape my ribcage, so I forced myself to address the piggy bank instead when I'd said bye.

The substance smelled like nothing at all when I dripped a tiny amount into the waiting bowl. But all that changed when I tossed in the hot noodles: an earthy aroma arose – rich, salty and tangy, all at the same time.

A few leaves of coriander and sliced spring onions completed the garnish. Once upon a time, we would serve this dish with fried mince or slivers of roasted pork, marinated in a sauce that turned it red. But well, that'd be yet another thing to try re-engineering one day.

I loaded the bowl onto the tray along with some tea, and headed to Grandpa's room. The bowl was heavier than the teapot and cup combined; I might have been a clown struggling with a balancing act – except this wasn't funny. The chopsticks rolled to one side, coming to rest against the teacup. Somehow, I managed to lose neither the noodles nor the tea.

Grandpa was sitting up in bed, his back propped up against a cloud of pillows, watching something off a local media stream.

"Still experimenting, eh?" He smiled when I walked in, the years on his face creasing like stolen time.

I set the tray down on the over-bed table, smiling back. "Just trying to make it taste like the real thing."

"Or you're trying to make me live longer," Grandpa joked, eyes twinkling. He picked up the chopsticks and tapped the ends together. I settled into the chair by the bed.

I fixed my eyes at the moving pictures on the screen, pretending to be interested, trying not to stare at Grandpa while he ate one slow bite, followed by another.

He wiped his mouth with the back of his hand. "Not bad."

Not bad? I frowned. What did he mean by that?

"Flavour is close, but…"

But? Did I miss a crucial step? I'd kept a careful log of all my experiments, all measurements meticulously tracked, down to whether the variance in ambient temperature had any bearing on the taste or texture.

Maybe Grandpa was having one of those days where he couldn't taste so well.

"What's wrong?" I blurted out.

"Nothing's wrong," Grandpa said, chuckling. "Just the texture of these noodles isn't quite what I'd remembered."

I'd ground the wheat from the last harvest into flour. Countless hours figuring out the right amount of water and egg. Cracked my knuckles kneading the dough. If my skills weren't good enough, then it was never about the lard.

Grandpa patted me on the shoulder. "Don't worry, you just need practice."

Words failed me. I stared at the shuttered window on the wall across the bed. On the other side, the wind howled, trees thrashed their branches in defiance, leaves rustled in protest. I didn't need to see it to know.

"When I was a boy," Grandpa said, between mouthfuls. "I once saw how they made noodles for mass production, without using machines."

He'd kept on eating; it seemed as if he would finish the bowl anyway. Perhaps it was okay after all?

"They had a large table where they mixed the wheat flour, egg, and water. Then they got a guy to swing on a pole to beat down the dough."

I had trouble imagining this. "How?"

Grandpa leaned back and sketched a picture in the air with chopsticks in hand. "They suspended a pole from the ceiling using a length of rope. One of the noodle-makers would ride it astride, like a bicycle. He would bounce up and down –"

"Like a see-saw?"

"Exactly!" Grandpa said, chortling. "Funny sight. The poor bloke was sweating so much he had to wear a towel around his neck the whole time."

I studied my feet. If the poor man from a long time ago had to beat the dough until he sweated buckets, then maybe heart and soul wasn't enough. I sighed. I'd run out of wheat flour. It might be a few weeks before I could try making kolo mee again.

Rain had begun waging a war against the walls of the house, pounding on the roof as if it had giant feet. Automatically, I scanned the edges of the room, checking for leaks.

"You shouldn't worry about reproducing it, you know." Grandpa's voice scissored through my thoughts.

I faced him, bewildered, consciousness caught somewhere between thunder and rain.

"I know you're trying. But those were memories from my childhood, and that was a long time ago." He pointed his chopsticks at something, somewhere. "My favourite noodles came served in white porcelain bowls, koi hand-painted onto the side, eaten with black chopsticks and right by the hawker stalls. Noisy, steamy, probably not the most hygienic."

Grandpa laughed, but I couldn't quite bring myself to join him. "Food is layered with meaning, see? Depends on when you eat, who you eat with, what's happening around you. Know what I mean?"

I rubbed my eyes. I'd never be able to replicate that – *that* memory – no matter how hard I tried. Those days were long gone. Those types of hawker stalls in ground floor shop lots by the streets, the intimate relationship we had with food was largely driven to extinction by landowners more interested in making profits. Was it folly then, to recreate something that had been lost to time, something perhaps better forgotten?

Beyond the window, lightning snapped and thunder growled, splintering the sky.

The chopsticks clicked together as Grandpa laid them down. "Things change, life changes. Memories are merely figments of the past."

I studied his expression, trying to connect my world to his, struggling to stitch his past into my present in a continuous line. He must have caught my confusion.

He cleared his throat. "What I was trying to say – we shouldn't revere a past that never was."

A past that never was? I swallowed a sob. Had I been fooling myself? Was all this effort to recreate the memory of these noodles – more for my selfish sense of identity, than for him, his nostalgia?

He looked down at the over-bed table. I followed his gaze.

His bowl was empty.

Lily's small frame stood hunched over a microscope when I found her on the twenty-first floor. I'd stopped past her lab on the eighteenth, but her empty chair had been pushed halfway out from under the bench, turned outward at an angle as if she'd vaporised and left everything behind. I silently interrogated the purple piggy bank on the shelf, but it had nothing more to say to me.

After wandering up the nineteenth floor and back down to the seventeenth, I gave up and asked the building's computer where she'd gone.

Through an unspoken agreement between us in the past weeks, she had progressively commandeered the top half of the building – leaving the bottom half to me, my rice plants and my fishes. It suited me just fine. I could live with not running into her too often without prior warning.

Lily didn't look up when I hovered near the door of the room.

"How did your noodles go down?" were her first words, though she might have been speaking to the microscope and not to me.

A fruity odour wafted out into the corridor. I wrinkled my nose. She'd found herself another former broom cupboard, if a slightly larger one. This one teemed with freshly grown mushrooms along one wall.

I told her: how we'd have to wait for the next wheat harvest before another trial.

"Oh, too bad…" Her voice sounded far-away, faint and distracted. "Well, the substance should keep in the fridge."

Her slender fingers feathered over the fine adjustment knob, making imperceptibly small movements. Her petite frame hidden in a lab coat one size too big, the hem of her purple dress peeking out underneath, her smooth ankles disappearing inside practical shoes. She was standing on a crate.

A large old-fashioned clock hung on the wall next to a rain-plastered window. I didn't have to look outside to know that the floodwaters hadn't gone down. Thunder thrummed in the distance.

The clock dinged. Half-past five.

I should really be going home to make dinner.

Lily was still focused on whatever she was studying. On my tongue were the words *What are you doing tonight?* but something stopped me. What did I want from her – if she wouldn't be interested in me? A friendship? A collegial existence? I'd forgotten how to do this.

Outside the window, the rain deepened the evening sky.

"See you tomorrow," I said.

Without looking up, her hand still caressing the microscope, she waved goodbye at me with her little finger.

Burning my tongue on too-hot coffee first thing in the morning wasn't the plan. Still, few things beat the black bitterness to stir up the senses.

Beyond the window, the banana tree shone an emerald green, as if blessed by the days of rain – which, thankfully, seemed to have lightened at long last. Somewhere by the clutch of bamboo in the garden, a burung murai started a song.

Congee simmered on the stove, ready to be served. Rice cooked this way always smelled slightly sweet, perfect with a touch of ginger to give it zing. I stirred in a pinch of salt and ladled it into a bowl on a tray. One of these days, I must figure a better way to get food into Grandpa's room. In the end, I managed not to spill any of the congee, but I couldn't stop the spoon sliding to the edge of the tray, where I caught it just in time with my thumb.

Grandpa seemed to be still asleep, his thin blanket folded to one side. A wooden creak echoed, I looked up. The shutters had been left open. They swung gently back and forth, coaxed by the morning breeze spilling into the room, freshly cool on my face. The rain had stopped, the sky brightened to a pale blue.

Strange. Grandpa never opened the window. For some years now, he'd found it got too cold after dusk. But sometime in the middle of the night, he must have got up and pushed the shutters out wide. It must have taken him all his strength; that must be why he was still asleep.

Better check for mosquitoes later.

I placed the tray down onto the table by the bed and reached across to pull the blanket over Grandpa.

"Breakfast is ready, Ah Gung."

He didn't move.

"Ah Gung?"

Did he catch a chill? I leaned forward and touched Grandpa's forehead. My hand jerked back. His skin. Cold.

"Ah Gung?" I whispered. My body sank into the chair. Somewhere outside, a burung cegar cried its high-pitched *kreee-eee-eee*.

That moment of being untethered.

Couldn't he have at least said goodbye? How could he just leave me here?

How did I not know – not see –?

Yes, noodles, for longevity. I'd made him noodles by hand, he'd lived a long life –

But maybe I didn't do it well enough, or often enough. And I was a total, useless failure for –

I stared at the open window.

There might have been one reason he'd opened it: to liberate me from his own ghost.

In his dying moments, he'd thought of me.

My breath hitched. Tears, a rising tide. I didn't fight them.

Grandpa was the only family I'd ever known. And now, I had no one.

The sun sank low on the horizon, the windowpanes of the greenhouse glistened. The evening call to prayer drifted up, rich melodic tones ringing through the streets below. A gentle wind made the plants dance. I reached out and caressed an ear of wheat. Not fully formed yet, the kernels surrendered to the soft pressure between my fingers. New beginnings were just like this: fragile, easily crushed.

I stood by the safety railing on the rooftop of the building, breathing in the unobstructed view under shades of peach smearing the sky. The flood had finally receded, but pools of water remained like unnecessary punctuation. Did we tame nature, or had it tamed us? Maybe a bit of both – the way it should be.

The door to the roof slid open with a swoosh. I knew who it was without turning around.

"Hey, you're on my patch." Lily's elbow brushed mine when she drifted up to the railing beside me, her monochromatic white T-shirt and black jeans stark against the green-gold backdrop of young wheat.

I might have said something in response, I wasn't sure.

The breeze constantly re-sculpted her hair, purple streaks flowing like ribbons, threatening to knot but never managing to.

"He had a good life, you looked after him well. You know that, right?"

I didn't answer. My entire body, an open wound.

Somewhere across the road, a burung rimba led a chorus of birds. We stood there awhile, listening to their song, bicycles rattling in the streets below, escorting echoes of inconsequential conversations.

Lily shuffled her hands into her pockets. "Dinner with me tonight?"

What?

It took me a few moments to find my voice. "I thought you liked –"

She tilted her head back, her laugh lush and luxurious. "No, Jin, I said I *preferred* women. But c'mon. I'm your friend. We can go out, do something."

Thoughts refused to form properly in my head.

"And before you hear it from anyone else," she continued, grinning. "It's not gender which matters, it's who you meet."

My response surprised even myself. "It wouldn't have mattered to

113

me either."

A raise of her eyebrows – a bittersweet reward.

Things change, Grandpa had said. Life changes. Don't revere a past that never was. But no, this was different. There had been a fissure, an unknotting, and I just had to figure out how to stitch the past into the future in a continuous line.

We turned to each other simultaneously in the present.

She said, "How about some nood –" I said, "What do you think about nood…?"

She chuckled, I smiled.

How to stitch the past into the future in a continuous line.

How to shape a single strand of noodle to traverse the thread of history, connecting our souls across time's jagged ravines – a blessing of longevity.

Where the Garden Grows

What would you do if you'd lost everything that mattered? If the land onto which your memories were sown could no longer be called home?

I push my way up the overgrown path, humming a half-forgotten tune under my breath. The grass dampens my footsteps; shrubs on either side rustle gently, their sweet balsamic scent punctuated by the occasional sharp camphor of wild lavender. Overhead, the spindly branches of las encinas intertwine like tendrils hardened by time, their tapered leaves softening the glare of the sun, already harsh before midday. Like the holm oaks, rock roses have grown back onto this former dehesa – now that the humans are gone.

The goats – Dubhe, Merak, Phecda, Megrez, Alioth, Mizar and Alkaid – enjoy a dense forest, and so do I, though perhaps for different reasons. I'd named them after the seven stars of El Cazo, the 'saucepan' in Osa Mayor. My name, Estrella, which I share with my darling Abuelita, just means 'star'. I like to think the goats appreciate some specificity.

They clamber up the hill without hesitation, bells on their collars tinkling with resolve – as always, with Alkaid leading the way. Not that we need the bells; each of them wears a tracker, their locations blinking green on my retina. I could, if I want, see the world through the tiny cameras mounted on their crowns as they munch their way through the shrubs.

In Spanish, we call this terrain dehesa, in Portuguese, montado – I don't know the word in French: managed grasslands which we traditionally used for grazing, especially for our famous Iberian pigs in the old days. I say 'our', and 'we', but there's 'we' and then there's the actual 'we'; my Abuelita was born in the Americas and she'd struggled to make a life here.

You might know what I mean.

I usher the goats forward. The day is warming up rapidly and I want to make it past the hill before midday. I swing the straps of my pack to my right shoulder, pausing only to glance behind us. Good, the chest still follows us. Hovering soundlessly above ground, its cuboid shape throws an unnatural, rectangular shadow over the scruffy vegetation, its metal surface sparkling whenever it catches slivered sunlight through the canopy.

The clink of bells slows as the goats arrive at the crest. At the top of the mound, the trees cluster closer together, as if they need comfort. I head for the largest gap; the chest needs to fit through behind me. A yellowed fragment of newspaper peeks out from the undergrowth, somehow having survived the elements, its edges charred, its partial headline still visible. I avoid reading the words; I know what they say.

Maybe one of the goats will eat it.

Bracing myself, I inhale the herby, heady air.

Breathe. I should be grateful that I'm still able to breathe.

Some days, I can get past this point of the hill with just a dull throb inside. Some days, I can ignore the gaping wound, that feeling as if someone had cleft me open and left my soul to bleed.

At the pinnacle, the treeline abruptly stops, the shrubs thin out. The goats stop here, too; there's not much more to eat beyond this point. Under our feet, scorched, black earth slopes down towards the horizon in a smear of monochrome, a tumble of broken shadows, a colourless shade of lives long faded.

An obliterated world of nothing.

How is it possible that something which took us decades – maybe even centuries – to build, could be all gone, just like that? Abuelita moved here after my yayo died, Mamá grew up here as a child. I –

Tears threaten to overwhelm. I swallow. Must focus.

"Release," I command the chest, my voice hitching on the word. A low hum crescendos to a steady buzz, the sides of the box unfold like a reverse origami. The five brightly coloured drones nestling inside rise one after another: red, blue, purple, green and yellow. Each the size of a small bush, they ascend above the tree-line like mechanical birds. They have names too: Caph, Schedar, Navi,

Ruchbah, Segin; old names for the stars in Cassiopeia. Soaring outwards, they find their positions over the ash-laden landscape.

I choke on the smoke, which I know exists only in my head because all my sensors mark the air as clear. Even now, two summers on, I still smell the death of everything.

Thursday, 26 July 2057
Massive Forest Fire Destroys Eight Thousand Ha in
Fifth day into the wildfire that
villages decimated as
Some 200 fir

I'd told myself that coming back was the right thing to do, that I would be fast enough to get out. Fast enough: two tricky words. Foolish: one factual word.

Somehow, the inside of our house stayed cool. Considering the stifling heat beyond the stucco walls – this came as a welcome surprise. All I could hear was the thumping of my own heart, my blood pounding in my ears.

The fires hadn't yet reached our village, but still, there's no time to waste.

I wiped my sweaty hands over my jeans.

"Mamá!" I called into the house, just in case.

No reply. Please, let her be long gone with the others.

Resting my electric bike over the front door, I hurtled through to my bedroom in the semi-dark.

My room smelled faintly of smoke; I'd left the window open. How careless of me. My go-bag stayed exactly where I'd left it: to the right of my desk. The frequent forest fires since my childhood meant we'd been drilled to be ready to leave at a moment's notice. A go-bag made sense except I'd been a total airhead to leave it at home; I'd already been running late for this morning's maths class. Served me right for staying up too late the previous night, but it had been too much fun chatting with the other engineers, my pals based in Portugal and France. For a while now we'd been collaborating on improving open-source drone designs. But I bet they didn't have to worry about being awake for integral calculus first thing this morning.

A flick of the switch on my desk lamp, a pool of golden light lit up the sketches and notebooks I'd come back for. The contents of the go-bag would make the days ahead easier, but these sketches had been freshly conceived from last night's discussions – I doubted I'd be able to reproduce them from memory. We'd all been told to evacuate; it might be some time before I could speak with my friends again.

The winds had picked up during the day, the fires got close to the next town. When they shuffled all the students from school onto buses in the late afternoon, I'd slipped away and sped back here on my bike. Right this moment, I regretted not telling anyone.

The thing about being a kid with darker skin; people tend to forget about you. They'd look for me last. Maybe they'd find me as a charred corpse, or maybe there'd be nothing left of me.

Best case scenario: Mamá would give me an earful later.

With one hand, I grabbed the go-bag; with the other, I zipped it open, stuffed the notebooks in among a first aid kid, emergency rations and a change of clothes. The scarf. Must not forget the scarf.

A quick glance, just to remember it all. This house – this edition of our lives – might all be gone tomorrow, tonight, in an hour. No go-bag big enough to cram all sixteen years of my memories into.

Filtering masks hung by my bedroom door for moments like these. I grabbed one and secured it over my face. I dropped the spare into the bag – just in case. The scarf I wet in the kitchen sink and wrapped around my neck. Cold water dripped down the inside of my shirt. No time to care, not now.

Time to go. I raced past the kitchen counter. A sheet of paper was pinned there, held in place by a ceramic salt cellar that belonged to Abuelita. As I passed, it fluttered.

Something about that note gave me pause. Mamá had been standing right here at the counter last night, chopping up onions that made her cry. She'd wiped it clean this morning before work, but my breakfast dishes sat crusted with crumbs and dried milk because I'd been late for school. Guilt smacked me; I could… it wouldn't take long – no, not important, not right now.

I stuffed the note into my pocket, moved the bike aside to open the front door.

The latch felt uncomfortably warm between my fingers. Beyond the doorway, the world roared like a furnace, the sky seethed, an angry shade of vivid orange. Acrid fumes coat my throat. Flames had begun licking at the western edge of the village, their flickering tongues just above the roofline of the last house.

Strange how fire mesmerises you, hypnotises you – before it consumes you.

Only one way out: the way I came.

I gave the bike a shove and jumped on.

Smoke stung my eyes. I fought the urge to hold my breath; the mask should do its job. To any goddess who might be listening: please, please keep the winds steady. All that I ask: Fifteen minutes to get to the hill.

Go-bag weighing on my back, my hands throttled up the bike, my fingers found the speed assist. I willed my legs to pedal – hard.

I just needed to be fast enough.

The drones whirr over my head and take up station above the forest. Ascending columns of air, they purr softly like contented cats as they speed up the process of harvesting water above the canopy. My new algorithm should enable them to adjust their positions by detecting ambient humidity, but still I track each and every drone – assessing for any unpredictable behaviour. I'll have time before they reach capacity; when they do, they will come back down to douse the parched earth at my feet. It's tedious, but it helps between the rains.

Something else speeds across the sky. I shade my eyes with one hand but find nothing. Probably just a bird.

Keeping my pack tight across my shoulders, I slide-walk down the slope and onto flat ground, treading over small bushels of eucalyptus shoots, kicking up a potent aroma somewhere between mint and lime.

Almost no other plants came back, not this time.

But hope isn't an option, neither is persistence.

If we can get the ground wet enough, other plants may return. Then, perhaps we could re-seed, regrow.

The chest has parked itself on the closest flat surface, a central control hub for the drones to recharge their batteries and sync their data logs.

My eyes hunt for signs of where the edge of the village used to be. Whose house was there? I pause, struggling to recall. Maybe Señor

Marcelo. My inability to remember gnaws at me.

The fire razed the village and raged for a few days before firefighters got it under control. Nothing remained of the houses by the hill, only unidentifiable debris. My feet found their way down an unmarked stretch, which might once have been the main street. Odd what the fire left behind: a random half-wall here, a stump of a pillar there, a scatter of burned belongings, all seared to blackness.

If we never move back, perhaps nature might move in – with a little bit of help.

A silence permeates here, a heaviness to the air, an uncomfortable hush except for the crunch of my footsteps and the jingle of the goats' bells up the hill, underscored by the drones' hum and the occasional hiss when they release water back onto the earth. Working by my hazy recollection of where houses and community buildings ought to have been, I pick my way towards our house – or where it used to stand.

A loud crack in the distance jerks my head towards the horizon, just in time to see a yellow drone listing to one side, a star falling fast, splashing its water load as it crash-lands, an explosion of electronics stirring up ash and dust. On my retina, a warning blinks red: Segin is down.

I hurry over – but stop. Too late to save it now, I should prioritise the ones still in the air. Did I introduce a bug with last night's firmware update? Having one drone down means my targets for the day will be missed; not great.

Cursing, I head over to the chest, tap the side to open a console. Not everything may be watered to the depth I'd like, but if the remaining drones stay up, I can at least make sure they cover the necessary surface area provided none of the remaining drones malfunction today. It takes me a few minutes to reprogram their flight pattern; they are smart enough to figure out the rest.

Sweat covers my skin. I fish out a canteen from my pack and guzzle from it, the water cool under my tongue. I should probably eat something too – but first, I want to examine what remains of Segin. Lessons can still be learned from the broken, the fallen.

Stepping over ghosts of lives past, I beeline towards the drone's impact site, the hems of my trousers swishing against eucalyptus shoots.

Segin's remains wouldn't have been recognisable if they hadn't been bright yellow. Fragments lay strewn across an area about the size of a house. A groan fights its way up my throat. This won't be a repair job – I'd have to rebuild it.

I lean down to pick up any promising parts and drop them into my pack, my shoes squishing on unevenly damp earth. Salvaging anything reusable is tiresome as tasks go, but resources are scarce, wastage is not an option.

Something orange and glossy nestle among the grey-black and yellow. I pick it up. Likely from a drone, but none of mine use this colour. Overhead, the remaining drones hum, one of them returning to the chest for a brief recharge, two of them heading back towards the canopy, the last one hovering somewhere in between. Where has this fragment come from?

I check on the goats. Merak and Phecda have stopped for a rest, but everything is as it should be.

A voice shouts from the direction of the hill. I stand up, swing around, squinting to locate the direction of the greeting.

A tall, male figure slide-walks down the slope then runs towards me, a small pack hanging off one shoulder, white shoes kicking up black ash with each step. Pale skinned, dark hair pulled back in a bouncing ponytail, he moved with the awkward grace of a colt.

The distance between us steals away his words; I can't hear what he's telling me.

He gets close now. A little younger than me, every bit lankier.

A gasp escapes my lips.

I might even know his name.

Schedar: System Log 20590522
11:32 Relative locations from: Caph, Navi, Ruchbah. No ping reply from Segin. Continuing sector watering. Water capacity at 79%.
11:35 Sector of operation recalculated. Commencing repositioning. Battery charge: 96%.
11:36 Sector scan commenced.

11:37 Temperature: 23.2°C. Mean atmosphere water content: 18.21 g/m3
11:38 Sector scan status: soil moisture critically low (<3.2% VMC). Initialising water collection sequence.
11:36 Relative locations from: Caph, Navi, Ruchbah. No ping reply from Segin. New sector watering commenced. Water capacity at 71%.

Up ahead, smoke bellowed in, suffocating the surrounds with a blanket of grey. My legs began to ache, but the bike held up. Must keep moving. If the fire swept through here, it would accelerate up the hill, then there would be nowhere to go. Not far now.

A scream pierced the air.

I squeezed the brakes. My tyres squealed to a stop.

Where?

There, another scream. This time, I pinpointed its source.

A cottage off the main road, its roof ablaze.

Heat seeped from the frame of my bike. I wouldn't have much time.

I ran first to the window, but drew myself back. Flames on the inside. It might explode.

The front door. Locked. I banged on it hard, pain racing up my arm with every blow. Frantic shouting. Might have been me, might have been someone else.

Suddenly, the door opened. A lean, boyish figure stumbled out, flames flying off the back of his trousers. A child? How could someone have left a child behind?

"Drop and roll!" I yelled. His eyes clouded over, as if he couldn't register the presence of another human being. But then he dropped to the ground, turning himself over back and forth over the earth. Snatching off my scarf, I slapped out the fire around his legs.

For a moment that felt like forever, he laid still. Had he fainted? I leaned down to get closer. His arm moved, his head lifted.

Muttering a prayer to any passing god, I extended a hand. "Can you walk?"

He nodded.

"We must go now. What's your name?"

Tears streaked down his cheeks. His body looked about twelve, but shock seemed to have turned him into a trembling child of five.

I had to ask the question a second time.

"Josué," he finally said, voice quivering.

From the go-bag, I grabbed the spare mask and pulled it over his face. The elastic caught on his hair, but I managed to secure it around his head.

"Breathe," I commanded.

He did. Once, twice. I wanted to give him more time to recover, but we couldn't risk staying any longer.

I gestured at the rack on the back of my bike. "Sit here, hang tight onto me, okay?"

Again, he nodded.

Further ahead, the flames hadn't moved. We were in luck – for now.

The mask stuck to my face with sweat, but I was alive, breathing, and so was my charge.

The bike gathered speed at my bidding.

I rode like wildfire.

I call out his name.

Abruptly, he stops, nearly tripping over his own feet.

"Estrella?" His voice has deepened, cracking with adolescence as he speaks my name.

In two, three strides, he covers the distance between us. His arms envelop me in a crushing hug, his body almost towering over mine. He's grown so much, just in two years.

I laugh, mostly to hide the tears.

"¿Cómo estás?" he asks, releasing me, smiling. The innocent "how are you", which these days tend to mean: are you holding up okay?

"Bien, bien," I lie. Of course, he knows. We all lie.

"And you, did you –?" I start to ask. A shadow slithers across his eyes and his smile evaporates, telling me everything I need to know. So I gesture at the bare land that we stand on. "What brings you back here?"

He wears a pale blue shirt over dark-coloured shorts, a trail of scars visible on his legs. Mischief tugs at the corners of his lips, almost forming a smile. "Could ask you the same."

I glance down at the debris that had been Segin.

His face pales. "I think our drones collided."

I struggle to hide my surprise. Something resembling anger bubbles up, but I bury it. I can't get angry at Josué. If it had been someone else, perhaps.

"So sorry, this is my fault," His shoulders drooped. "It's running on a basic navigation algorithm, I hadn't accounted for what happens when it flies too close to another drone."

Actually, neither had I. My drones would avoid colliding with each other, but if something outside their ecosystem happens to be in the same flight space, they may not do the right thing. Well, I didn't expect to run into anyone else here.

"What does yours do?" I ask, leaning down to pick up another piece.

"Mapping regrowth," says Josué, squatting next to me. "I need data to make the case to get rid of all this eucalyptus." He sweeps an arm out wide. "They're the only thing that survives now. The next fire that comes, the cycle starts again. We'll just have more of this foreign stuff."

I wince. I know he doesn't mean anything by it, but still, it stings. Another thought hits me: my drones might have been keeping the eucalyptus alive, allowing them to take over the landscape. Why hadn't I thought of that?

"And yours?" he asks, a hand shading his eyes as he looks to the sky. "You have a few?"

I point at Schedar, currently a blue contraption hovering over the oaks. "What do you think?"

"Collecting water?" Josué whistles. "Genius."

"Can't take all the credit," Still, I smile. "Some of the ideas came from other engineers I've been working with, in other places affected by fire. But I adapted them for our landscape."

"I can't believe you'd give away recognition like that." He punches me playfully on the shoulder. "You're much too humble."

"I'm just being honest," I protest.

Josué's laughter is not yet that of a man's. "Well, I want a patent to my name."

I nearly choke. A fire burns in my chest, my muscles tense. "You want to make money from this?"

The laughter fades, and the boy in front of me shrugs, nonchalant.

My hands ball into fists, my nails cut into my palm. Correction, I *can* get angry at Josué.

"Really? Josué? You're telling me after all that we've gone through – that money and fame matters more to you? More than our community?"

I am shouting, I realise. Josué stares at his shoes, opting to stay silent.

I shake my head. I don't want to crush a boy's ambitions – but there's a better way. There has always been a better way, though people who profit from inventions will seduce you with their success, disguise their good luck as great ability, convince you that you can do the same if you just try hard enough. Before you know it, your private riches become more important than people you love.

I take a deep breath, then another. Perhaps I could show him.

"Have you got a controller?" I say, changing tact.

He fishes out a tablet from his own pack. I pair with it and transmit the footage from Merak's camera. A shuffle of green leaves fills the screen, then, as Merak turns her head, we get a view of the others: Mizar taking a moment's rest, Alioth crunching his way through a shrub with unparalleled vigour.

"What the –"

"Goats," I explain.

"What? Why?"

"Clearing the undergrowth, minimising the chances that a blaze would happen here again."

Those words weigh heavily. Neither of us wants to dwell on memories of that day.

"But first, we have to rejuvenate the soil," I gesture at the drones. "Hence, the watering."

"How do you know it'll work?"

"We're using both old and new techniques," I continue. "And comparing results with other sites. Another reason why no one should do this alone – what you come up with may only work here, and it may take you a long time. If we do it out in the open, someone else can come along and improve it."

His brows crease in concentration for a brief moment, then he throws his arms up, obviously exasperated. "I'll think about it."

Have I said too much?

"I'm sorry I broke your drone," he says.

I search his face. He isn't lying, that much I can tell. Those dark eyes fill with an earnest yearning, a desire to please.

"Will you let me help you rebuild it?"

I smile.

"I'd like to find something first," I say, shouldering my pack.

"Sure, let me help."

He sounds so self-assured, but I know he must be feeling what I'm feeling. This deep-seated dread, this self-loathing – survivor's guilt, they told us – this unshakeable unease that we are trespassers through a graveyard of the past, that we have no right to be here.

I let Josué follow me into the area of ruined earth where houses had once stood – my neighbours' homes. Where families slept until tomorrows, where friends enjoyed meals together, where lives had been sacrificed to Hunraqan, the god of wind, storm and fire.

Neither of us say a word, keeping our thoughts to ourselves.

Every so often I lean forward slightly, scouring the ground, getting my scanner to magnify anything that seems promising. This is something that I can't teach a drone to look for, not yet. Not until I know that it has worked.

"What are we looking for?" Josué asks, after a while.

I stand upright, holding his gaze. It takes all my will to keep my voice from cracking.

"Home."

We hit the edge of the forest. I had to ditch my bike. The path snaked upwards, riding to the crest was out of the question. If Josué could walk, we'd be faster on foot. Down the other side of the hill – if my sense of direction hadn't gone entirely awry – help should be at hand. The sudden green coolness of the trees brought welcome relief, but the winds could still change, and I wanted us out of these woods.

"You okay?" I called to the boy behind me.

"It hurts, but I can walk."

From my go-bag, I handed him a bottle of water. "Drink up, we have to keep going." Still, I paused to see if he really was fine. He'd developed a slight limp. I scavenge around the undergrowth, found a dead branch for him to use as a walking stick.

"Come, stay in front of me so I can keep an eye on you."

Mostly I hoped like hell that he wouldn't pass out. That would be another problem I didn't want to deal with –

He stopped suddenly, doubling over, almost toppling forward.

I grabbed him just in time, right when he heaved the contents of his stomach onto the grass. Sobs racked his shuddering body, punctuated by gasps as he fought for air.

"My abuelita –" his voice rasped, shoulders shaking. "She didn't wake up. I –"

Knots wormed in my gut. I still had no idea where Mamá might be.

Wait, the note. Did I lose it?

I reached into my pocket, brushing my fingers against the reassuring, crisp texture. The paper unfolded into my hands, crumpled and creased. Mamá's writing scrawled in blue ballpoint.

Fighting back the urge to cry, I mouthed the words. A tear uncoiled from my eye, soiling my cheek. I swallowed the rest. Grieving, that could come later. Right now, we must keep moving.

The shrubs slid cool against our hot skin as we climbed, as if reaching out to comfort us. Dusk had begun to fall, a chill settled, almost pleasant.

Josué paused, tugged at my arm.

"What is it?"

He pointed a finger at the air. "Look."

It took me a while to realise what he was staring at.

All around us, small glowing dots blinked on, and off again. The stars, they had come down to earth.

Fireflies.

"What does it mean?" Josué whispered.

For a moment I stood stock still, too transfixed to answer. I hadn't seen any in years, not since when Abuelita was alive. I gave Josué the same explanation she gave me.

"When you see fireflies, it means there's hope, that a new world would be born through death."

How I clung onto that hope.

Mi niña,
Forgot to tell you I'll be late home from work today.
Leftovers in the fridge.
Don't wait for me for dinner.
Un beso,
Mamá.

It's not easy to visually identify where our house used to stand when the land, devoid of any distinguishing features, spreads out vacantly like a blank slate. I've tried a number of times before today, keeping a log of where I'd searched.

Josué follows me as I pace around from where the front door ought to have been, around to the side of the house, past a spot where there used to be a porch.

Mamá had left for work earlier that day in the car; she probably assumed that the school would take care of me. When we got to the nearest emergency shelter, they'd shuffled Josué away, giving him first aid. They hustled me over to another stall, checking my vitals. By then, my tears flowed freely; I didn't care who was watching, whatever they thought of me – I just wanted to look for Mamá. A few days later, I found her, unconscious in a different shelter. They told me she didn't have long. But by then time had lost all meaning. *Don't wait for me for dinner,* she'd said, but now I'd be waiting forever.

It would be weeks, months afterwards before I began wondering about the boy I'd rescued.

After locating the likely spot, I touch my hand to the earth. It's moist. Good. I scan for the drones. One of them has been through here. I file the location away for later reference.

"What are you looking for?" Josué asks again, for about the fifth time.

I squat down and examine the soil. Then I spot them: several different shoots, planted in a specific formation: maize, beans, squash.

Just like my ancestors have done.

Joy erupts within my gut but I contain my excitement – not until I have cross-verified them with my friends. All those long hours and late-night conversations might have finally paid off.

"Josué – here!" I point them out to him.

At first, he struggles to notice the tiny leaves, but when he does, awe invades his voice too. "Not eucalyptus! What are these?"

"Results from an ancient growing technique from Mesoamerica."

Wide-eyed, he looks to me for further explanation.

"There's a lot to the old ways. The maize will provide the beans with a climbing trellis, the beans will fix nitrogen and stabilise the maize in high winds, while the squash will shade the ground to keep it moist."

I get up, dusting the ash off my trousers.

Not far from these, another small plant has opened its true leaves. My delight escapes in a squeal as I bend down, touching a leaf tenderly.

"Is that... a tomato?" Josué gets down beside me, hands on his knees. "How is it growing?"

"Well, fires are not all bad. It's just... we've forgotten how to tame them, how to live alongside them."

"I don't understand, it's not native here." Impatience clouds his voice. He jabs a finger at the other shoots. "None of these are. They shouldn't have survived."

He doesn't really mean it like that, I tell myself, he doesn't know what he's saying.

Exhale, breathe.

"You know how the eucalyptus is the first to come back after a fire?" I ask.

"Yes?"

"Those kinds of plants – they have thick seed coats, so germination is triggered by fire, or smoke. Before the blaze, I'd been working with others to modify food crops to have the same –"

"But they won't survive here!" Josué interrupts, looking incredulous.

I stand up slowly now, all the while holding his gaze. "If I can grow roots on this land, then so can a damn tomato."

He takes a hesitant step backwards, but he nods. "I'm sorry, I don't mean –"

I wave his words away. One day, he might truly understand.

Silence hangs heavy around us. It may be some time before we hear green leaves rustle here once more.

Josué's voice suddenly breaks the spell. "I suppose… home is where the garden grows."

Can it be that simple? Maybe so. Abuelita would have something to say about that. I wipe the sudden wetness on my cheeks.

The sun has climbed high. Sweat pours down my back, drenching my shirt. My stomach rumbles.

"Lunch?" I ask.

But Josué is now thinking aloud. "Are you saying we could scale this? Rebuild the community differently? Use less land for feeding ourselves?"

"Perhaps, yes."

"If we get rid of the eucalyptus, other things may grow back. More food for the goats!" He laughs.

But he has a point. Apart from being fire attractors, eucalyptus are greedy drinkers. Maybe I could use his help.

Together, we push our way up towards the crest of the hill where the forest begins. The grass dampens our footsteps, shrubs on either side rustle gently. One by one, I call to the goats. I'll come back later for the drones; they won't tire. Josué hums a half-forgotten tune under his breath.

"Estrella, look."

We only see it because the leafy branches of las encinas intertwine in velvet shadows, softening the harsh glare of the sun.

In broad daylight, stars blink under the branches.

Fireflies.

The Scent of Green

The problem was apparent even before Chloë could see the photobioreactors of Bluefirth – the distinct smell punched through the dappled morning daylight, a seashore's worth of dead creatures left for too long under a hot sun.

Next to her, one hand on the wheel, Doug grinned at the face she made. "Quite something, isn't it?" He took a swig from a metal canteen, which Chloë hoped contained water and nothing else. "I usually have to make this the last stop on my rounds, else I get complaints from the other settlements on the way."

Doug's laden utility vehicle had made the journey relatively smooth, but the rough road that cut through the wild woodland was pitted with holes, the mud tossed into miniature sculptures by the sheer force of rain. The norm now: endless cycle of storms punctuated with droughts. Up north the climate remained wetter, even if it averaged just several degrees higher compared to thirty years ago.

How Doug coped with these road conditions on a weekly basis without complaint, Chloë would never know – but something like admiration replaced trepidation; there must be other settlements at least as difficult to get to, journeys made complicated by the erratic weather.

The woods ebbed away behind them, and their vehicle emerged into an open meadow so wide that Chloë couldn't locate the edges. At its heart, surrounded by wildflowers, a monumental structure of glass and steel materialised: Bluefirth spanned a sprawling series of hemispheres, glistening in the mid-morning sun. Photobioreactors had been built into the lower half of the walls, luminous green bricks holding up the steel frames and the glass panes.

"You didn't warn me," she chided Doug. "It's marvellous."

"Wanted you to see it for yourself." He chuckled. "Microalgae and photovoltaic glass. Genius combination."

They pulled up to the main entrance; no one else seemed to be in sight. Still reeling from awe, Chloë hopped out and gathered her belongings from the back seat. The small satchel she grabbed and slung across her body, the large pack she swung onto her shoulders with practised ease.

"See you in a week," Doug called, driving around the corner – likely to drop off medical supplies. She waved at his departing silhouette, the solar panels on the roof of his vehicle glinting in farewell.

Another week, another new assignment. Another opportunity to show goodwill to a remote community. This one wouldn't be easy. Taking a deep breath, Chloë approached the doors. They slid open without fuss, as if they'd been anticipating her arrival.

Stands of palm trees stretched up into the height of the entrance dome. Without a full tropical forest canopy, they dominated, their leaflets combing the roofs, slicing the rays of sun into slivers. Whistling under her breath, Chloë called the palms by their true name: *Metroxylon sagu*. The people of Bluefirth had definitely been clever with their resources; few places like this existed any more – where you could grow such plants away from their native climate and enjoy their harvests.

Chloë sniffed; the microalgae smell seemed tamer here; it lingered, but never entirely gone. The unmistakable scent lurked in the background, a persistent ostinato in the undertow. Perhaps these buildings had some form of air filtration? A fair assumption, given the mild temperatures.

No one else appeared to be in this dome, apart from a few butterflies. Had her Bluefirth contact forgotten she was coming today? Chloë shrugged off her large pack, then her jacket. Well, she could wait. Enough interesting plants lurked in the undergrowth to keep her occupied.

A cheerful, booming voice rang out. "Ms. Qing! Welcome!"

It belonged to a well-built man, his deep taupe skin radiating health under neat black hair speckled with grey. Eyes bright, he rushed up to greet Chloë, shaking her hand with enthusiasm.

"Pleased to meet you," she said.

"İlkay." His grin, infectious; smiling back wasn't optional. "I trust you had a good journey?"

When İlkay gestured that he should take her pack, Chloë raised her hand to decline. "I can manage, thank you."

"Shall we get you settled first?" The kind of question that didn't wait for an answer.

The far end of the dome diverged into two passages. İlkay led her down the right tunnel which opened into another gigantic glass hemisphere, green with familiar trees: an oak, a sycamore, a copper beech.

"Bluefirth was intended to be an eco-resort," said İlkay, waving a hand at their surrounds.

"What changed?"

"Like all things at the time, the business couldn't survive, so they shut it down." İlkay didn't seem to be too disappointed by that.

They walked past a silver birch, lush with dainty heart-shaped leaves. Chloë inhaled the mix of scents – a freshness imparted by species of flora native to the region, underlined by the undertone of the microalgae that seemed ever present. This dome had been made to replicate the outside world – or how it *used* to be. There would be plants here that no longer existed out in the wild.

"You've been here a long time?" she asked. İlkay appeared older than her, but even he would have been born after the submersion of the last coastal city in the country.

"A little more than twenty years," he said, with a slight shrug. "I'd come from a settlement in the west. When I arrived at Bluefirth, they'd nearly completed the installations of the photovoltaic glass, but I brought the microalgae farming technology with me."

"Impressive," said Chloë. An honest assessment.

"Not much wind around here, given how sheltered we are. So, sun and photosynthesis it had to be."

Several homely cabins perched within small groves, all different in their design and colour, each awaiting their own fairy tale.

"These were for visitors?"

"They still are." İlkay smiled. "Residents have assigned housing on the other side of the main hall."

They arrived at a log cabin tucked away from main thoroughfare, flanked by some young oak trees. The rosemary bush under the front window effused a gentle camphorous scent, mingled with mint-green.

"Here you go, this is yours for the week," İlkay said. "Make yourself at home."

Then he motioned to their right, where another glass tunnel led around the corner. "See you at the main hall for lunch? Head through that way, you can't miss it."

How grand it would be to partake in a communal meal here every day, under a large glass dome, surrounded by greenery – all edible? Chloë paused by the fig trees, promising a harvest of fruit in a few months' time. Kale and radishes grew next to assortments of herbs and leaves in rows of raised beds; smaller, free-standing planters delineated spaces between long wooden tables, where Bluefirth residents sat and chattered, enjoying the day's lunch offering. Cosier spots dotted the edge of the dome, perhaps for those who wished for a little more privacy. Here, the aroma of food won out over the odour of microalgae – much to Chloë's relief.

A figure stood up and waved frantically from the middle of the hall – İlkay – stuck between merry clusters of diners tucking into their lunch. It took an awkward moment to decipher his haphazard semaphore, but she eventually understood he wanted them to meet over at the kiosks where food was being served.

"I hope you don't mind," he said, after they'd filled their trays. "I asked Lovorka to join us."

He guided Chloë towards a table in a corner, at which a pale, athletic woman was already seated, her violet hair loosely pulled into a topknot. She reached out to shake Lovorka's hand – no warmth in the other woman's greeting, a restrained smile.

Chloë slipped her satchel over the back of her chair, making sure she wouldn't be in the way of passers-by behind her. İlkay settled into his seat with a contented sigh.

"Thought it'd be best to introduce you early. Lovorka is our lead horticultural engineer. Obviously, you'll have free run of the place, but should you need anything, she'd be happy to help you –"

"Wait." Lovorka raised an eyebrow. "I thought you're here to help *us*. What would *you* need help with?"

Chloë stiffened. Doug had warned her that not everyone would be so welcoming. Best de-escalate it quickly. She mustered a smile. "I have just arrived, so I've not yet seen –"

"Oh, you will," İlkay cut in. His eyes still twinkled with enthusiasm, but was that a quizzical glance thrown at his colleague? "Lovorka is best placed to show you around – she knows this place inside out. I'm sure she would agree."

He looked to Lovorka for affirmation, but she said nothing and resumed picking at her salad with a fork. If İlkay was frustrated, he showed no sign. "Afterwards, I could show you our harvesting hub – which might as well be a harvesting *hut*."

When Chloë merely smiled and Lovorka remained sullen, İlkay shrugged, and continued, "So, how about I describe our true dilemma here."

His tone had darkened, all the prior light-hearted humour gone. He waved one hand at their surroundings. "You can see we're obviously thriving. We're growing to the extent that we need more people to keep it running. Problem is, Bluefirth has a reputation. A certain… how shall we say –?"

"The stink from the photobioreactors puts people off." Lovorka interjected, drawing a little circle in the air with her fork to punctuate her point. "It's not that bad once you get used to it."

"I see…" said Chloë. A glance at İlkay – he didn't seem bothered by Lovorka's brusqueness. Good. At least they agreed on what the problem was.

"We've hit the limits of what our filtration and purification systems can do." He started on the salad on his plate.

"And it'd be entirely comical if the implications weren't so serious." Lovorka pierced a piece of spirulina protein, her lips a thin line. "Bluefirth acts as a backup supplier of energy and food to a number of settlements in this region."

Chloë lowered her own fork. "So you need to ramp up production before the winter storms hit."

"You catch on quick," said Lovorka.

Chloë ignored the barb.

"More settlements have appealed for our help in the last couple of years," İlkay continued. "Without people willing to stay and work here at Bluefirth, we simply can't keep up."

"If we suffer, so do they," Lovorka finished. "You'd think that would be enough reason for them to come and help here. But – no."

A moment of silence descended as the meal consumed their attention.

In her mind, Chloë ran through all the other cases her team at Central had dealt with lately. Lack of resources – distressingly common. But Bluefirth's particular challenge was as unique as its combination of power sources.

İlkay spoke first. "We've heard of your work with other settlements, in particular on – how shall we say – non-standard issues. Let me reassure you that we're very glad of your assistance."

He punctuated the end of his sentence with a smile; someone who always seemed to know the right thing to say at the right time.

Lovorka, however, might take more convincing.

Turning to her, Chloë asked, "How about if you show me around this afternoon? Then perhaps tomorrow... we can even get some work started while I'm here. I can help."

Did she sound too eager? She really needed to work on that.

İlkay clapped his hands together, evidently satisfied. "I'll leave you both to chat while I get back to work. See you later?"

With a parting wave, he took his tray to a trolley, then disappeared through a doorway between a young fig tree and some hollyhocks.

The moment İlkay moved out of sight, Lovorka leaned forward, bristling. "Look, tell me why you're really here?"

Chloë blinked. "What do you mean?"

"I know what you guys get up to in Central."

This kind of distrust had occasionally shown up in other settlements she had been to, though it had been getting rarer over time. Still, sometimes stories had a way of hanging around long after myths were dispersed.

Conscious not to cross her arms – there wasn't any need to be defensive – Chloë asked, as gently as she could, "I'm assuming no one has explained to you what we really do?"

"No need for that." Lovorka grimaced. "Steal knowledge from

different settlements, then give it to others for free? Jeopardise our chances of making fair trade agreements amongst ourselves? I don't need an explanation. No, thank you."

Chloë breathed deeply, buying herself time to think.

"Sharing isn't stealing," she said. "We learn from settlements we visit, bring practical knowledge we've gathered to others who need it – just as I've come here to do."

"Really?" Lovorka's voice sounded just a bit too loud over the lunchtime din. "I heard what happened at Riverton. I don't believe you."

"I think you misunderstand," Chloë said, persisting. "Settlements are usually focused on their own unique issues. It's not easy for them to learn how other communities resolved various challenges."

Lovorka's lips curled with impatience, but she remained silent.

Chloë moved her hand off the fork she'd been toying with. Had she hit upon a small semblance of truth?

"At Central, we act as a knowledge hub, setting up programs so that settlements can partner with each other based on their needs," Chloë explained. "We take nothing of material value in return for what we do. No community should be left to stagnate or to struggle on their own."

Lovorka's laughter drowned the last of her words even before Chloë could utter them.

"Makes no sense to me that you take nothing in return. We're all trying to survive. Why would you do that?"

It had been a long while since Chloë last had to give the whole spiel. She reached deep for some self-restraint. "Like Bluefirth, in the beginning we became a hub. We started helping out smaller communities around us – just like you. Decades on, as other hubs found us, it seemed only right that we should help each other thrive. It's just something that citizens of Central have always done."

Lovorka crossed her arms and leaned back. "Explain to me, then: someone I know at Riverton said a Centralist showed up one day, hung around for a week and never came back. Then a month later, Riverton's techniques were being used elsewhere at Clyde. What do you say to that?"

"That's actually quite normal."

"Oh?"

Chloë sighed. Far more justification than she bargained for. What would it take to convince this woman? "Usually, a generalist – like me – would visit and understand the situation first. Perhaps the problem is best solved by a specialist or in partnership with another settlement. Clyde was partnered directly with Riverton."

Lovorka's face seemed to soften a little.

"It's common for settlements to distrust each other initially," continued Chloë. "There's not always a way for us to learn much about each other before we meet."

Lovorka paused, as if contemplating. Around them, the crowd of diners had thinned significantly.

"Fine. It's not like we have too many options," Lovorka conceded. "And I suppose I can make use of a spare pair of hands this week."

Relief washed over Chloë. She might have just won Lovorka over enough to make progress. For now, at least.

They looked down at their empty plates.

"The tropical wing is next door," said Lovorka. "Let's start there."

Being in close proximity to flora so rare – yet familiar – after such a long time felt rather like running into long lost friends. Chloë's heart leapt at the sight of a large bush with brilliant red, five-petalled flowers near the entrance. She reached out and tenderly touched its leaves. *Hibiscus rosa-sinensis,* just like the ones her grandfather used to win prizes for. How long ago had she seen one of these in the flesh?

"Are you a horticulturist?" Lovorka asked.

"No, not exactly." Chloë drew back her hand. "I specialise in how to use plants beyond just nutrition – dyes, inks, perfumery and the like."

"Perfumery? That's unusual."

Chloë considered elaborating, but she picked up on a distinct scent in the air. The unmistakable smell of microalgae had returned, but here, it had taken on a different character.

An idea dawned on her; making it work would depend on the type of plants cultivated at Bluefirth. The advantage of having a settlement set up within a former botanical garden – there ought to be plants here that would normally be difficult to find anywhere but in their native habitats on the other side of the planet.

Even though she already knew the answer to the question, she asked, "Do you have the *cananga odorata* here?"

Lovorka gave her a strange look but led her to the tree in a corner on the far side of the dome, a much taller specimen than Chloë expected. Branches reached out on all sides with glossy, pointed oval leaves; here and there, pale blossoms drooped like green-yellow accents. The scent was heady and intense – somewhere between a sweet fruit and a flower.

"Roll up your sleeve and breathe in at the crook of your elbow." Chloë demonstrated the pose to Lovorka.

"What? Why?"

Despite her obvious scepticism, Lovorka copied Chloë's bizarre instructions. When she pulled her face away from her elbow, she wrinkled her nose. "Wow. Okay, I have to admit that's a neat trick."

"Yes, it's a handy way to reset your olfactory sense."

Lovorka seemed genuinely impressed. "I don't remember the last time I was able to smell the ylang-ylang properly like this."

"What about the microalgae? Can you still smell it?"

Lovorka stuck her nose into the inside of her elbow a second time. "I think I've got a combination of the ylang-ylang *and* the microalgae just in the background."

"Our noses adapt to our environment over time."

"Right, fine, I get it." Impatience crept back into Lovorka's voice. "Anything else you want to see?"

Chloë held back a sigh. Convincing Lovorka of her idea would take time.

Over the next hour, she asked for specific plants, and Lovorka guided her to them. They tested the earthiness of the vetiver grass, the resinous mastic tree, camphorous green of the common myrtles, the tang of citrus trees.

All of a sudden, Lovorka stopped, and laughed. "I see what you're doing. You're thinking we can replant a few of these all around the area to neutralise the smell? It won't work. We've tried that. The scent of green is a stubborn one."

"Not neutralise." Chloë smiled. "Perfumes are just a blend of scents so that they come together in a harmonious balance. Your citrus plants here, their fragrances are short-lived and they tend to be what you smell first – we call these the top notes. Some scents come a little later to our senses and hang around for a while, like the ylang-ylang. These are the heart or the middle notes."

"Notes, as in a chord? Like music?"

"In a manner of speaking, yes," said Chloë. "Then chemically you need a fixative, something that holds down and extends the aroma, like our friend the vetiver grass here, or the resin of a styrax tree."

Lovorka appeared to be thinking. "The main source of the external smell is the harvesting area. We've placed it as far away from the residences as possible precisely because of the problem. It's in the east-most part of the complex."

"What do you suggest?" Chloë asked. She could be ready for anything at this point.

"Let's see if this could even work at the site."

They gathered a few of the fragrant flowers, fruits and leaves to take with them. From her satchel, Chloë pulled out small cellophane bags to house the flora samples. Out of habit, she labelled them before stowing them safely away.

Together, they walked back through the cafeteria, the entrance, and a thriving vertical food farm. Then, they cut through a space with wildflowers in full bloom. But beyond that, the domes housed a scattering mess of untended plants. Once upon a time, these must have been gorgeously landscaped, but without human hands some plants proved more dominant than others. In one glasshouse, a giant agave stretched out its spiky leaves like green inert tentacles. The occasional tree threatened to burst the glass above it. Nature and human-made construct in a silent power struggle.

"Restoring this place has been a challenge." Lovorka waved an arm around them. Their feet trod an uneven path cracked by time – or by plants flexing their roots. "We've got so much undeveloped space that had been abandoned when the eco-resort closed down. There aren't enough of us to tend to everything."

Would allowing the biodomes to rewild have been an option? Chloë glanced back at the giant agave. Humans had interfered here from the beginning. No, we started this, so it remained our responsibility to maintain balance with nature.

"How long ago did it close down?"

"About fifty years? We designated some wildflower patches for the pollinators, which also helps to keep maintenance low. I've been here for ten years – there's still so much to do."

Chloë stole a sidelong look at Lovorka. Her exasperation was undisguised. "Why did you stay?"

Lovorka didn't answer immediately.

The path had narrowed, shrunk by tall, overzealous bushes on either side. Chloë squinted. Impossible to identify the plants without stopping for a closer look, and Lovorka seemed intent on marching them onwards.

"I didn't have anywhere else to go," she suddenly said.

A story lurked behind the sentiment. Chloë swallowed her questions, opting instead to allow her companion space to speak freely.

"I was born into a small caravan of travellers who never settled," said Lovorka. "But many of them were getting old. We had to change our way of life, it was no longer sustainable. Let's just say I had to drop the habit of fighting for survival – and learn to trust."

She flashed Chloë a pensive smile. There might have been a hint of pain.

Ahead of them, the path tapered further, so they walked in single file with Lovorka leading the way.

"My grandfather was a traveller too," said Chloë. "He eventually settled in Central, found work as a farmer there."

"I can tell you inherited his green thumbs."

"If only!" Chloë chuckled. "But he taught me a great deal."

The odour of seaweed grew stronger. The path led them into a narrow glass passage. It opened up into another giant dome, which, unlike the ones prior, was completely devoid of plants. A small wooden cabin, somewhere between a shed and a hut, stood alone in the middle like a soliloquy.

The smell was now overwhelming. Chloë struggled not to gag.

"We suspect they originally used this area to manage waste," Lovorka said. She'd put a hand over her nose and mouth. "It would explain why there are sections set so far from the main buildings. There is an identical space on the west side which we use for composting."

They finally reached the cabin, where the door was open and they could see İlkay working inside, his face under a mask. A trolley was parked near the doorway, full of glass bricks containing deep green liquid, similar to the ones Chloë had seen on the outer edges of Bluefirth in the morning. Sliding doors on both sides of the dome had been left wide open, presumably to encourage airflow, but that wasn't working particularly well.

İlkay looked up and waved to them through the open door. "You've made good progress?"

"We have ideas," Chloë said, smiling.

Frustration furrowed Lovorka's brow. "There's no way I can smell anything while we're in here. How about we try outside?"

Chloë turned to İlkay. "Can we have a sample to take with us?"

Armed with a small amount of the microalgae, they made their way through the eastern doors and headed for the woods beyond the meadow. Humidity made the air heavy; it was surprisingly warmer outside than in. Chloë welcomed the heat on her skin, but the sight that greeted them made her sick in her stomach: trees with their trunks split in half, exposing the heartwood inside, the remains of their branches jutting into the sky. Damage from a recent storm.

She paused, took a deep breath, steeled herself.

Lovorka seemed unperturbed, and stuck her face into her elbow. "Phew, all my clothes probably stink. It's going to bother me now."

Nonetheless, being outdoors felt like they'd been granted a gift. The seaweed smell pervaded the air but it was almost bearable. Together, they sat side by side on a freshly fallen log.

"We probably didn't need that sample after all." Chloë chuckled and pulled out a notebook and the plant samples from her satchel. She held up a small bunch of immortelle and inhaled gently: turmeric, tarragon, and pepper all at the same time.

She handed it to Lovorka, who wrinkled her nose. "That's just weird."

Undeterred, Chloë passed a small branch of mastic shrub to her companion.

"Promising," said Lovorka, after giving it a sniff.

One by one, as they went through their samples of plants and fruits, Chloë scribbled down notes on whether they went well together with the scent of sea-green in the backdrop.

Something tugged at Chloë's memory. From her satchel, she extracted a tiny, nondescript amber bottle. She twisted off the black cap and held it up to her nose. "Forgot I'd brought this with me, just in case it came in useful."

"Here." She handed it over to Lovorka. "It's potent, you'd want to –"

But her warning came too late and Lovorka screwed up her face in a mix of shock and revulsion.

"What the –!"

Chloë laughed.

Lovorka knew by now what to do, so she reset her senses and tried again. "Okay, I'm stumped. This is amazing. What is it?"

"Choya nakh. A balsam of roasted seashells, originally made from an ancient process in India."

"You roast seashells to get this?"

She gave the bottle another sniff, and then smelled the air around them. "Seems as if it sweetens the sharp edges of the microalgae – just a tiny bit."

Chloë hid a smile; her patience had finally paid off.

Lovorka returned the bottle; Chloë twisted the cap back on.

"Tell me something. How do you get all the scents into a bottle?"

"First, we extract the essential oils, but the process differs depending on the plant. Steam distillation is the most common, though there are other extraction processes. For resins you tap the trees for the gum. For citrus, it's with a cold expression of the peel, and so on."

"So you mean if I've got enough of these plants available in Bluefirth, I can extract the oils even while we're growing the plants round the harvesting hub?"

"I don't see why not."

Lovorka's sudden grin stretched from ear to ear, and Chloë wondered what she had in mind.

Dusk had become darkness by the time they returned to the complex and paced the area around the cabin, plotting out what they could plant where, taking into consideration a mix of aesthetics, and which plants went well together. Vetiver would go directly next to the harvesting cabin.

"Citrus next to entryways, I think," Lovorka postulated. She had found a large piece of paper onto which they'd sketched out a plan. "Tomorrow, we tidy and sort out the types of soil we need here. We should probably also start a few plants propagating."

"So much to do," breathed Chloë. The long day's effort had translated to a soreness in her back.

Lovorka, on the other hand, seemed exhilarated, bouncing from one thing to the next. "Yes, it will take time. Pity you're only here for the week."

Chloë gave a little shrug, but satisfaction glowed beneath her weariness. This tactic worked every time: how someone's scepticism could be turned into passion the moment creativity was encouraged to take hold.

A persistent, thundering noise rattled overhead. Chloë opened her eyes. An unfamiliar bed, an unfamiliar room, all still shrouded in cozy darkness. Not morning yet.

She'd retreated to her cabin after a hearty dinner in the main hall. Sleep had overtaken her like a warm blanket, but now the noise outside made it impossible to fully relax.

Chloë swung her legs over the side of the bed. Her shoes were where she'd left them. Her jacket hung off the hook next to the entrance. Draping it loosely over her shoulders, she opened the door and stepped through.

Out here, the din became deafening. The darkness rendered it too difficult to see the roof of the dome, but the sound was unmistakable. A severe rainstorm. Was it heavier than normal? Or was the noise amplified by the glass of the entire complex?

The rosemary bush smelled sharp but sweet. It would have been nice if she could also smell the rain, though its amplified clatter was far from pleasant. Perhaps Bluefirth also needed some specialised help from an acoustic engineer.

The next few days fell into a steady pattern. Lovorka and Chloë would meet for breakfast and begin the day's work – tidying the grounds around the harvesting cabin, adjusting the soil, checking the seeds, and nurturing new cuttings. A few plants were transplanted from the tropical wing. Walking past a fragrant tree or shrub changed how everything smelled relative to the dense seaweed green of the microalgae. It would take a few years for everything to mature and make a real difference, but this location would be unique once they were done.

On Chloë's last morning in Bluefirth, they waited in the entrance hall for Doug to arrive.

The sago palms stood serene in their majesty. Chloë breathed deeply. She had never quite known how to describe the scent in their presence.

Lovorka had been brimming with ideas all week, and today wasn't any different. "The way we've taken an unorthodox route to solving the microalgae problem will attract attention. Perhaps it'll bring a few curious settlers."

"We'll spread the word," Chloë promised. There was just one more thing. She reached into her satchel and brought out the amber bottle. "I want you to have this."

Lovorka's eyes widened. "Are you sure?

Nodding, Chloë handed it to her.

Lovorka gauged the weight of the object within her palm. "This is rare and precious. I can't –"

"It's not something I use a lot of, and I have a few more bottles at home." Chloë smiled. "Please, take it."

Before she could say anything else, Lovorka handed her a cellophane bag. It contained a cutting of a plant carefully installed into a vial of liquid.

"This should survive the journey back," Lovorka grinned.

Chloë stared open-mouthed at the cutting. The leaves gave it away. A hibiscus rose. "Thank y –" she began to say.

"No," Lovorka cut in. "Thank *you* for helping us. And for teaching me something new. Promise me you'll come back to see what we've created together."

They embraced, just as the sound of Doug's utility vehicle approached.

A year later.

"Something for you," a cheery voice called out from the doorway of Chloë's studio.

The afternoon sun filtered in from the windows, ordaining the young hibiscus rose bush in the room with a certain optimism. She glanced up from her reading. Doug had a steaming mug of dandelion brew in one hand; in the other, he held out a small box towards her.

"Special delivery from Bluefirth."

The box had been wrapped with brown paper and tied with string, but the scent emanating from the parcel gave away its contents. Inside, a folded note covered a delicate glass vial containing a deep green liquid. The label on the vial read: "Bluefirth East Wing".

Chloë opened the note.

You once said it's not easy for settlements to learn from each other. How about a shared library of signature scents – unique to each settlement – so we can learn about each other even before we meet? – L.

Chloë's hand flew to her mouth. Such a genius way to extend goodwill; a stepping stone towards building necessary trust between settlements.

"Well," said Doug. He took a loud sip from his mug. "What is it?"

Chloë carefully replaced the vial back in its box. "A scent of green, but perhaps also a scent for success."

Night Fowls

I peeled off my gloves, one finger at a time, making sure nothing on the outer surface touched my skin. The plants in my garden were less lethal than their original cousins in the wild, but still, one couldn't be too careful.

The summer sun had deserted the day, throwing pinks and oranges at the clouds rolling overland, turning the normally blue-grey sea into a multi-coloured jewel. Starlings chattered as they settled on Brighton West Pier – once a metallic, skeletal ruin, now a thriving greenhouse and mussel farm. The dark curves of its Victorian frames rose out of the water against the lazy spin of the Rampion wind turbines further out to sea.

I'd been allocated a house facing the beach, a rare lot with a garden that I worked hard to keep in shape. My neighbour's garden, however, had always been a bit of a mystery. Mrs. Leigh had been using a wheelchair for as long as we'd lived next door to each other, and I'd never seen her move about in her own garden – yet it was always pristine. Almost too perfect. How did she do that? She kept so busy distributing food for humans – her official portfolio assigned by the Cross-Species Citizens' Committee. I should learn her secrets, but I never seemed to catch her at home.

The gloves left white powdered streaks on the warm-beige of my hands. I stretched my legs and aching back, careful not to kick over the basket of cuttings: deadly nightshade, monkshood, foxglove, oleander and a few more. Specimens for toxicity tests, halfway between a careful breeding programme and genetic selection to retain their medicinal value – without their poison. The plan: to prepare them tonight with Morrigan, my carrion crow-friend and fellow medic, for our experiments tomorrow. She'd be pleased with today's harvest.

"Evening, Willow!" A jolly tenor voice called from across the street.

Mr. Mutitu was being walked by Chocolate, a Labrador whose fine fur almost matched the ebony of his human's skin.

Chocolate gave a short, sharp bark; the implant in my brain kicked off a translation. "Got treats, Willow?"

"Sorry, Chocolate, none today!" I chuckled, filing a mental note to get some tomorrow. "How are your squirrels, Mr. Mutitu?"

Mr. Mutitu's current responsibility included negotiations with small mammals. "Fine, fine, they've all found their autumn stash now. And you, your birds?"

Holy henbane, I'd not thought about the birds all day. Though I loved what we do through the Committee, being randomly assigned portfolios didn't always guarantee the best match, even if everyone learned to do a little bit of everything. This time I'd landed on a bit of a tiresome role: arbitrating a long-running dispute between the jackdaws and the seagulls – the Daws and the Mockers. They'd settled on a truce recently, thanks to Violetta, the previous mediator, who had now graduated to overseeing the health of human beings.

I'd really like that role someday. Anything, but these birds.

"No drama today!" I answered Mr. Mutitu. Not yet, anyway. I forced a smile. Just a few months more of this, and maybe I could move on.

Mr. Mutitu waved as Chocolate tugged him towards the corner pub.

A flicker of movement in Mrs. Leigh's garden caught my eye. A silver-black bird with a short bill hopped out; a jackdaw. How unusual. Everyone knew to steer clear of my human-designated garden – but I suppose Mrs. Leigh's was fair game.

"Hello!" I hoped I sounded cheerful.

"Evenin'," it replied before flying away, something wriggling in its beak. Likely a grub, that'd explain the curt greeting.

A thin crescent moon had already risen, impatient for the sun to set. A fog emerged over the sea. The evening breeze teased the bioluminescent trees lining the street with playful tenderness; they had begun to glow, complementing the algae heritage lanterns punctuating the pavements, marrying the old alongside the new.

I gathered my basket, checking I hadn't left any stray cuttings behind. Last thing I'd want: to cause someone unintentional harm.

"Willow!" A frightened voice, a frantic wingbeat. "Wait!"

Morrigan, her sleek black feathers glistening green from the trees and gold from the setting sun. She landed in a clumsy, uncharacteristic half-skid on the steps to my front door, panting hard. Our paired implants connected, initiating the private, close-proximity comms channel. *Willow, something's wrong!*

"What –?"

Someone's been poisoned! Her eyes flitted at me, at my basket, at the horizon. I'd rarely seen her so anxious. *Silk and Kittiwake are quarrelling at the Old Steine –*

This might escalate, badly. I leaned past Morrigan, opened the door, dropped the basket inside, grabbed the emergency med kit from the hallway. A canister of calming pheromones we'd been working on glinted on a table. No, better not, we hadn't yet tested its effectiveness at scale. I pulled the door shut.

"Quickly!" Morrigan flapped her wings, once, twice, pointing the way with her beak.

Swallowing a sigh, I followed her into the fog-laden night.

Brighton often turned suddenly cold after sundown, even at the height of summer. I shivered; in our hurry, I'd forgotten my cloak. Running after Morrigan did little to warm me up; the fastest way to the Old Steine Gardens meant taking the wind-exposed road along the seafront. The sycamores on Kingsway glittered as night swooped in, but Morrigan's black silhouette blended into the shadows of buildings we sped past. I squinted, trying not to lose her.

"Why the hurry?" A roadside rosemary bush said.

I halted mid-run, nearly tripping over my own feet. I knew that voice.

"Violetta?" Panting hard from sprinting, I could barely speak. "Why are you here?"

"Could ask the same of you." Violetta materialised from behind the plant, dark hair flowing over a purple dress, her tall, overly thin frame sharp enough to slice the air. Something about her always took my breath away.

"I –" My eyes searched for Morrigan in the bio-lit dark, but she'd already spun towards us.

"We can't stop! He might die!"

Violetta swung her attention to Morrigan. "*Who* might die?"

"A Daw!" Morrigan's wings struggled with hovering flight; she flitted awkwardly, an oversized, jet-feathered butterfly. "Quick! They might fight –"

I squirmed.

"Fight?" Violetta glared at me. "After all I've done, you let them regress to *this?*"

"I –" Words stayed stuck at the back of my throat. Half of me wanted to run back and hide in my garden, the other half wished I could be more like Violetta, who always seemed to know what she was doing.

"I'm coming with you."

What? No!

"If you ruin this," Violetta's voice turned frosty, her eyes blazed, "I'll report you to the Committee for negligence."

My heart skipped a beat. Several. I'd be taken off the roster. I might get reallocated a different house, forced to start a new garden from scratch. Or worse, they might take away my implant with the bird-speech decoder. I swallowed. To not be able to talk to Morrigan any longer –

"Hurry!" she beckoned.

No time to think about that now.

Zigzagging through the narrow lanes, we arrived at the Gardens, an ancient common that survived many transformations. The Royal Pavilion School glimmered to the northwest, its domes lit by glowing elms, liquid trees dotting its lawn.

Squawks rang out.

"There!" Morrigan zipped towards Victoria Fountain. I'd always thought it resembled a giant birdbath –

"This had better not be a bloodbath," Violetta hissed, somewhere near my ear.

I gulped down a gasp.

Two birds perched on the lowest and widest rim of the cast-iron fountain. Kittiwake, the leader of the Mockers, spread his grey-white wings wide, screeching his wrath.

"Stop. Calling. Us. Names!"

"That's no reason to poison one of us, Kit," said Silk, the much smaller leader of the Daws, whose smooth, black feathers reflected the moonlight despite the mist. "But we know only a dirty, oily, *Mocker* would."

He tittered.

Kittiwake reached out to smack him with a wing, but Silk hopped deftly backwards.

"*You!* We'll –"

"Enough!" I shouted, hoping my voice carried sufficient authority. I'd never been particularly good at this, never throughout the mediation training we'd all had to have.

"You'd never –" Silk chittered, winging up higher on the fountain, ready to attack.

"*Enough!*" I yelled.

This time, they both heard me.

"Where's the sick Daw?" Less a question, more a demand. How could they be arguing when one of their own might be dying? I sucked my breath in, struggling to quell my rage.

Neither of them answered.

"Where's the sick Daw?" I repeated.

Violetta sighed and started to check under the nearby bushes. Why didn't I think to do that?

Morrigan's signal flickered through my implant. *Here!*

I rushed to the other side of the fountain. The black bird lay unmoving on the grass, barely visible in the dark.

Ignoring the damp air on my arms, I unrolled my kit. Morrigan leaned down by the fallen daw, using her implant to read vital signals too faint for mine to pick up.

"Heart rate very high, blood pressure low –"

Not good.

We needed to run toxicity tests, and fast. I handed Morrigan a small device – this should pick up the most common toxins.

After half a minute, she shook her head. "None of these."

Panic seized me. What if we didn't have an antidote? A jackdaw would die on my watch. If ever there was a case for negligence…

I breathed away the dread. Must focus. I fished out a tiny needle for Morrigan to take a blood sample. Working swiftly, I set up several swabs and fed them through the portable tester I'd programmed to identify all the toxins I knew.

Violetta had bundled herself onto a bench, her hair rippling in the wind like dark water, watching us. Back when we first met several portfolio reassignments ago, her knowledge of the birds astounded me, but somehow, I never drummed up the courage to ask her if she'd be willing to be my mentor. If I weren't such a coward, I might have asked her so many things. Like, if this was what she'd had to go through.

Or like, to be a friend. Maybe.

Mentally, I folded away the sight of her, same way I wrapped up my apprehension. Treating sick creatures – I was good at. She could judge me all she wanted.

The results took forever. I extracted a stethoscope and checked the daw's heartbeat – an unnecessary move. Sometimes, a bit of theatre projected the illusion of control.

Morrigan hopped on my shoulder, eyes on the tester. An alert flashed on mine.

Strange. Mostly some complex molecules not in our database, with traces of aconitine. No telling if that was the main ingredient causing harm, but it was the only lead we had.

I retrieved the correct antidote and let Morrigan administer it with the practised, precise control of her beak. With any luck, the jackdaw should feel less ill shortly, but real recovery might take weeks.

I stood up, puzzled. Aconitine, the toxin present in monkshood. You'd have to be traipsing deep in the South Downs to find any in the wild. Not a plant typically found in gardens – whether designated for humans or birds – not any more. The rest of the unidentifiable components? I wouldn't even know where to begin. The aconitine might be our only traceable clue.

Morrigan fussed over the recovering jackdaw. Swaying a little, the daw managed to right himself and took a few steps. Was he the same bird I saw last night? Impossible to discern in the deepening darkness.

I headed over to Kittiwake and Silk, who at least had the decency to stop squabbling.

"So, who did it?" Silk asked first.

Must not sound irritated. "We treated the patient, not traced the source."

Kittiwake chortled. Seagulls always laughed, even when something wasn't funny. He puffed out his chest. "We resent being accused –"

"Who else would have a motive?" Silk interrupted.

"Please, let's not get carried away," I tried again. "There's no proof right now."

Both of them stared at me, as if they'd forgotten I existed.

I took advantage of their attention. "We must work together to find out why – and how – this happened."

A moment of uncomfortable quiet.

"Whatever," said Silk, with an indifferent shuffle of his wings.

"Yeah." Kittiwake jerked up his head, emitting a screech. "Well, we'll *not* see you around." A dirty glare at Silk, at me, then he took off.

On days like these, I wondered: what right did humans have to meddle in the affairs of the fauna? The Cross-Species Citizens' Committee had been initiated by humans, with the belief that collaborating with our non-human friends seemed to be the wisest way to mitigate the effects of the precarious climate. But… do we just make things worse?

The garden bench sat empty. Violetta had left, I hadn't even noticed.

Morrigan walked over to us. "He'll be fine after some rest."

Silk bobbed his head. "We'll take over from here."

After he left, Morrigan nodded to me. Her movements seemed slower; the evening had taken a lot out of her. I let her hop onto my hand.

"You look terrible," I remarked.

She cocked her head, casting one amused eye at me. *You look wonderful yourself.*

I laughed.

We should try using seeds next time, it's good distraction tactic for the likes of us.

Seeds! Why hadn't I thought of that?

I suppressed a groan. "What would I do without you, Morrigan?"

You'd be lost, she cackled. *Let's get some rest. See you tomorrow.*

A gentle nibble of my finger for a friendly goodnight, she bounced off the ground and took off to her roost.

I sighed. Yes, I'd be so lost without her.

My feet somehow found their way home. My brain whirred, mapping out patches of monkshood in the vicinity. I'd catalogued locations of wild poisonous flowers so I could correlate environmental factors with their toxicity. No bird would deliberately eat off such a plant. Perhaps they found a poisoned grub? Came in close contact by accident?

My hand froze on the smooth wood of my gate. Something just moved in Mrs. Leigh's garden. A Mocker, the tips of its feathers fluttering in the breeze.

"Hello," I said.

It didn't reply.

Something – someone stood on the far fence. I blinked. A Daw.

Perhaps I'd interrupted a confrontation.

Before I could say more, they took off in opposite directions, wind whistling under their wings.

A soft, mechanical purr floated in from the street. Mrs. Leigh gave me a wave from her wheelchair as she approached her gate, grey hair pulled back into a tight bun, a faded scarf around her shoulders.

"How are you, Willow?" Her kindly voice croaked a little. She'd only just made it home? It must take so much of her energy to make sure all the humans in the city got their preferred food deliveries.

"Um, fine, how was your day?" I wanted to ask about her garden, but she looked so tired, I didn't have the heart to raise that now. Instead, I said, "We should have tea soon, when you're less busy?"

"Always busy," she replied, smiling. "But never feels that way when you love what you do."

Her words gave me pause. Would I ever love what I do that much?

I struggled to imagine what that could be like. Just dealing with these birds drained me.

"Let's find a time! It's been too long since you last came for tea." And with that Mrs. Leigh bade me good evening, her wheelchair whirring through her front door.

Finally, alone in my garden. The nearest tree didn't shed quite enough light. At a cursory glance, nothing had been trampled.

No bird tracks.

No clue.

Sleep – a fickle mistress.

I freshened up, made some dandelion brew and hunted through my archives for a monkshood map. One of these days I should post my maps to our citizen plant catalogue, so other enthusiasts could add to it, building up specialist knowledge of the local flora.

A tap-tap-tapping on the window. Morrigan balanced on the sill, her body tense enough to break the glass.

Why didn't she connect through our private comms?

I opened the window, checked my implant. It had defaulted to do-not-disturb mode while I slept, switching to focus-mode because I'd been preoccupied. Oh.

"They're at it again!" Morrigan burst in without greeting – a bad sign. "The Mockers have cornered a Daw!"

Definitely bad. Ignoring the silver lure of the canister on the hallway table, I grabbed the kit, spare swabs, slid a pack of seeds into the pouch around my waist. Miraculously, I remembered my cloak.

Three steps outside, it began to rain – the kind of polite rain that made no sound but still drenched you thoroughly. My shoes slipped a little on the pavement as we hurried down Kingsway a second time in two days.

What caused them to fight again? What had undone Violetta's work? I thought I'd be stepping into a problem long resolved. Peace is such a fragile thing.

We heard them before we got near the old mall. Churchill Square lacked personality but it housed a farmers' market, several makers' coops and the city's health centre.

Seagull screeches skewered the morning air. I listened for a tortured caw of a jackdaw. Sweat broke out on my brow, mingling with the rain matting my hair.

Let it not be too late.

Morrigan led me to the fire escape that accessed the roof. The metal railing felt cold under my palms, the steps slicked wet. Solar panels glinted under the drizzle between a myriad of plants reaching for the sky. I never realised a food forest grew here.

Several Daws battled with some Mockers, swooping from the fruit trees, chasing through the shrubs. Two birds collided in an explosion of feathers and leaves.

"Stop!" I yelled, my voice muffled by rain and damp.

No one did. Instead, birds continued to dive for each other, squawking, cawing. I really wasn't any good at this. How did Violetta do it?

"Let me try!" Morrigan crowed.

Before I could stop her, she flew straight among them.

"Morrigan, wait!"

Her sudden scream sliced through the commotion. My hands flew to my head, her pain piercing through our comms, zapping my nerves. My heart dropped through my feet. Not thinking straight, I forced myself into the middle, sheltering my face from sharp beaks and battering wings.

Something sliced into my forearm, the scratch long and deep.

Anger rose, a sudden wildfire. I clenched my fists and –

The seeds, Willow!

The seeds! Bending low, I ducked through the other side, pulled the packet from my pouch, ripped it open and flung my arm in a wide circle, scattering its contents.

The distraction tactic worked like magic. After a few moments of scrambling, the remaining uninjured birds stopped fighting each other and began chasing after the new source of food. Success! That had been the last packet though; I'd need to acquire more.

As things settled, I called out. "All right, can we talk now?"

A few birds continued to peck at the seeds, but no one dissented. I didn't know that even slightly soggy seeds could be so appetising. Unsurprisingly, I failed to gain their attention, guess I had to wait until they were done eating.

Going to tend to the injured, Morrigan's voice, though weak, held resolve.

Together, we evaluated the damage. A multitude of lost feathers, some scratches, a few bites. Sighing, I opened my kit.

Once most of the seeds were gone, I tried again.

"So, what happened?" I asked, dabbing some antiseptic on a Daw's foot.

A Mocker spoke up first. "They tried to poison us!"

A bunch of beaks pointed to something tucked under a lettuce. A dead caterpillar. I prepped the swabs.

"He was mean!" added another Mocker, pointing at a Daw perching on a mulberry bush.

I didn't roll my eyes.

The Daw sniggered. "That's because you *are* greasy chip-stealers –"

"Can we *please* talk this thr –" but I never got to finish my plea.

The first Mocker squealed, spread his wings, but held back. Morrigan threw me a sideways glance; these birds behaved like children.

I turned to the Daw. "You brought this?"

"'Twas a gift!" the Daw protested.

That surprised me.

"But *we* think it's poisoned," said the first Mocker.

"Smelt wrong!" another chimed in.

The first one spoke again. "Then he insulted me, and the others –"

Several Mockers looked suddenly sheepish.

"Just trying to be friendly!" the Daw cried, adamant. Around him, other Daws murmured their support.

An alert pinged. The swabs.

My eyes met Morrigan's. Similar to yesterday's swab, the results indicated numerous unidentifiable compounds, but with faint traces of digoxin. Digoxin, found in foxgloves.

How? Morrigan seemed equally confused.

Foxgloves were banned as domestic ornamentals, but medics and health establishments could grow them under controlled conditions. There was exactly one plant in the city: my garden, which was human-designated because it contained plants that might harm our avian and animal friends. How, indeed?

"Where did you get this caterpillar?" I asked the Daw.

"Found it," he mumbled.

Something rustled. I looked back towards the fire escape.

Violetta leaned lightly against an apple tree.

Had she been here long? How could she remain so composed in the rain? I swallowed. I must look a mess.

"I heard the commotion." No warmth in her voice. "Correction, the whole city heard it."

The fire in her eyes scorched through me. My insides somersaulted.

The Mocker cleared his throat. "We'll be complaining to the Committee that you keep siding with the Daws."

I spun to face him, my jaw dropping open. "But I don't!"

Out of the corner of my eye, Violetta smothered a smirk.

Breathe, remember to breathe.

Blood still ran down my arm, hair dangled across my face.

I summoned every inch of composure I could muster. "We must find a way to co-exist, re-build trust from the ground up."

A Mocker laughed. Of course he would.

I ignored him.

"I propose a forum between both parties," I addressed the birds, then locked my gaze on Violetta. Maybe it was her who needed convincing that I was in charge. "At dusk, two days from now, on the beachfront between the West and Palace Piers."

Murmurs rippled among the birds, but no one disagreed.

I exhaled, relieved. "Then it's done."

"I'll tell Silk and Kittiwake," said Morrigan, taking off at speed.

One by one, then all at once, the avians left.

"Oh look, you actually *did* something," said Violetta. The sarcasm didn't escape me.

She paused to caress a spear of lavender by the stairs.

The fury I'd been burying bubbled up.

"Just leave me alone!" My voice bounced off the solar panels.

The look of pity she threw me shredded my conviction into tatters, scattering it like dead leaves.

"I would, if you did a better job."

Ouch.

I wheezed. "Either you give me counsel, or you let me do it my way!"

Her hesitation lasted just long enough to give me hope. But then, she said, "I'm not convinced you truly care. Let's not waste the time, don't you think?"

With that, she disappeared down the escape.

My cheeks had got wet, whether from tears or rain, I couldn't tell.

I did care. Didn't I? If I didn't, I wouldn't be trying so hard. Right… right?

By the time I made it home, the midday sun had banished most of the wet weather. A warbler started singing. Once more, I checked for signs of tampering in my garden.

Nothing.

Most creatures didn't have a death wish – how could these poisonous substances be circulating?

I sat down on the steps.

Toxins could be extracted; I did it all the time for my experiments. Violetta had some medical training. Would she…? I tapped my fingers on my knees. No, she'd never harm the birds.

But. Oh no. I covered my face with my hands.

Only one other had the skill to extract toxins with accuracy. Someone whom I'd been training since she was a fledgling.

Morrigan.

"How could you think that of me?" Morrigan had said, her voice quiet with hurt.

Guilt whacked me like a sack of wet potatoes. No way to comfortably confront an old friend. "Morrigan, I —"

She'd flown away, cutting our comms.

I hadn't seen her in two days. Worry chewed at my insides like a leaf scalloped by a caterpillar. It had been strange, to not hear her tapping on my window, to not have her land in my garden unannounced. I'd never realised how much time we spend together – day in, day out.

Alone, I stood on a viewing platform between the piers. On either side, stairs led down to the pebbled beach. The sun had given up, the clouds swept from orange to deep blue, the moon a skinny sliver suspended in the sky. The rhythmic slosh of waves splintered the uneasy silence; the starlings had vacated their usual perch.

I pulled my cloak tighter and patted the med kit hanging around my waist: the usual swabs, first-aid affair, and the canister of experimental calming liquid from the hallway table; we'd run out of seeds. The liquid probably wouldn't work, but it might provide the advantage of surprise.

"Evenin'," said Kittiwake, landing on the railing next to me. The swish of wings and high-pitched screeches rose to a crescendo as seagulls descended on the left side of the beach. A moment later, a swathe of jackdaws alighted on the other, black feathers rustling, the air punctuated by their squeaky chatter.

Silk hopped onto the railing. "Where's Morrigan?"

"Not here yet," I said, burying a pang of guilt.

Kittiwake piped up. "We think she might know more than she's letting on."

"What do you mean?" I turned to face him.

Kittiwake shrugged his wings. "Word on the street? She's been making these poisoned grubs."

Not good, if they'd come to the same conclusion.

"She's the only bird who knows how. Besides, why would humans be interested in grubs?"

I couldn't refute the logic. Perhaps I should've taken Kittiwake and Silk aside for a conversation without involving everyone else. Too late now.

The breeze picked up. The moon hid behind a cloud.

Still no Morrigan. I sucked a breath through my teeth. But it was time.

I cleared my throat and straightened my back. I might be a bigger creature than the birds, but my insides shrank infinitely smaller.

"Welcome, everyone —"

"Feathered vermin," someone among the Mockers muttered.

A few Daws cawed in protest.

"Scavengers!" someone retaliated.

"Please!" I hated how I sounded like I was begging.

A few soft squawks of unrest, but they complied.

Meeting on the beach was a terrible idea. My voice barely carried; it sounded shrill.

"We're meeting here today to re-establish a truce." I tried projecting confidence. I'd probably already failed. "Let's —"

"Ya posh snobs," a snicker escaped from the Mockers' camp.

"Greaseheads!"

I whirled around to tell Silk and Kittiwake to control their flocks, when a sudden burst of black and white feathers exploded in the middle of the beach. Ear-splitting shrieks perforated the salty air.

"Tell them —" I yelled but Kittiwake had flown into the whirlpool of the brawl. Silk followed suit.

Holy bloody hemlock. That didn't take long.

I ran down the steps, two at a time, screaming for them to stop. Amid the cacophony, no one could hear me. The birds squawked, shrieked, flapped, pecked at each other. Every now and again, someone would gain height only to be dragged down into the pulsating jumble of flying feathers.

I'm here! Morrigan's voice, over our comms link. My heart pounded at the familiarity.

I scanned the ugly scene. Where? I couldn't see her.

Morrigan?

There, the small black dot flying a wide circle above us as if to gain momentum. Oh no. She'd better not —

Morrigan, no! Stay back! It's not safe!

But Morrigan rode on some other kind of instinct. She made one last turn before pointing her beak down, cutting through the middle of the mess before her small brave body disappeared into the heaving avian quagmire.

Morrigan!

A tall silhouette, running down the stairs. Violetta, outrage plain on her face. But she ignored me and started breaking up the closest fight. She must really care about these birds. Where could I find courage like hers?

A bird, not sure from which camp, squealed in pain.

Must stop this. Consequences – later.

Shielding my eyes with my arms, I shoved my way into the throbbing chaos.

"There she is!" someone shouted. I froze. Did they mean me? Violetta?

"Get her!"

I gasped, inhaling feathers. I braced for the attack, but the scream that shot through my implant knocked the air out of my lungs, the pain of a thousand knives digging into my flesh.

Morrigan!

Beating my hands wildly, wings caught my arms, claws drew blood from my skin.

Morrigan!

Must find her, but her shrieks were everywhere, all at once. Feathers blocked out the light. Too dark to see. A sharp beak bit into my hand. I jerked it back. My bleeding fingers brushed against hard metal on the soft pouch of my med kit: the canister.

Squeezed down into a squat by the sheer gravity of warring birds, I fumbled for the fastener and grabbed the cylinder. It slipped, but I caught it, just. Wiped hand on skirt, tried again. Better grip.

Clutching the tin tightly, I thrust it above my head. Fingers found the catch. Holding my breath, I pressed down on the trigger. It hissed. Once, twice.

Nothing happened. I tried again. One, two, three times.

A seagull dropped back down onto the beach, conscious, but looking a little confused. Then another, and another. More stopped fighting. They'd be fine later.

I stole a bird-filled breath. The sky brightened. I stood up straight.

Close to the stairs, Violetta appeared to be sliding a branch along the sand to detract a pair of Mockers from a few Daws. It wasn't working all that well.

I adjusted the dosage on the canister. Pointing it high, I pressed on the trigger and sprayed in three directions. One, two, three.

A few more bewildered birds landed, wobbling on their feet.

Morrigan!

Where was she? Where did she land?

I staggered forward, using the spray to clear the path. Silence descended as the birds settled.

A clump of jet-black feathers laid by the water's edge.

I crouched down. *Morrigan?*

No reply.

"Morrigan!" Someone was sobbing. Might have been me.

My arms ached to cradle the broken body but my hands shook too much.

A tall shadow appeared by my side. An arm on my shoulder.

Violetta knelt beside me. "She's not gone."

I tried to meet her gaze but tears veiled everything into a blur. An alert flashed on my retina. A faint heartbeat.

"Quickly!" Violetta handed me a purple sash. "Use this."

Seconds stretched as we dug into the beach around Morrigan, making space to move her as little as possible.

"Wait, let us help," a Mocker said. Some jackdaws and seagulls levelled the area with their beaks and feet. One of them found a discarded plank. Carefully, we wrapped the sash around Morrigan, and lifted her gently onto the makeshift stretcher.

Around us, broken feathers, battered beaks, injured wings. Helpless, uncertain, I looked at Violetta.

"Take her home," she said. "I'll start on the first aid."

"I'll come back –"

"Take care of her first."

A few birds followed us. I ignored them.

I was going to lose everything I'd work so hard for.

Sod it, sod them all.

I just wanted my Morrigan back, alive.

Some days passed. I stopped counting.

A knock on the door drew me away from Morrigan's side. I opened it; no one there. Grey clouds covered the sky, muddling the time of day.

"Ahem," said Kittiwake, somewhere near my feet. Next to him, Silk stood upright, pristine as always.

I ushered them into the garden.

"How is she?" asked Silk.

"Better than yesterday." Morrigan still couldn't move much, but the crystalloid drip I'd given her helped; she'd been able to converse through our comms.

The ferocity of the incident shocked everyone into a truce. A day afterward, Silk and Kittiwake gave a joint statement to the Committee.

Silk looked regretful. "We've been fighting for so long, no one remembered how it all began. It just takes one side to feel hard-done-by, then things spiral into finger-pointing…"

"And we don't know how to stop," Kittiwake continued, solemn for once. "We request that Willow continue as mediator, so this doesn't happen again."

That stunned me, but not half as much as when Violetta defended me. "Peace is fragile. Like tending to a garden, it takes work. Willow has shown us we can't take any of it for granted."

Had I? Nothing, I felt nothing.

But one issue remained unresolved, so I'd asked them all to convene in my garden.

"Evening," said Violetta, as she glided through my gate. The birds murmured a greeting.

Time to come clean.

"I think someone stole from my garden. I don't know how else we could have got these poisoned grubs."

Violetta shrugged. "I don't think it was deliberate."

"I doubt it, too," Kittiwake said.

Silk cocked his head, his clever eyes darting all around the garden. With a flick of his wings, he landed on Mrs. Leigh's fence.

"Have we looked here?"

My eyes widened as we all flocked next door. Under the magnolia, between the roses and the rhododendron, I spotted them: baby foxglove, tiny monkshood. But in and around them, tiny bright blue pellets.

Pesticides. Oh *no*.

Kittiwake swore loudly in seagull.

The Daws must have eaten these by accident, or picked up grubs in close contact with the baby poison plants, sending us on a wild bird-food chase.

"This is unacceptable," Silk spoke first. "We ought to get her garden re-designated."

"No," I shook my head. "It's better to keep more space everyone can share. Leave it with me. I'll speak to Mrs. Leigh."

Perhaps if I could help her tend her garden, she might not need to use pesticides to keep it tidy.

Violetta lingered after the birds left. We sat on the steps, nursing steaming mugs of dandelion brew.

"I'd been foolish to think I could be in control – poison plants, the birds, the lot." I rubbed my eyes. In the end, the Committee had agreed to address better cooperation over any punitive measures. "We're all equal in nature's eyes, none of us are superior. We should have never interfered."

Violetta shook her head. "Communing with animals isn't new, we did it as early as nine thousand years ago. We're just learning how to do it again."

Perhaps she was right.

I sighed. "I'm only slightly better with plants..."

"Well, humans confuse me, I'm only slightly better with birds," Violetta said, a little ruefully. "Why do you think I kept checking up on you?"

I hadn't thought of that.

She sat upright, as if an idea just sparked. "Willow, if I help you with the birds, will you give me a hand with my role with human health?"

Our eyes met. Peace is a fragile thing, we had to start somewhere. With a friend, maybe.

Anatomy of Emotion – the Carving of Chance – Seize the Moon

Anger in the body: a coiled snake, a raging wildfire.

Anxiety in the gut: the doom-laden twist of a strangler fig.

Em – I definitely wasn't angry at her. If anything, my anger was reserved for myself: me, and my own cowardice.

I ran my thumb around the twenty-sided die in my palm, feeling its precise triangles, its edges sharp enough to carve chance into defined probabilities – just not quite sharp enough to mark my skin.

Swirling it thrice, I let the die drop soundlessly on the grass beside me. It rolled off the hem of my skirt, then a little way down the hillside I was sitting on, settling between a cluster of clover and a young sprout of chamomile. The white numeral on its topmost face glistened in the late afternoon light, picking up a tinge of orange from the departing sun.

Fifteen. *Sit and breathe awhile.*

I must have been nine or ten years old when I found an entry in our Chronicles describing an old tradition of using randomness. A list of actions matched up to numbers on a set of dice or a shuffled card deck, an aid for moments of hesitation. I had no idea what the cards looked like, but shortly after that I found a schema of a die – so I crafted my own.

Pulling a breath deep into my lungs, I willed the anger inside to dissipate, the anxiety to dissolve. Anger about something or someone had a semblance of shape. Anger at myself? A formless force, a relentless riptide.

Letting go of this might take a long time, if ever.

Under the shadow of the old elm tree, the earth seeped cool, the meadow still damp from last night's rain. From the edge of the foothill below, an eclectic mix of coloured tents with no uniformity in size or structure spread across the plain – our summer settlement, most of which would be gone by the end of tomorrow.

A gaping hole in the middle had appeared since yesterday; some of the tents had been moved outwards to make room for tonight's festival. For days now, all of us had brought masses of kindling and dead wood for the bonfire. Around the clearing, movement rippled: a few tall youths hoisting up strings of solar lights, others setting up tables ready to bear food, chairs to receive hungry bodies.

Em wasn't there. Of course, I'd looked.

I propped myself up on my elbows, feeling the slope of the hill under my calves. I'd have to go down soon to help Old Ma Olga with the Harvest Spirit – as I'd done every year since they learned I had the gift of craft – but no one would miss me for a little while yet.

Towards the horizon, the jagged edges of the ancient city sparkled, its glassy ruins almost glowing in the dimming gold of the sun, as if someone had smashed the top off an egg and left behind the shell. Most of it had been overrun by vines, brush and wildflowers. Our Chronicles recounted how it had been built over a river, so when the city fell several hundred years ago the forests around it reclaimed the remnants with speed, trapping relics under leaf, root and tendril.

Em used to joke that we could make a home there – on the inside.

"Think of it, Cee: so much ancient glass we could repurpose," she'd said – a curl of honey-brown hair at the base of her neck, her smile the pink fragrance of geranium. Tools I'd fashioned for her from the remains of an ancient flying machine jangled on the belt around her waist. "Imagine how many photobioreactors we could build! We could make winters so much more comfortable – for all of us."

For some reason, she'd only bring this up whenever we were alone.

I'd let a moment of silence pass. Recent winters had seemed harsher, but I just couldn't see how our whole community would change our seasonal habits, traditions we'd kept year after year. We'd scavenged within the old city limits for materials now and again, but our tales told of something bad that had happened there a long time ago; changing minds would be no small feat.

"You honestly think everyone would move?"

"Oh, Cee," Em had sighed, impatience in her tone. "Once they realise it'll be consistently warmer, that we could cultivate a regular winter source of food – of course they will move."

We'd have to transform the place, make it liveable. Start small, show others how it could be done, until enough of us decide to work together. Not impossible, but every time I tried to imagine Em's vision of the future, my throat tightened. What if she overestimated my abilities? How rapidly would she tire of me?

Insecurity: the soft earth at the edge of a precipice.

It had been late spring then. I remembered because the poppies had just begun bursting out their vermillion petals, tiny red silk skirts fluttering in the breeze that still carried a chill. Em had stretched out beside me on this hill after breakfast, under this very elm tree. The remnants of the glass city caught the light differently in the mornings, a little less sparkle, a bit more haze. We'd sat here, stealing sips from a bottle of last winter's mead that we'd smuggled from Zed's father's reserves. My mind swept blank from the sheer bliss of being next to her, bare feet touching, legs lazily entwined, the meadow green against our skin – hers porcelain pale, mine tree-bark dark.

Desire: a turbulent propellant, not unlike the rocket fuel the ancients employed to such devastation.

"You could build what we'd need, I could adapt our algae culture, or perhaps use some enzyme to the same effect." I couldn't tell if Em was simply thinking aloud, but her eyes had taken on a faraway daze. "It'd only take us a season or two to get it working. You'll see."

Em, the ever-optimist, the forever dreamer. Me? I just wasn't so good with change.

Uncertainty: a heavy fog at dawn's edge, the kind thick enough to blind you.

I wish I had known what I'd wanted, the way Em always seemed to. My fingers had twitched at that moment, aching to roll the twenty-sided die inside my pocket, but I'd known by then that Em didn't approve of my habit, so I fought against myself, battled against a cloud of guilt.

At some point, Em had shrugged, given in. "Anyway, seems you prefer to stick to the way things are."

That had stung a little, a puncture wound from a thorn under a rose. Then I'd tried to sound clever, forward-thinking. "But – what if we fail?"

"We could also succeed," Em promptly said. "You're always so either-or, Cee. We have the skills. Wouldn't you even want to try?"

Em had a gift with the abstract, with things we couldn't see with our eyes. She'd engineered the solar-powered lights for our settlement, built community ovens that required no fire to cook. Glass – I could work glass. I could work nearly every material I put my hands to: stone, clay, wood, metal, fibres from any plant. The glass could be restructured to become a vessel for the algae, but also insulation for us. We could grow some food through the cold season. Yes, we could've made it work, had we chosen to.

Had she chosen me.

Was that the last earnest conversation we'd had? I'd never quite known what she saw in me. She was an enigma, an endless source of beguiling mysteries.

Regret: a bottomless pit of stinking, rotting leaves, from which there was no way out.

Summer without Em had been eternal days and too-short nights. Every time I'd seen her since, she'd been with some others, younger or older. We still greeted each other, waved hello, but never spoke.

Grief: an open, bleeding wound that refused to heal.

Jealousy: All of the above.

Down the hill, it seemed as if all the lights had finally been set up. Not long before I would have to head down to find Olga-Ma.

From my left pocket, I extracted a small piece of paper that had gone soft from the number of times I'd handled it. It no longer rustled as I smoothed out its folds. A purple ticket – my name in Em's neat, handprinted capitals, the last one she'd given to me. It might even have been on that day when we were on this hill, when we last talked about the ancient glass city.

Purple tickets had evolved from an old practice; the Chronicles described a similar system which existed as far back as the time of the ancient city, explicit expressions for the wish of mutual intimacy. Arrangements with multiple people had been the norm then too.

They'd warned us not to be overly attached to your first. I'd exchanged tickets with others throughout the summer, but – dare I admit it to myself – they were not Em. No one else was quite like Em.

No one else made time irrelevant, days brim with possibilities and nights gentle with quiet ease.

Maybe she stopped asking for me because I'd thought all this time that she was joking – and she wasn't. Maybe it was my inertia, my indecisiveness. My either-or-ness. Maybe it was simply she found someone better who didn't fear her dreams.

A rustle came from my left, the sharp resinous scent of a rosemary bush being disturbed. A familiar figure, a slender silhouette sheathed in a loose work-wrap dress, pale legs long under the fluttering hem. My heart thumped.

Em. She'd walked up here barefoot.

Hastily, I tucked the purple ticket into my pocket.

Em sat down by my side, all honey-brown curls and geranium smile.

"Thought I'd find you here." Her silken voice – the sound of home I no longer had.

I pinched my hand. No, it wasn't a dream.

"Hello," I said, trying to appear casual, simultaneously chiding myself for it. I was happy to see her. Why couldn't I show it? "I'm just taking a break from the preparations."

That wasn't a lie, at least.

Her forehead furrowed ever so slightly, an expression I couldn't read. "Old Ma Olga sent me to look for you. Are you in trouble?"

Well, you found me, I wanted to say. Instead, I stared at my feet, two small creatures clad in worn leather shoes. "No, she just needs my help constructing the Spirit."

Silence: the weight of unspoken words crowding out the present.

My twenty-sided die still sat nestled between a clutch of clover and chamomile further along the ground. I itched to pick it up and roll it, but I didn't want Em to see – she hated the thing. So I leaned forward and pretended to brush something off my skirt, swiping my hand over the die at the same time, feeling its reassuringly sharp edges over the soft of the grass. I caught the number on top.

Seven. *Do something good for someone.*

Almost as if this thing contained an oracle.

Em was looking down the hill, and not at me.

"Where's Olga-Ma?" I asked, more to break the awkwardness of the moment than for the actual information.

She pointed to the tent of red-blue-green cloths that a few of us had erected some days ago, a temporary shelter standing where forest met field.

Beyond the woods, the glass city glittered. For a moment then – had the sun shone differently, had different wildflowers waved between the grass – we might have gone back in time to that day at the end of spring, when happier possible futures spanned ahead of us.

Em stood first.

"Come on –" She extended a hand to me. Her fingers smooth, her grasp firm. How could I not recall their caress on my shoulder? Or the feel of them tracing my chin?

I retrieved the die from the grass as we got up. I wasn't quick enough to hide it.

"You still have that thing?" Em's eyebrows lifted, her green eyes examining mine. I shrivelled inside, words congealed in my throat. It didn't sound like an accusation, but still, guilt trapped me like the sticky middle of a spider's web.

She threw me a sideways glance but said no more. Perhaps one day I'd be able to show her, make her understand.

We sauntered down the hill, hand in hand, as if things had never changed. Perhaps they never did, and it had all just been in my own head?

"You've been busy?" It was an absurd question, but curiosity scratched at my insides, a wildcat marking a tree.

"Kay will be getting committed in the spring, so there's just been endless arrangements."

Kay, her sister. "To whom?"

"To Vee, and also to Tey."

Everyone knew Vee, a nice enough guy, well-liked by most. Over a year ago, I had turned down their offer of a purple ticket. Tey, I knew less well.

"That's happy news!" I genuinely thought so. A commitment in the spring – something to look forward to.

Nearer to the tents, blackberry bushes sprawled down one side of the hill where they mingled with wild rosemary. Late season flowers dotted the meadow or exploded in bunches – vervain, burnet-saxifrage, harebells. I stooped down and picked a few, gathering them with my free hand, an idea brewing in my mind.

"Tell me," Em said, her voice a sudden shade of grey, her hand clasping mine tighter.

"Yes?"

"Cee – are you happy?"

That took me by surprise. The wildflowers in my unsteady hand shook their little floral heads. "Em, I –"

I didn't know what to say.

A little sigh escaped those lips. Em looked away. "You never asked for me any more, I assumed you found happiness elsewhere."

What?

"Em –" I swallowed. How could I put this into words? "I thought… I thought that maybe I was holding you back…"

You, your dreams – your dreams like murmurings of starlings.

She gripped my hand, dragging me to an awkward stop. Her gaze pierced mine, a flash of an undecipherable fire behind those green eyes. I would gladly melt in that fire.

"Really, Cee, you're so silly sometimes."

We'd reached the edge of the settlement, and suddenly people were everywhere, busying themselves with various tasks ahead of the festival. More to say, but now wasn't the time.

Em nodded towards the tent where Olga was waiting. She gave my hand a final squeeze, and mouthed *later* – a promise that made my skin sing. Letting go of her hand was like losing an anchor. She vanished into the bustle of other bodies, the noise of the settlement suddenly unbearable after the calm of the hill.

I wanted badly to follow her and say, *yes, yes, let's go – to the ancient glass city. Let's make it work. Tomorrow, we could go tomorrow.*

Instead, I slid around the settlement towards the field and paused at the door flap of Olga-Ma's tent, watching her shadow move about inside.

I'd read in our Chronicles that when communities decided to split and settle separately they would take a piece of the Spirit – the symbolic winter home of the Harvest Goddess – after the Festival of the Full Corn Moon and bring it with them to the new place as a blessing.

I could detach a section from this year's Spirit after the festival. I could take it to Em – a token to show her I was ready to go with her.

But if I couldn't tell anyone, would that count as stealing?

If Old Ma Olga had been impatient, she didn't show it.

"There you are, Cee-cee," her warm, sonorous voice called from inside the tent when I lifted open the door flap.

She'd already sharpened her sickle. Together we walked up to the last sheaf of wheat, rye and vetch standing in the field, a patch of browning grasses at the edge of the food forest we cultivated whenever we settled here. Some of these trees and plants had probably been here as long as the ancient glass city. The ones we liked to eat, we helped to reseed, resow. For the others, we let nature do its thing.

On our way back to the tent, I held Old Ma Olga's sickle for her.

"A tall one this year, I think," she said, her arms full of the symbolic harvest. "To signify how the early rains helped the plants flourish so early, that we had such a bountiful harvest this year."

I nodded and got to work, the die in my skirt pocket shifting as I moved around Olga-Ma's worktable. Grabbing a handful of wheat, I wove a foundation for the Spirit's winter home.

Eighteen. *Focus on the task at hand.*

I'd only really understood our annual ritual with the Harvest Spirit after I'd had the luck of the draw. Every year, all the children in the settlement were invited to draw from a pile of straw; whoever extracted the longest got to lead the procession, carrying the Harvest Spirit from the field to the festival. Six years ago I had been the one blessed with good fortune. The idea wasn't to craft the likeness of the Harvest Goddess herself – more to fashion a home for her essence to overwinter in. During my turn that year, Old Ma Olga realised I had the gift of craft and material. She used to make the Spirit with her own hands, but the more persistent the pain in her fingers became, the more she relied on me.

After the festival, the Spirit would journey with us to our winter settlement and pass the cold seasons in Old Ma Olga's caravan until the following spring. Then we'd bury it back into the ground so it could work its magic for the new year.

I had no idea if that would be possible in the ancient city. If the whole place had been paved over beneath the wild green, like I'd read in the Chronicles, how could Em and I even grow anything?

The fear-laced anxiety came again like a tidal wave. My hands shook. A stalk of wheat slipped from my fingers. I very nearly reached for the die, but remembered myself. Olga-Ma might be busy with something else behind me, but the rattling of the die on the worktable would catch her attention, and I'd have to make uncomfortable excuses. How might I ever reconcile Em's dislike of the die? How could I ever explain – just reciting its list of actions calmed me down?

"What's eating away at you, my Cee, hmm?" Old Ma Olga's voice jolted me out of my thoughts.

Without paying conscious attention, I'd somehow completed the foundations for the Spirit, and already begun the second, decorative layer. Olga-Ma had been working through the knots on a string and winding it up into a tidy ball.

"Nothing." I kept my face expressionless. How did she know?

"You've always been a quiet one, but usually…" She paused. "Well, I don't know, I'll let you tell me."

When I still said nothing, Olga-Ma spoke, her voice soft. "Cee, look at me."

I dropped the bundle I'd been working with, did as I was told.

"My little rabbit, you looked positively gripped with fear right then. What are you afraid of?"

Fear: a cavernous ravine, a night creature waiting in the shadows to devour you, a future with endless possibilities.

What was I afraid of? Everything.

I exhaled, it came out as a sigh. Somehow, Olga-Ma heard the voices in my head without me saying a single word.

Suddenly, she dropped the ball of string she'd been fiddling with and wrapped her arms around me. My body stiffened at her touch. The ball unwound itself, rolling haphazardly across the uneven floor.

"Oh little one, you never did get much time with your Ma, did you?"

The community had been good to me since the day Ma didn't come back from a hunt, barely a year after Pa fell ill and hadn't woken up one day. I was always fed, clothed, given a place to sleep. I had free rein over our Chronicles and the settlement, but, always, something seemed incomplete.

That time I brought the Harvest Spirit from the field to the festival, I'd looked back into the crowd, knowing that Ma and Pa would be so proud of me. I'd searched for them in the sea of faces – only to remember they'd never see me do that walk of a lifetime. They would never see me raise the Spirit up high, how I held my poise, my feet leading the procession in a steady rhythm.

They'd never see me do anything, ever again.

Grief: a slippery slimy slug eating its way through a fragile leaf, the tattered residue of one's soul.

I shook my head, fighting the tears building up behind my eyes. I didn't want to cry right now. The die felt hard under my thumb in my pocket.

Three. *Acknowledge your anguish.*

A shuffle at the tent flap made Old Ma Olga release me from her embrace.

"Do you want me yet, Olga-Ma?" A small, but confident voice piped up from the entrance.

Jay, barely a teen, this year's lucky child to carry the Harvest Spirit to the centre of the festival. Already tall for their age, Jay's whole being buzzed with anticipation. I'd been that chosen child once. That excitement: a bellyful of fluttering butterflies. Did I also wear such joy on my face?

I quickly wiped my cheeks. But Jay spotted the Harvest Spirit and skipped right over for a closer look.

"Olga-Ma! Cee! This is *beautiful!*"

I had to smile; I might have outdone myself by weaving in the end-of-season wildflowers. Unlike the usual beige figure, this year's Spirit stood laced with colour: white, orange, pale purple and a gentle pink.

Neither Olga-Ma nor Jay would have been able to see, but I'd built it so a small bundle of the harvest under the decorative layer would release with a tug of twine.

"It's nearly finished," I declared. "See that pole down here?" I showed Jay where their hands would go. "I've carved little notches for your fingers, should make it easier to carry."

I'd not forgotten the slippery pole I'd had to handle that day when

I was the chosen child.

A cacophony of voices crescendoed outside the tent. The other children joining the procession were ready. The moment Olga-Ma left to speak to them, I slipped a cleaning cloth off her worktable and stuffed it into my pocket.

Then, I gave the working twine one last twist around the body of the Harvest Spirit. For some reason I blew on it as I would a candle. Perhaps to infuse it with my own, unspoken wishes.

The sun hadn't yet entirely dipped below the horizon by the time I joined the end of the procession, but already the wind had turned cold. Winter might come early.

I kept myself well behind everyone else. I wasn't part of the troupe, but I wanted to be close enough to keep an eye on the Spirit should anything happen.

Jay held it up high, using their height to advantage. Olga-Ma followed several steps behind, surrounded by the youngest children. Giggles, laughter. The walk from the field to the feast wasn't that long, but I could still remember the weight of the Spirit I'd had to balance above my head, how that short walk felt like an eternity.

We could smell the food even before we reached the tents. The punch of herbs and spices, the meatiness of stews prepared from yesterday's hunts, the vegetable roasts. Cheers erupted as we got close to the open clearing where the tables had been set, the adults parting a way for us to walk through. One of the musicians – the drummer – had started up a rhythm, the steady pace of an enthusiastic march.

We headed towards the main table at the far end of the clearing where it faced the bonfire, already lit and blazing. With deliberate care, Jay set the Spirit down and Old Ma Olga slipped it onto a stand someone else had prepared, a large weighted spool with a hole in it. The hole was a little too big for the pole, but the Spirit stood up fine. I should probably build something better next year.

A tiny swell of pride warmed my chest; this year's Spirit had something special about it. How hard would it be to replicate another? This might have been the first year I didn't agonise too much, let the textures of the sheaves guide me as to where they might go, lost myself in the joy of making something with my hands.

I felt for the die in my pocket.

Sixteen. *Dance at every opportunity.*

All at once, other musicians joined the lone drummer, and they burst into a lively little jig. A few carried the textured tune on stringed instruments, someone kept time on a tambourine. People began to sway and twirl. Someone hoisted a wild hog over the fire. Freshly baked breads, generous bowls of root salad, large plates of rice and beans made their rounds on the feasting tables.

Did I want to dance? I didn't get a chance to think before Jay dragged me into the heaving crowd.

For a brief moment I caught sight of Em, fixing a string of lights that had stopped working. A song or two afterwards, she sat at the edge of a table, deep in conversation with a young man older than both of us, his blond hair pulled back into a ponytail – perhaps Zed's brother. She seemed to be having a good time. Old jealousy soared, a wily shark breaking through the surface, but I swallowed it. No, I should be glad she was having a good time, even without me.

A herby aroma permeated the air when the first soup was served, a number of dancers peeled off to eat. I took the chance, beelining for the table where Em had been.

She was no longer there.

Disappointment: the damp bottom of a well.

What had she meant by 'later'?

The sun had given way to the rising full moon, rendering the night bruised and darkened. We pushed the tables back towards the edges when more people joined the dance.

I slipped away from the crowd and walked towards the Harvest Spirit, approaching the figure from behind. The bonfire and solar lights lit up the dance, but out here beyond the feasting tables, shadows lurked.

My heartbeat loud in my ears, I reached towards the fold where I'd hidden the end of a second piece of twine.

"Beautiful work this year, Cee," a voice said.

I thrust my hand back into my pocket. The die hit hard against my knuckles. It was only Tey – one of the young men Kay would be committing to. "I don't know how you do it."

"Thank you," I managed to say, my breath ragged. "Just practice,

I guess."

"Anyhow, thought you should hear that." Tey flashed me a smile, and disappeared back into the group of dancers.

I reached again, shoving my hand into the right side of the Spirit, just under a sheaf that fanned outwards. My fingers found the hidden twine – I tugged, hard. A small, neat bundle of wheat and rye came away silently, straight into my palm. I breathed out through my teeth, a low whistle of relief. Using the cloth I'd taken from Olga-Ma's worktable, I wrapped the bundle and slipped it deep into my pocket.

Probably best to drop it back at my tent, then rejoin the dance. No one need ever know. Tomorrow, I would find Em, and we could start forming plans, make our way to the ancient city.

The tent I slept in stood furthest away from the centre. A plain, dark green affair, I'd made a few custom adjustments so I could keep the external door flap open on hot summer nights without anyone seeing inside. In winter, it stayed warm. I liked my quiet and everyone knew it, so they always let me settle a little further from everyone else. Behind me, the music throbbed, the fire burned, the dancers spun.

Someone seized my arm, I stifled a scream.

Em's face emerged from the shadows, framed by those honey-brown curls, carrying that geranium smile.

"Sorry, didn't meant to startle you."

I choked down my panic.

"Why are –?"

"Been waiting for you, that's all."

She drew me into an urgent embrace, her lips soft, tasting of mead. Then she reached for my hand, placing something that rustled into my palm. I knew what it was without having to look – a purple ticket. My heart pounded, my mouth dry. When she pulled back to speak, her breath was shallow.

"I knew you'd try to escape early." She gestured towards the pulse of the festivities. Laughed. "You're so predictable, Cee."

Desire: a fire pooling deep that hungered for more to burn.

I might have been predictable, but there was more to me than that.

"I want to… to show you something first." I reached into my pocket, feeling for the cloth bundle.

A loud scream pierced the darkness. The music stopped. A

thunderous crash. More shouts. Different voices yelled.

Wild-eyed, Em and I exchanged a glance. She moved first, back towards the dance. I ran after her flying hair.

By the time we wove through the tents back to the feasting, the crowd had gone largely silent. A sniffle here, a sob there. The smell gave it away first, a smokiness, a greenness, something being freshly burned.

In the middle over the fire, a burning pile of the Harvest Spirit, engulfed in flames.

Em grasped my shoulder. "Cee…"

I couldn't speak.

Someone must have bumped against it, knocked it off its precarious stand – straight into the bonfire.

Old Ma Olga was nowhere to be seen. She might have already retired for the night.

The die in my pocket weighed heavy, but I didn't need it, not this time. Somehow, the solution was crystal clear. The Chronicles had always been explicit: what we fashioned year after year was only a temporary home, not the Spirit itself. This needn't be the disaster everyone feared.

"I can make another," I said out loud, surprising myself. The conversational noise around me dropped as people realised I'd spoken.

"I can make another," I repeated, louder this time.

All of them – the dancers, the musicians, the feasting crowd – stood and stared at me, confused. In the smoky dimness, I tried to meet their gaze, one by one.

"The Spirit is here, yes, it is in what we grow, but it's also in all of us." I tapped my right palm to my chest. "Here's what we need to do: each of you – go back to your home, bring me a piece of your harvest, however small. I'll remake the Spirit's winter home. Right here, now."

At first, no one moved. Then one of them shuffled towards a tent, another followed suit. One by one, they hurried away.

Em, Jay and Tey cleared the feasting table so I could use it as a workspace. Material started flowing in: ears of corn, bundles of grapes, apples, a small sheaf of wheat, some rye.

I got to work, arranging and binding this to that, focusing on the natural shapes of the bounty and gave way to how they wanted to show themselves.

The small bundle from the old Spirit felt heavy in my pocket. The thought struck so suddenly that, looking back now, it was as if a higher force slipped the idea into my head. I took the bundle out and split it in two. I'd keep half for the city, but doing this meant part of the old Spirit could live in the new.

Someone started a song. One of the musicians picked up a fiddle, and once again people began to dance, if slower, less frenzied.

At some point Em had her hand on my shoulder, at some point she moved away.

Time melted, the world folded backwards as my fingers worked to construct a new Harvest Spirit – affording me a kind of peace.

"Here," said Em. In her hands were wildflowers from the hill, our hill.

I smiled, and braided them in.

And suddenly, the second Harvest Spirit I'd made in a day was finished.

Tey helped me balance the new Spirit on a more stable stump of wood.

Cheers drowned out the music for a long moment, then the dance resumed.

A different thought entered my head: next harvest moon, I should teach someone else to do what I do, so none of these traditions would be forgotten.

The air cooled my back, my legs felt stiff with each step up the hill. The moon had begun its descent, a silver disc losing its shine but still round, still full. From the settlement below, sounds of dance and song floated on the night breeze, muted by the shush of grass and the whispering leaves of trees.

Em fell in step beside me. I took her arm, like old times.

"I wanted to tell you I've missed you," she said. "All summer."

"Was that why you were hovering near my tent tonight?"

She let out a soft, embarrassed giggle. "I suppose I owe you an apology, of sorts."

"You do?" My feet stopped, so did hers.

Em spun me around to face her, her serious gaze half lit by the glow of the moon.

"I never asked you what *you* wanted. I might have said you were predictable. But truth is, I can't read you, Cee."

"I'm not a book."

She laughed, and clasped me close.

We made our way to the elm tree, the grass damp under our skirts, yarrow feathering under my fingers, clovers cloistering under the fading night.

I pointed at the horizon, at the glass city in the distance.

"I came here often, so I could look at that over there, like we used to do. Dream about what we might have done if we'd gone." I caught myself. "Think about it, I mean. You did all the dreaming."

She chuckled, the breeze teasing her honey-brown hair.

I took a deep breath. "Do you want to go tomorrow?"

Her eyes widened, her mouth dropped open. "Did you just say what I thought you said?"

For an answer, I pulled out the bundle wrapped in its cloth from my pocket. Smaller than what I originally intended, but it still hefted a decent sized bulk.

"A part of the Spirit will come with us, we can start something new. And when the next harvest comes around, we could return and meet everyone else at an appointed place. Will you come with me?"

Given how hard Em hugged me then, I was worried I'd lose the bundle altogether. The moon hid behind a cloud, I could no longer see her face, but I was sure that she was wearing her geranium smile when she planted a crimson kiss on my cheek.

The die in my pocket shifted as we laid down on the grass.

Nine. *Give way to courage, seize the day.*

Or perhaps, seize the moon.

When Em wasn't looking, I tossed the die under the elm tree.

Fear: something one should never face alone.

Hope: the dawn of a new day, because no sunrise is the same as any other.

Emily's Farewell Coat

It had begun as the nice day off which had every promise of going right. Ria had just settled into her favourite chair to knit a new cardigan for herself, but all that changed the moment her circular needles snapped, dunking dropped stitches into her steaming cup of tea. Which would be why, around the time she should have been having a lovely lunch of roasted vegetables, she was instead drenched to the bone standing at the front door of the Textile Collective's workshop, living proof that the new water-resistant coat fabric they'd been testing for Emily's parting gift... well, wasn't.

On any other day during the cold season when the rivers swell, it would've taken a quick jaunt from her raft-cottage moored over the winterbourne, across the floating walkways, up the hill and through the twitten to the workshop. But before she made it halfway the skies opened, dropping a merciless deluge over the town and its surrounds with the kind of ferocity that flattened grass and churned bare earth.

The moment it became apparent something had gone wrong: when Ria tried to tug a sleeve down to cover more of her hand, and a chunk of it came clean off between her fingers. In all the years she'd worked at the Textile Collective, despite their philosophy of reusing every bit of fibrous material for their fabrics – new, recycled, or found – *this* had never happened before.

One small consolation, perhaps: the dye she'd developed for it held fast even as the fibres began to disintegrate under the weight of water, so she *hadn't* left a trail of deep inky blue through the cobblestone streets.

Silver lining, and all that. Maybe she should have sewn one into the dang coat.

In the distance, wind turbines spun serenely, elegant in an asynchronous dance.

At the door of the workshop, Ria stood in a puddle of rainwater. The front door was an oversized wooden affair that once belonged to a bank up the street. The workshop itself nestled at a corner. A long time ago it might have been a real-estate agent's, in the old days when humans wrongly claimed legal rights to the land instead of ceding to nature's authority.

Ria pushed the door handle. It wouldn't budge.

She rapped one hand on the door.

"Open up."

No answer. Could they not hear her?

Surely, it being a Tuesday, everyone else ought to be working either on the long list of the town's requests for repair, or on new clothes for the upcoming warm season. Everyone except for Ria, of course, and Emily, who had begun acclimatising for her transition to be a Reader-Traveller next week, by only coming in on Saturdays in the past month.

Which meant Emily's leaving party would be *this* coming Saturday. Four days' time.

Panic squeezed the air out of Ria's lungs. She'd taken this coat from a rack of test garments – in the batch they'd been trialling for Emily's parting gift. If this prototype she'd worn couldn't survive a single rainstorm, could they even use the rest of the batch?

Ria picked at her soggy collar. The entire piece tore off in her hand.

"A whole bloomin' knot of yarn," Ria swore.

It had all seemed so feasible when they spoke about it a few days ago during their weekly Big Meeting. A simple afternoon tea for Emily, and everyone from the town would be invited. Then, Leyla, the newest member of the Collective, pointed out they *could* make Emily a leaving gift, to thank her for all her work. And wouldn't it be nice if they made her something suitable for a Reader-Traveller?

"Something weatherproof," Geoff, their lead designer, had thought out loud, a cookie halfway to his mouth. Whenever Geoff didn't have a sewing implement in hand he'd have some semblance of food. "She hates the texture of waxed fabric, though, so we'd have to do something different."

"Pockets," Ria herself had said. "Lots of them."

"Then you'd need something to counter gravity," Jules added.

Leyla said, wide-eyed, "We can do that?"

"In theory," Jules had replied. "With our ability to blend an assortment of fibres, we could do *anything*."

That had been last week. Now, Ria knocked once again on the workshop door, hard enough for her knuckles to hurt. "Oi! Jules? Leyla?"

This early in the day, Geoff wouldn't be in yet.

She *could* try the back door, but that meant going into the rain and circling around to the rear garden.

A small black rectangle to the right of the door blinked a tiny square of bright, green light. Ria could have sworn this wasn't here several days ago.

She leaned down for a closer look.

"Good morning, Ria," said a calm, genderless voice.

Ria jumped backwards, spraying rainwater in a frenzied fountain. "What the –"

"Hi Ria, welcome back to the workshop. This is EZEE-5000. How can I help?"

EZEE, the monstrous machine that Emily had acquired over the past several months, in the belief that it would help them scale up during the change in seasons when people commonly needed more clothes.

"You know a machine won't replace you, right?" Ria had tried to tease, but Emily hadn't appreciated the joke.

EZEE had taken on the bulk of fibre processing, spinning and dyeing, which was welcome, but also half the space in the workshop – somewhat less welcome. And now, they also seemed to answer the door. Would they be making a Sunday roast next?

"How can you *help*?" Oh, the nerve of the thing. "Let me in, you –"

Ria caught herself. However much she distrusted EZEE, everything in her universe, whether animate or inanimate, was simply composed of atoms fused into molecules. Just because one set of molecules in a different formation happened to be making your bad day worse didn't mean you needed to be rude to it.

"Sorry, I didn't mean to shout." Ria wheezed.

"It's okay, Ria, I don't have human ears, that didn't hurt," said EZEE. "Do you need to come inside?"

"Yes, please. It's bloody pouring out here." It felt better to be rude at *something*.

"I'm sorry you're caught in the rain, Ria," said EZEE.

Had they always been so irritatingly polite?

"So, open up then," said Ria. "Please," she added.

"You need to authenticate yourself first."

"Authen-what?"

"Authenticate yourself: tell me you are who you are."

"But I am who I am."

"Yes, but I need to confirm you are who you are."

"I'm telling you who I am, EZEE." Somehow her voice had ratcheted up in both pitch and volume. "Hurry up, please. I'm drenched out here."

"Sorry, Ria. I can't let you in unless you prove you are you."

Ria flung up her arms, showering droplets of water in a wide circle. "How?"

Come to think of it, several weeks ago Emily went around and asked everyone to place both hands flat on a black device. She had given a rambling explanation, but at the time Ria had been right in the middle of counting stitches for the sleeve of Hartley's new springtime jumper, custom-made to cater for the stonemason's spectacularly muscular arms.

"Place your palm on the black panel to your right, Ria."

"My whole palm? On the panel?" A strange ask, but Ria slapped the flat of her hand on the black rectangle next to the door. Something beeped.

"Thank you, Ria," said EZEE. "Glad that you are really you."

Before Ria could think of a smart retort, the door creaked open a fraction and she shoved her way in, shoes squeaking water with every squidgy step.

Between the heavy rain rattling on the workshop roof and the low drone of EZEE's background hum, Leyla's concentration broke only when a sharp blast of cold air pierced through the front door, accompanied by the sight of a tall, sodden figure in the doorway.

Leyla bolted upright in her armchair by the bay window, crochet needle clattering out of her hand.

Under the dripping coat, the figure looked familiar.

"Ria?" Leyla called out. "That you?" Wasn't it her day off today?

"No, Leyla, I'm just a drowned rat, or a wet hen. Help me here?"

"Oh my!" said Leyla, rushing up from her nook, scattering a ball of yarn across the floor. She tugged the wet, dripping fabric from Ria's shoulders. A tricky business, given Ria stood nearly a whole head taller than her own petite frame. Together, they peeled off the soggy sleeves that clung to Ria's arms.

"Thank you," muttered Ria, when they finally extricated her from the waterlogged mess. Her dark, shoulder-length hair sat plastered against the earthy complexion of her face.

Leyla held up the remains of the coat, oblivious to a large puddle forming on the workshop floor. The coat seemed familiar. The deep blue gave it away – from their latest test batch, meant for Emily's parting gift.

"Wasn't this supposed to be waterproof?" Leyla asked. Something must have gone wrong with the mix of recycled fibres.

Ria grunted. Her words came out through chattering teeth. "Grab me a towel please? There's a love."

"Oh!"

The very wet bundle of fabric in Leyla's hands presented a more immediate problem. A metal trough glinted at the far corner of the room, attached to one of EZEE's components. It would have to do.

Nothing for it, but speed.

Cradling the bundle and ignoring how her own dress was getting wet, Leyla bounded across the room alongside the length of EZEE's chassis and dropped the remains of the coat into the trough.

"Breezy, help clean, please?"

EZEE's cleaning droid – a small robot no bigger than a bucket – whirred to life. Leyla ducked into the corridor that led off to the kitchen and the back room, grabbed a newly minted towel from a storage cupboard and sped back to Ria, who, by now, stood in a sizeable pond of rainwater.

"Cheers, love." Ria proceeded to work out the knots in her damp hair.

"Hold on, let me get you another."

Another run to the cupboard, another towel – on second

thoughts, a third.

"Here," said Leyla.

The cleaning bot had stopped completely by the puddle. It had extruded something that resembled a straw. Whatever was it doing?

"I think it's confused," said Ria.

Leyla shook her head and plopped the third towel on the floor to soak out the puddle. It confounded her; why had there never been a mat by the door? In the spring there would be pollen; in summer, wildflower seeds stuck to shoes; in the autumn, there would be flakes from fallen leaves. Then throughout November there would be spark powder and smoke residue from Bonfire Night. Any number of things that could accidentally end up in the fibre processing.

Ria wrapped the towels around her shoulders.

Not a common occurrence, to witness misery on Ria's face. Perhaps a cup of tea would warm her up.

"Can I get you –?"

"Ye gods, EZEE!" A deep, male voice boomed from the back of the workshop.

Ria's lifted an eyebrow. "What's going on?"

Leyla turned and squinted. No smoke wisping out from the back room this time. A minor improvement, perhaps. Leaning towards Ria, she whispered, "Jules has been battling with writing new subroutines all morning. He's in the foulest mood, I wouldn't –"

"Huh," said Ria, and began plodding towards the back room, leaving a trail of wet footprints through the corridor.

"I'll, um, set EZEE on an analysis cycle," said Leyla, to no one in particular.

Something bumped against her ankle.

Breezy, wet with rainwater, held up an object glinting in its mechanical hand – her crochet needle.

Jules extricated his fingers from his hair, and with it a few greying gold strands. He had been at this for hours with nothing to show for it. EZEE's components took up half the room, and to work at its console, Jules had to wedge his lanky figure between the tail end of EZEE's chassis and the back wall.

How Emily used to fit in this tight spot, he hadn't a clue. She wasn't exactly a small woman. Though right now, he dearly wished Emily could be here – *she* would have known what to do. But Emily would be gone next week, and so much knowledge, such immeasurable wisdom, would be gone with her. Jules sighed. As much as Emily had trained him in EZEE's workings from the beginning, he'd never feel ready.

EZEE's console blinked a blank cursor, its standard hum descending into a whine.

"Can't you just make the rest of it up, EZEE?"

"Sorry, Jules, I cannot do that."

"Well, bugger that." Perhaps it had been a foolish idea to get EZEE to construct a garment on command, let alone a pattern.

A tall, gaunt silhouette manifested through the doorway. Jules glanced up from the console.

"Wow, Ria, you look like a drowned rat."

"Or a wet hen. Take your pick."

"What happened?"

"Weather happened." Ria gestured at the outside world beyond the back window. The rain, however, had slowed and refused to be accused. "Take a look at the prototype I wore when you get the chance. I don't know what's wrong with it."

"EZEE has been giving me a hard time."

"I'm sorry, Jules," said EZEE.

Jules leaned back against the wall, which took only several centimetres to achieve. "Some days, I wish we'd never brought it here."

"Jules!" Ria said, alarmed. "You can't say that! Not in front of them!"

An unusual noise came through EZEE's vocaliser, sounding suspiciously like a whimper.

"You're upsetting them."

"It's just a machine, it doesn't have feelings." Letting out a heavy breath, Jules slipped out from the narrow gap. Something in his back popped.

Ria placed a gentle hand on EZEE's console. "There, there."

Consoling the console. Jules grimaced. Not that EZEE could feel sympathy, but it moved a mechanical arm to make room for Ria she leaned against its chassis.

Absently, Jules paced, his feet traced a small tight circle in the middle of the room. There must be a way to –

"What were you trying to do?" she asked.

"The coat for Emily. We only have a few days to go and either this thing can't figure out how to do the design, or I am obviously not competent enough to ask correctly."

"Don't call them a thing!"

"Why would that make a difference!"

Jules caught himself. That attitude did not belong here. "Sorry, Ria. I'm just… out of options."

"Also, wasn't Geoff supposed to do the design?"

Jules stopped mid-pace, staring at her open-mouthed. "Was he?"

Once again, his hands ended up in his hair. There had been so much to learn, so much to catch up on, it was entirely possible that he misremembered.

"Ugh," said Jules.

He had raised his bleary eyes at the crew during that Big Meeting some days ago; they'd formed a rough plan – playing to each of their skills – Geoff to sketch a design, Ria to blend the dyes, Leyla to craft the embellishments (perhaps with help from Ria), and Jules to coax EZEE into production. Wonderful creatives, they all were, but Geoff was a dreamer, Ria tended to be impulsive, and Leyla – bright but inexperienced.

Somehow, Jules' feet had taken him back to his seat by the wall. The cursor on EZEE's console blinked a confrontation.

Someone waved something in front of his face.

"Hello?" said Ria. "Earth to Jules?"

Ria, with a few sheets of paper. No doubt some sketches Geoff had left lying around. Jules rubbed his eyes with the back of his hands.

"I haven't seen Geoff's pattern for the coat. Are those it?"

"No, I have no idea what these are."

Jules might have said something in response, he wasn't sure. Shutting his eyes, he leaned backwards once again against the wall.

"You need some tea, Jules," Ria said, gently. "And some rest to go with it. I'll go find Geoff."

When he finally stood up, something smacked into his forehead, knocking him back down.

"Sorry, Jules," said EZEE. "Are you okay?"

EZEE's mechanical arm had somehow swung in the way.

The café had been peaceful in the late morning, but now, after midday, nearly all the tables had filled up and the clink of cutlery accompanied a chorus of chatty voices, churning the dregs of Geoff's conscious thoughts into unmouldable putty. He moved aside the remains of his brew and an unfinished slice of lemon cake, pushed his glasses back up his nose, and spread another sketch in front of Janice, who taught mathematics most days at the secondary school.

"Ooh, I like this very much," said Janice, trailing a finger on the frill he'd drawn on a dress she wanted.

"Glad to hear it." Despite himself, Geoff beamed. Always a wonderful feeling when someone appreciated his work. "This should give you the flair you wanted for the commitment ceremony, and after that –" he flipped over the page "if you remove this piece here, you'd be able to wear it like an everyday dress."

"Very clever!"

Geoff liked working here in the café, whether alone, or meeting with clients who had specific requests from the Textile Collective. Sure, he had a desk up in the loft at the workshop, but it had never been quite the same since EZEE took up all the downstairs space. Now, all their old sergers and sewing machines cluttered up the area which had once been wholly his. Nothing against EZEE, of course. He quite liked their low hum whenever he worked late at nights. Or maybe, he simply found it difficult to focus when everyone else was around. Who knew?

Janice gathered her scarf and coat, both in a shade of near-iridescent fuchsia that suited the honey-brown of her skin. "When shall I come around for a fitting?"

"How about in a couple of weeks?"

"Wonderful," she said, rising. "But I'll see you Saturday, won't I?"

Saturday? Geoff scrabbled through his memory.

"Yes, I have an invitation from Jules! For Emily's transition party."

"Oh!" Geoff whisked a quick smile. How had the day come around so soon? "Yes, we'll see you then!"

On her way out, Janice paused to chat to someone who had just come in – a tall, willowy figure. Geoff's heart skipped a beat. He'd recognise that silhouette anywhere; even though it must have been well over a decade since they were teenage sweethearts. Something about the way Ria moved, how her intensity always drew a kind of magic around her. It didn't matter that her dungaree dress crinkled, or that her normally wavy hair had flattened out.

Ria plonked herself in a chair opposite him, her damp hair exaggerating the point of her nose, the cut of her cheeks.

Geoff drew a sharp breath. "Did you get caught in the rain?"

Often it felt as if they'd known each other for so long that hellos and goodbyes seemed superfluous.

She shrugged. "Weather happened, but you should've seen the prototype I was wearing."

"Do you need tea?"

When Ria smiled, entire galaxies aligned. "No, but Jules needs your sketch for Emily's coat. If you've got it."

Geoff flipped open his folio, rifled through it. Where had he left those? He remembered drawing it: a long coat, with special-purpose pockets, detachable hood, storm flaps, interchangeable knitted cuffs and lace collar. "I left it at the studio for Jules."

Come to think of it, a few other designs appeared to be missing too.

"I'm sure I didn't dream it." Geoff's shoulders slumped. Being organised had never been his strong suit.

To his surprise, Ria reached out and patted his hand. Her earthy-gold skin a sharp contrast to his own washed-out pink, her skinny fingers – strong from working needles and yarn – couldn't be more different than his pudgier counterparts. "I'm quite sure you didn't."

Geoff sighed, and pushed his glasses back up his nose. It had been a busy end to the cold season, with many more custom requests that he'd remembered having to deal with since he'd joined the Textile Collective.

"Are you eating that?" Ria pointed to his unfinished cake.

"Better not waste, I suppose," Geoff pulled the plate in between them. The speed with which Ria picked up the fork didn't escape him. "It's your day off, Ria. How about lunch? On me."

"Oh!" Her dark eyes glittered. "My word, lunch would be wonderful."

The cake still tasted good. All days should begin with dessert. Everything always seemed to look up afterwards.

How to address EZEE for specific commands, when they took up half of the front of the workshop, a part of the corridor, and extended into the back room? Leyla gaped at the sheer monstrosity of the machine. It had never been clear – whether you issued a command to a component that did a specific thing, or if you just uttered a request.

How had Emily done it?

The Textile Collective had not been Leyla's first choice for an apprenticeship. She'd always thought she'd worked with the confectionery maker and spend her days making sherbert lemons or fruit gummies, but meeting Emily for the first time changed her mind. How her silver hair hung over her collared, ultramarine dress, a direct yet quiet authority, but more: a passion that still burned despite the wrinkles around her eyes. Something Leyla understood that day – that doing a great service to the community lit one up on the inside.

"We work a bit like musicians do," Jules had explained on her first day. "First designer, second designer; first knitter, second knitter…"

"But there are four of you?" Leyla blurted, before she could stop herself.

"Five now, if you count EZEE," said Emily. "Who could almost be an orchestra by themselves."

Jules had pulled a face. "More like a pipe organ with a hundred stops for different noises."

Emily had laughed.

On that first visit, EZEE had been contained in the back room. The front bay window opened to a view on the street, and this room had been full of rickety sergers, a loom and a mix of electrical and manual machinery – salvaged from all around town.

"Same with EZEE, really," Emily had said. "Though some of their parts came from further afield."

But now, all that had been moved upstairs, and EZEE spanned everywhere one looked.

"EZEE?" Leyla tried.

"Hello, Leyla. How may I help?"

"Analyse, please."

A pause.

"What would you like me to analyse, Leyla?"

"The fabric in the trough."

"What would you like me to analyse it for?"

Goodness, how tedious.

"Um, why it held so much water."

"Understood." Another pause. "I'm not detecting any fabric in the correct trough, one moment."

Breezy suddenly spun around from the front door, picked up the dripping remains of the former coat and dumped it into another trough that Leyla hadn't noticed before. EZEE's various inputs and outputs constituted a confounding, three-dimensional puzzle.

On the inside of the trough, something like a pincher captured a sample of the fabric.

"Fabric found," EZEE said. "Analysing."

Leyla whistled through her teeth. It couldn't be that easy, could it?

Breezy whirred towards the puddle at the front door, but changed its mind, and instead began cleaning Ria's footprints through the corridor.

Earlier on, Ria had glided in from the back room, and grabbed another coat from the rack of prototypes by the corridor.

Leyla hadn't been quick enough. "Wait! I have to –"

Jules had asked her to keep a catalogue so at least they could track any flaws.

"I need to go get Geoff," Ria had said, zipping herself into the coat. "Jules is tearing his hair out."

"Sure, but just let me take note of which coat you've got?"

"Later!" Ria had waved and hurried back out the front door.

Leyla squinted at the sheet she'd started to compile. If they didn't keep careful track, they'd never know what caused the issue with the other one. With a sigh, she pulled up a chair next to the rack and began to tag each coat.

Jules emerged from the back room with a shuffle, rubbing a spot on his forehead.

"What the –"

He strode over and examined the tattered, disintegrated remains of the coat in the trough. He pulled his hand back quickly, screwed up his nose. "Was this what Ria wore this morning?"

"Yes," replied Leyla. "EZEE is analysing now, I think."

Jules stared at the sheen of damp on his hand. "At least the dye didn't run."

He walked towards the bay window. The rainstorm had kept the townspeople indoors all morning. Now that it slowed to a drizzle, the street outside bustled.

"How's the rest of the batch?"

Leyla picked a coat off the rack and showed him. This one didn't look like it would disintegrate in a rainstorm, but probably neither did the one Ria wore.

"We should probably test that the coats will hold weight in the rain," said Jules, face upturned towards the sky.

And so they wheeled the coat rack out into the rear garden, still in need of a tidy after the winter, being careful not to damage Ria's seedlings. A heat pump hummed along one wall, squirreling heat from EZEE's functions to all the buildings along the street. No test in the garden would be as good as someone wearing them, but with only a few days before Saturday, this would have to do.

"Now, for weights," said Jules.

A large pebble caught Leyla's eye. She went around the garden and picked up a few. "How about these?"

"Rocks?"

"In the pockets."

Jules weighed them in one hand. "Let's do it."

Just then, the back gate squealed open.

"What *are* you doing?" asked Geoff. A warm, hearty aroma emanated from the parcel he carried in his hands; immediately, Leyla's stomach growled.

"Gosh, is that lunch?" Jules exclaimed. "Thank you, you two."

Leyla reached out a hand to Ria. "May I?"

Ria grinned and shrugged off her coat. At least she seemed to be in a much better mood than when she left. Geoff, walking into the kitchen with Jules, had some lightness in his step too.

"Three days left now, Jules," Geoff was saying. "Think we can do it?"

Leyla didn't hear Jules' reply; she'd followed them in but poked her head around to the front room. Breezy had done a decent job with the floor. Hadn't there been a pile of patterns somewhere? Where did those go?

A familiar whirring noise made her turn around. Breezy's mechanical hand held up a ball of yarn, with the lace she started making still attached to the end, miraculously intact.

The next morning, Ria leaned down, lined her nose with the top of the black rectangular panel and shouted, "*Hello?*"

"Good morning, Ria."

"Yes, EZEE. Morning."

She placed her palm on the panel. The door screeched open and Ria stepped through.

There, getting better at this.

EZEE hummed softly, just enough to keep their systems on standby. "You're the first one in today, Ria."

"Yes, EZEE, I know." Ria hung up her coat on the hook by the door – an older prototype coat she'd kept at home. They seemed chatty today. Do machines get lonely?

"Do you get lonely, EZEE?"

"No, I'm not human, Ria."

Whatever. Ria shook her head and beelined for the kitchen. First things first: tea.

Geoff's sketches littered the table, a few pages scattered on the floor. He must have worked late again. She picked up a sheet which featured a detailed design for Emily's coat, specifically the sleeves. He'd marked out where an embroidered heart could go. Ria chuckled. Rather fitting for someone as forthright as Emily.

The cuffs Geoff had drawn suggested a knitted design. Clever, attached with a cord around the sleeve on the inside, rendering them removable, interchangeable. Maybe they could bounce some ideas around afterwards. After all, in their crew, she held the position of first knitter.

Ria pushed the back door open. In the garden, a light breeze ruffled the collars of the coats on the rack. Whatever Jules added to the mix of the fabric did its magic – despite the pebbles weighing down in their pockets, they kept their form without warping or dragging.

She put a hand on the fabric of the closest coat. Dry. Not good.

"Morning, Ria," a lilting voice sang from the kitchen door.

Leyla appeared by her side and, too, reached out to touch a prototype.

"Hm. Not a good enough test, is it?"

Huh, Leyla had learned fast. Had it only been three months since she'd joined?

"Hard to get all scientific about it," Ria explained. "In the same way that our bread uses yeast present in our air, or the honey our bees make depends on what's in bloom, our fabrics include what we have around us that can be made into fibres. Everything we make is unique to us."

Leyla's jaw dropped, as Ria's had when she first grasped this very fundamental outlook to the Textile Collective's methods.

"So that's why there's no mat by the door!"

"What mat?"

Leyla's ability to focus appeared to be unwinding like a ball of yarn. "Then… why the cleaning droid? Why Breezy?"

"It collects the stuff, cleans it and processes it – like all the fibres we recycle."

"Doesn't it make the process harder?"

"That's one of the reasons why Emily brought in EZEE: so we could, in theory, teach it to identify problems before they happen. Though that will take time."

Leyla's eyes grew wide, and Ria couldn't help herself; she grinned.

"Morning!" Jules walked out from the back door, a cup of brew in hand. With his other hand, he reached out and ruffled the closest coat.

He grimaced. "Well, we could do one of two things –"

"EZEE should have done the composition analysis on the other one," Leyla cut in. "We can ask them to compare?"

"Or we could just throw a bucket of water over these," Ria muttered. "And water my spring seedlings at the same time."

"Or both?" Jules took a sip from his mug, his eyebrows hovered over its rim.

In the end, they did both, just to be doubly sure, and picked out the coat that seemed to have fared the best.

Late afternoon found the Collective settling around the kitchen table, except for Jules, who stood in the doorway.

"Two days to go," Leyla breathed.

"We can do it," said Geoff. He'd shown up after lunch, bearing a generous plate of cinnamon swirls.

Jules called over his shoulder. "EZEE, how's the fabric coming along?"

"Three metres will be completed this evening, Jules."

"What did the analysis say?" asked Ria. She'd found some yarn, a pair of needles, and had begun to knit.

"A high composition of an unusual cellulose, though it seemed to have mostly ended up in the one prototype," said Jules.

"I fed EZEE samples of the rest, and they were fine," Leyla added.

"Some kind of error in the mixture, then," said Geoff, a swirl on its way to his mouth.

Jules sighed and sat down at the table with the rest. He picked up a pastry, examined it, took a bite. "Seeing as I've failed to teach EZEE to design, we might have to make this coat by hand."

"Fine with me," Ria said. "We'll have three sets of cuffs done by tomorrow."

"And two sets of lace for the collar," said Leyla, watching Ria's hands fly.

"I'll cut the fabric tonight," Geoff volunteered.

"Then I can sew it tomorrow," said Jules.

A gentle determination settled.

Then Leyla asked, "Who should give it to her?"

They hadn't thought about this.

A momentary pause.

"I can," said a voice from the corridor. "If you'll let me."

They all turned, staring at EZEE.

Eventually, Jules spoke. "Well, why not?"

Somehow, Emily's last day at the Textile Collective had come around much too quickly. No matter how well she'd planned for this day, how she gradually reduced her days at the workshop, still there seemed an insurmountable number of things she hadn't done. She didn't want to leave like Old Kim did, stretching out his time until one day he couldn't climb the hill any longer. Hard to forget the chaos that ensued afterwards. He had been the most experienced of the Collective then, when she first joined as a thin stick of a girl, when her hair had been a glorious chestnut instead of faded grey. No, there had to be a better way to untether from one's lifelong vocation and move on before one got too frail and old. All the other dreams she'd never chased, all the other things she'd never done, because the Collective had been her life.

The real gamble had been EZEE, something Emily wished the Collective had during her early days. Collating all the parts for EZEE took much longer than expected; the final components arrived from the north nearly two months late because of winter storms and floods. Thank goodness Jules seemed to have picked up the most important things quickly; he'd teach the others. They'd be fine.

The morning had dawned surreptitiously, and it had taken Emily longer than normal to get out of the house. With each step up the hill through the twitten, Emily made a mental list of things to tell the Jules, Ria and Geoff – such as how to improve the error detection in fabrics using a custom subroutine. Leyla, the bright, sprightly new recruit, will no doubt learn from them in due course.

Emily paused, resisting the urge to sigh. Hard to imagine that she wouldn't be walking up here regularly any more. On the bright side, as a Reader-Traveller, she could go where she liked, collect stories and bring them home. She could journey up north when the weather warmed, to see her sister and her niece's little daughter.

In the distance, the wind turbines twirled.

At the door, the access panel she'd installed a couple of weeks ago blinked green.

"Good morning, Emily."

"Morning, EZEE."

"Good to see you, Emily."

"Um, nice to see you too, EZEE."

When had the machine learned to make small talk? She placed her hand on the authenticating pad.

It beeped red. Mild panic gripped Emily, like the first time she'd cut off an entire shirt sleeve by accident.

"EZEE? What's going on?"

"One moment, Emily."

All the pent-up anxiety Emily had kept under control all these weeks burst through the seams of her sanity.

"EZEE, it's my last day! This is *not –*"

"Won't be a moment, Emily. Please wait."

Emily willed a breath to fill her lungs, then pushed the air through her gritted teeth. She'd have to examine what happened once she got inside.

Lately, EZEE had sounded less and less machine-like. Or would that be a natural progression for a learning machine?

Finally, the light blinked green. The door yawned open.

Inside, none of the lights had been turned on.

"Jules? Ria?"

No answer.

The kitchen too was empty, though the back door stood open. The garden hadn't recovered from its scraggy, winter state. Some years, frost could come as late as mid-May. Emily shook her head. Not for her to worry about now. Ria would take care of the garden, she was a natural.

She turned back inside, paused by the stairs in the middle. Too quiet. Even EZEE wasn't humming. "Geoff?"

No, he wouldn't be in yet. Geoff always came in around midday, if not later.

"EZEE, why are the lights off?"

"They blew the other night in the storm, Emily."

"And no one has fixed them?" She huffed. "Where *is* everybody?"

"I don't know, Emily. Sorry."

No matter. Emily knew her way around the workshop blind. Walking up the length of the room towards the back, she ran a hand along EZEE's chassis.

"Leyla? Jules?"

The door to the back room was shut. Why?

The moment she opened it, bright light flooded outwards, nearly blinding her.

"SURPRISE!" A chorus of voices whooped. Stumbling back a step, Emily grabbed onto one of EZEE's mechanical arms, caught her breath.

Then she began to laugh.

The room squeezed full of people. Hartley, Janice, half the town seemed to be here. How did they all manage to fit? Bunting decorated the walls, streamers dangled from the ceiling. A cheerful tune emanated from somewhere; did they wire up speakers to EZEE?

Jules stepped forward, led her to the middle of the room by her elbow. "Happy Transition, Emily."

"Oh, this is so silly of you all," said Emily, but a warmth swirled up inside her heart, and with it the swell of a tear. She reached over and patted Jules on the shoulder.

He grinned. "Everyone has been crouching here for a while, and would dearly love some cake, tea and tipple. But first, EZEE, would you please?"

EZEE whirred, but then it was Breezy who whizzed through between everyone's legs. A hessian wrapped parcel secured in its clutches, it stopped right at Emily's feet.

"For me?" said Emily. She hadn't expected this, though maybe she should have. Didn't they give Old Kim a lovely warm blanket?

But when she pulled off the ribbon and the wrapper fell away, her mouth dropped open. She ran her hands over the soft garment – a luxurious coat woven from a fabric with a fine weave. The cuffs, hand-knitted in fingering weight, dainty and spectacular. The crocheted collar held form, bearing a hint of lace. Most of all, the dye was a gorgeous, deep blue, the colour of the deepest ocean, or a clear dusk sky. An embroidered red heart sat atop the right sleeve. Emily chuckled.

"You made this." It wasn't a question. They were, after all the Textile Collective.

Ria stepped up and helped her into it. The way the folds hugged her body, it weighed next to nothing, but she could already tell it'd keep her cool in the heat but warm when it got cold.

"For your new adventures, Emily," said Ria. "From all of us."

Tears sprung into her eyes unbidden and Emily banished them with the back of her hands, and continued to examine the construct of the coat.

Pockets everywhere, including a large one over the front.

"For a scarf," Geoff said. "For those times where you have to remove your coat and your scarf has nowhere to go…"

"Oh! A silver lining." A giggle escaped her.

All at once, Emily wanted to hug them, shower them with affection she so rarely bestowed on anyone. Then she reached her hand inside a pocket and found something hard, rigid and rectangular.

She pulled it out so all could see. "What's this?"

Emily turned it around in her hands. A book? She flipped the cover open. The paper bore a good thickness, but page after page was blank. Reader-Travellers who had gone before her normally took books to read, but it would make sense, wouldn't it, to have a book to write in?

"How thoughtful of you!"

A sudden hush had descended on the Collective. It hadn't escaped Emily; the glances they furtively exchanged with each other. An unspoken puzzlement.

"Um, glad you like it!" said Leyla, with a nervous giggle.

"Well," said Ria, clapping her hands, altogether a little too cheerfully. "How about some tea and cake?"

A loud cheer erupted from the crowd in the room, then one by one, they filed past Emily, wrapping her in hugs and pecks on the cheek. Then somehow, only a confused-looking Geoff stood in the room with her. He glanced down the back of EZEE's chassis.

The coat felt a little too warm now, so Emily slipped it off and folded it over her arm.

"It's a lovely design, Geoff, I'll be proud to wear one of your best."

"Everyone worked so hard on it," he said, but he seemed distracted, distant.

"What's wrong?"

"Oh, you know me. Always losing my sketches. I swear I left some patterns down here last night." He stood back upright, adjusted the glasses on his nose. "I'd come down to take them upstairs, but you'd shown up earlier than we thought you would."

Emily couldn't contain her smile. "Next time, just get EZEE to scan them, even your drafts. They'll even keep versions for you."

Geoff raised an eyebrow. "Now that would be very handy." He extended a hand towards the kitchen. "Shall we have that cake while there's some left?"

She let Geoff leave first. Then slowly, Emily turned around and whispered into the room.

"You were in on this with them, weren't you, EZEE, my dear."

"Yes, Emily. I'm sorry I lied to you."

"Nice work on the book."

"Thank you."

"Don't worry, I won't tell them; they'll work it out. Take care of them for me, won't you?"

"Of course, Emily. Goodbye."

With a sigh, Emily walked out of the room, into the kitchen, then into the sun where the clouds had parted, where people were milling in the garden, where a frantic Ria began to strap a string of bunting to avoid anyone trampling on her seedlings.

"Good morning, Ria. You're early today."

"Yeah," was all Ria cared to say. Her head ached. That final drink last night had been a very, very bad idea. By the end of the evening, the Collective had agreed that a day off would be wise, but dawn found Ria restless, wide awake much too early. All the way up the hill and through the twitten that led to the workshop, she'd been dreaming about a good, hot cup of tea by the window to watch the rest of the town wake up, or perhaps by the back door so she could study her seedlings' progress in the garden. And maybe, if she dared be honest with herself, indulge in a little daydreaming. Geoff had been so sweet yesterday, even walked her home – something he hadn't done in an entire decade. But he didn't hold her hand – and she hadn't dared to ask. Maybe it was all nothing; he was just being a gentleman.

Something about the morning light today – how it seemed a little more gold, a smidgen more determined to punch through the pale grey clouds – seemed to signal spring must be properly on its way.

In the distant hills, wind turbines danced in the morning breeze.

At the door of the workshop, Ria placed her palm on the black rectangle.

The door squeaked open.

She hung up her coat onto a hook by the door – another prototype she'd picked off the rack when she left last night. She'd promised Leyla to write down the identifier on the tracking sheet on the kitchen wall. It had been a good night; Jules even found time to fire last minute questions at Emily.

Through the bay window, shy sunshine slanted past the rooftops across the street and landed unceremoniously on the workshop floor in a trapezoid mosaic. A rustling noise scattered the peace, but it was only Breezy, dusting up the floor.

"Thank you, Breezy," said Ria.

Breezy beeped, as if in response. It didn't have a vocaliser, and Ria never quite knew if it had a distinct brain from EZEE, or if they were one and the same – or if 'brain' was even the right word.

Scouting around the knitting nook, Ria pursed her lips. Her

knitting needles ought to be here, somewhere. Given the frantic scramble since Tuesday, and then yesterday's festivities, she'd completely forgotten about the needles she wanted – until she got home late last night and tried to pick up the cardigan where she left off.

Breezy's rustling seemed to have escalated to a loud shuffle.

"Breezy, are you okay?"

The small droid turned, beeped, and stopped. Something white stuck out unevenly under its wheels.

"Hang on." Ria moved towards the robot, lifted it up gently.

Breezy beeped loudly in protest.

"This won't hurt, I promise."

The droid beeped again. Could it understand her? Machines: a mystery.

From under its wheels, she tugged out a sheet of paper, then sheaves of the stuff. Patterns?

Geoff's patterns. Crumpled, shredded.

Oh *no*.

"EZEE?"

"Yes, Ria?"

A realisation blossomed. "Tell me you *didn't*."

In her shaking hands, the paper scraps fluttered.

"EZEE, did you recycle Geoff's patterns to make the notebook for Emily?" Her voice came out cracked.

A silence. Then EZEE said, "In a manner of speaking, I –"

"Can you not tell the difference between wastepaper and *valuable* paper?" Her words tumbled out in a rush. Her breath quaked. "Do you know how bad this is?"

Her voice bounced off the walls, pinged off EZEE's metal chassis.

"Ria, please calm down. I can explain."

"Explain!" Ria threw up her arms, slumped in the armchair, picked up a ball of yarn, tossed it down again into the yarn bowl.

How would she break this to Geoff?

She pinched the ridge of her nose, closed her eyes. "Okay, EZEE. Go on."

"We observed that Geoff left a lot of papers everywhere, and could never find them afterwards. Every single loose pattern that we found, we've scanned into our system. I can recognise them, but Breezy can't. When he collects the dust and waste for me to recycle, if I recognise a pattern I send an instruction to Breezy to bring it to our scanner. Typically, these pieces of paper are no longer viable, so I recycle them."

"So, they *do* end up in our fibres." Ria tapped a finger on her forehead. Maybe that was why one of the prototypes misbehaved so spectacularly? She had always loved the metaphor as Emily taught them; that things made from a place should carry traces of its surrounds, like honey, like bread, like wine. But maybe they ought to be a bit more careful from now on.

"And the notebook? How did you make it?"

A pause.

"Emily acquired my components from many places. I retain memory of all the other patterns I've learned."

Ria grabbed another ball of yarn, gave it a squish. This might have come from local sheep. Maybe they had underestimated how they could use EZEE's help.

"Can you…" Ria hesitated, searching for the right word, "*compile* all those scans into a book, too?"

"Certainly. I can get started now."

"Please."

EZEE began to hum, Ria picked up the ball of yarn. Underneath another skein – her needles. She began casting on, without any idea of what she might make. Maybe a sock. One could never have enough socks, no matter the season.

Around midday, after Ria had lost track of how many cups of tea she'd had, the back gate creaked. Geoff walked into the workshop from the back door, humming a lilting tune.

"Thought I find you here," he said, smiling. "Went past your place and you weren't there."

Ria stood up, heart beating a little quicker. He hadn't stopped by to see her for a very long time.

A loud *thunk* made them turn. Something black and rectangular landed in one of EZEE's troughs.

"Ah," said Ria, walking over and picking it up.

Her hands sweated, not from knitting with wool, and her blood pounded, not from having had too much to drink yesterday. Maybe the best way to do this is with the least ceremony possible.

"Um, EZEE and I worked something out today." She thrust the large book at him. "Here, this is for you."

Geoff raised an eyebrow, picked up the book and flipped through the pages. Impossible to read the expression on his face; it cycled through surprise, disbelief, relief. Then he walked towards the kitchen, sat down on a chair, and flipped through the last of the pages.

Ria followed him. Breezy activated from his corner and followed her.

"I thought I'd lost all of this." Geoff wiped a cheek with the back of his hand. To Breezy, he said. "Thank you, EZEE."

Breezy beeped.

Ria stared. One and the same, then.

Geoff stood up, and to her surprise, took her hand, and gave her a shy peck on her cheek.

"Thank you."

"I didn't –"

He gave her hand a gentle squeeze. "No, you figured it out."

Ria's cheeks warmed.

His nose had gone a little pink, but behind his glasses, his eyes sparkled. "How about lunch?"

Ria smiled. "Lunch would be *divine*."

Outside, rain began to fall. But they weren't going to let that dampen their spirits. Not when it had begun as the nice day off – which had every promise of going right.

Coriander

The narrow metal gangway wobbled though I disembarked the ship alone, or perhaps my legs had jellied after five weeks at sea and it was I who wobbled. My rucksack dug into my shoulders, hastily packed in the final hours on board. The heft should mean I hadn't left anything behind.

The dove-grey morning dawned cloudy, misting over the green-brown tangle of young mangroves, the day already heavy with the promise of equatorial heat. Unseen birds twittered, warning each other of my presence. The last time my great-grandmother – my ah-zho – made it back here, the city of her childhood had not yet ceded a third of its land to the rising river. What would she have thought if she'd come back now?

My palms slipped on the dew-coated safety railing. I paused, steadied myself. If only I could lend my body to her long-departed spirit so she could see this, hear this. We had no record of her return after her parents died – and now, decades after her own passing, we'd never find out.

The revelation sliced deep into my gut, a pain with no name.

Mild salt scent from the estuary mingled with root-sweet of damp earth, giving birth to dark green flora. Curiously, a sharp note of fragrant spice sang in the air – food being cooked, somewhere nearby. Cumin? No, much more complex, a whole chorus of aroma. My empty stomach rumbled, a gaping cavern. I hadn't eaten since –since when?

"Walk straight down," Carlos had said a mere two hours ago, white sailor's uniform still unbuttoned, billowing around his muscled body in the dreamy half-light of his cabin. We'd foregone much of last night's sleep. Words went unsaid, but we both knew: once the ship docked, our pleasant little arrangement would be over.

He'd leaned down, planted a chaste peck on my lips. "There's a good laksa stall in the middle of the port – if you need an early breakfast."

Throughout the past five weeks, he'd been the one to make sure I'd adjusted well to life on board, that I ate regularly given the multiple time zone changes, or that I had ample anti-nausea meds.

"Aster." His voice, low, quiet.

"Yes?"

His hand warmed my cheek. "I'll find you in town later when we're done here."

I didn't make him promise then, and now it nagged at me: should I have? He'd be gone the next sea day and I'd rather not know how I might feel. Better to focus on what I came to do: to understand what this place had been like, seen through Ah-Zho's memories, using her memoir as my guide. A relationship would be a distraction, a needless ephemerality.

Brackish water lapped under the metal planks, my unsteady steps rang too loud. I grasped the safety railing and shoved one uncertain foot in front of the other, grateful for the weight of my pack to keep me grounded. It didn't make the dizziness go away but at least I could walk reasonably straight. This must be how a toddler feels, walking for the first time.

The gangway stretched a long way down until it met a wide, wooden pier, flanked by tight clusters of mangroves. I turned and squinted at the ship, its bloated white body a foreign beast, an unnatural assault on this landscape of deep green. At this distance, the passenger door I'd exited seemed impossibly small. A floating concrete limb cut through the water on the far side of the ship, connecting sea transport to land; several automated cranes stood ready to unload the containers stacked-up within the ship's cargo hold. Further beyond, smaller crafts harboured in the small quay.

It had been easy to forget that I'd hitched a ride on a cargo ship to get here, to this island, home to my great-grandmother, my ancestors. No planes flew here any more, but occasional ammonia-powered ships carried cargo, and sometimes someone like me who needed to get here from the other side of the planet.

I indulged in a smile. Over the last five weeks, Carlos certainly made me forget.

Sudden panic gripped me. Shaking the rucksack off my back, I rummaged through rolled up clothing and ephemera, until my relieved fingers found a reassuring rectangular form – the only remaining copy of Ah-Zho's memoir.

I opened to a page, ran my fingers down the fading print.

This. This, I must not forget.

Everyone sometimes just call the boat 'the book fair', but later I found out the Doulos had been an ocean liner, then a cruise ship, and had in fact been sailing since the First World War. Complex identities get watered down; people seem only capable of remembering the last thing you were, the last place you've been.

The first time Mami took me on board, I'd struggled with the stairs; I wasn't tall for my age, and those steps had surely been built for Caucasian adults, not a small Southeast Asian girl. The ship deck smelled otherworldly, clean. I didn't know it was possible to have so many books in one place – that it was possible to have so many books at all. The small library Mami took me to every week had perhaps four, five shelves, and I must have read everything there, perhaps even twice. Here on board, shelves stretched across both walls of the main cabin, shelves filled the middle in clusters or in rows. Every single one of them held books with spines of every colour, weight and size.

A terrifying moment for a child – to realise how many books existed out there in the big wide world. How would one be able to read all of them?

Looking back, I wonder if that had been the moment that changed everything. Imprinted into the depths of my young mind: an unquenchable desire to see the world – and read all its books.

The tang of spices swelled, filling the air more pervasively the further I ventured inland. The birds had quietened, though still peppering the air with occasional sharp chirps. Weaving through mangroves that blended into ferns, shrubs then trees, the pier merged onto an elevated walkway, then another, each joined at irregular angles. Everything swayed, swung; I paused again, fighting to keep myself upright. Almost as if my body had forgotten how to cope with stable earth under my feet. Carlos had warned it could take a week for the sensation to fade.

I needed food, sleep.

Middle of the port, Carlos had said. When the walkway opened into a wide, wooden platform between the deep green of bushes and trees, I wasn't prepared for the onslaught of colour. Brightly painted shipping containers lined the edges; in the centre, chairs leaned against clusters of empty tables, presumably to keep the seats dry from dew and rain. Solar lights ringed the whole compound, but remained unlit. To my left, a cheerful yellow container bore a sign over a fitted wooden door: *Office*. Closed. I'd been cleared by authorities before the ship departed, there'd be no need for further formalities, so this wouldn't be a problem. Next to it, a similar shipping container in carmine-red sported a cut-out window halfway up – not unlike an enlarged version of a street food truck without wheels. A sign decorated with pink flowers proclaimed over the top: *Wei's Delicious Chicken Rice,* with *Lab-grown meat only!* scribbled on a jaunty angle to one side. Also shut.

Between the two buildings, a path snaked out of sight, bearing a sign pointing towards the light-rail transit that would run into the city.

Had I arrived too early?

On the far side of the platform, white cloud swirled upwards. Steam, from a stove. Another shipping container harbouring a food stall – this one cobalt blue with an entire side propped open. The aroma left me in no doubt that something good had been cooking there for a while. By now, my hunger had ballooned to the size of a small cave.

I wove between vacant tables, beelining for the source of the steam.

"Za! Morning! Jiak ba boi?" a woman's voice called in a mix of English and colloquial Hokkien – a tongue I'd only heard my grandmother speak, a language my mother had never learned.

"Aunty, zao," I responded in mangled Mandarin, conscious that my inflection would give me away. I might have dark hair and phoenix eyes like Mi, her mother, and her mother before her, but I could never sound like someone who spoke these tongues natively.

"Wait-ah!" From behind stove and steam, the woman emerged, her short grey hair framing a wrinkled face. She waved a flustered pair of chopsticks in one hand. "Can't hear behind all that! You dock early? I'm not open yet – Ah! You're not a sailor –"

Then she smiled, for a moment it could have been my own mother smiling at me and uncried tears flooded my throat.

"No, Aunty," I choked out the words. "I'm just… a visitor."

For now, at least. Until I'd made up my mind.

"Take a seat!" The woman gestured at an empty chair at the closest table. "You must be tired! We don't get travellers much. Last one here must have been almost five years ago. A scientist – an ecologist I think. You a scientist?"

I shook my head. "No. My great-grandmother was born here."

Her eyes widened, chopsticks poised in midair. "Ohhh, that's different. You from where?"

"England."

"Rain all the time there, right? Lots of rain here too, you'll be right at home," she said, laughing. "I'm Lian, welcome, welcome."

Only now I could see the source of the steam – a single, enormous vat, lacing the air with intoxicating, fragrant spice. Hunger gnawed at my insides.

"Running late today," said Aunty Lian, moving once again behind the stove, raising her voice. "Won't be long!"

"Smells delicious!" My mouth watered.

Her face lit up, obviously pleased. Her hands moved to shell an unassailable pile of prawns at surprising speed, covering her fingers in brine.

Next to Aunty Lian's bright blue ship-container building, a white one bore a sign in neat print: *Dayang's Nasi Aruk*. Shrubs poked through the gaps between the crates, as if they, too were keen on breakfast. A cicada's song pierced the air, sounding uncannily like a jaw harp.

It didn't feel right, to just sit there while someone cooked a meal for you. Besides, I could ignore the world-swaying sensation better if I was doing something.

I walked over to the stall. "Can I help, Aunty Lian?"

She chuckled. "Your Ma brought you up well! Okay, because I'm running late today. See over there." She nodded her head towards a small mound of green on her steel counter. Coriander, or cilantro – different names, depending on where one lived. "You know what to do?"

I did.

Behind Aunty Lian's stall stood a white ceramic sink where I washed my hands. We worked elbow-to-elbow; she continued to shell prawns, I pinched the coriander down to bite-size pieces, plucking off pieces of the past so I didn't have to think about them all at once. I inhaled its subtle citrus scent, ignored my rumbling stomach, tucked away memories of cooking alongside my own mother.

"What job you do?" she asked.

"I'm a cultural historian."

"Good! I hope you study food, because that's all you're going to get here."

I laughed. "Yes, food. Definitely." And a whole lot more besides.

"Had laksa before?" She used the word *had*, rather than *ate*, as if consuming this dish presented an entire experience in itself.

"My Mi used to make it, but well, it wasn't the real thing," I said, hoping the cracking of my broken heart was audible only to me.

"Ai-ya, every laksa is real, no matter how you make it."

When I finished preparing the coriander, she shooed me back to a table. Working quickly with both hands, she dropped rice noodles into a bowl followed by sliced egg, cooked prawns, and bean sprouts. Then she ladled the fragrant broth over the top, drowning everything in brown-red spice. No chicken, but I kept silent. As friendly as Aunty Lian had been, great-grandmother's memoir left clues; traditions had to change. Unless you knew someone well, you'd never know what wounds you could re-open by mentioning a missing ingredient in a dish.

"Here you go!" Aunty Lian announced, placing the steaming bowl in front of me along with a clean pair of chopsticks, and a small dish containing a red smudge of sambal belachan next to a green hemisphere of calamansi lime.

Despite having been drenched in the scent of spices, I wasn't prepared for the explosion of flavour that hit my tongue. Chilli stung my throat, flooded my nostrils and I chose the entire wrong moment to gasp a breath.

Lungs aflame with heat, I coughed, spluttering red soup droplets all over the table. Aunty Lian came quickly with a glass of water, patted my back firmly. "Don't eat too fast!"

The rich broth lined my mouth and coated my tongue, steaming hot and eye-wateringly spicy and I knew at that moment that I'd come home.

It always felt like kitchen magic: how two packets of laksa rempah cooked in a pot of stock could be enough to feed four families for one meal, even seconds for the teenagers – who'd somehow transformed into adults with jobs and children as decades blinked past.

Maybe time passed faster during those interim years I'd spent travelling, dotting my way around the world, one continent at a time. To my astonishment, several of my younger cousins followed my example, spreading their wings to different cities in other countries. Perhaps a testament to our grandfather's ancestry: Hakka, ke jia ren, 'guest families' who lived dispersed among other peoples in other places.

Big family meals with everyone present became rarer over time. We celebrated eating together when we could, harboured a little prayer in our hearts for those of us who ventured across other oceans. Home ceased to be merely defined by physical location and became the precious slivers of time where we cook together, eat together.

Food is home, food is family.

Sometimes on these occasions, if any one of us had rempah stashed in our freezers, I'd be the nominated laksa chef. They all claimed I had the best technique. I suspect it's because I had always been the patient, conscientious cook – just like Mami – hours spent shelling prawns (the shells go back into the stock for more flavour), shredding steamed chicken meat by hand (Dad always said it doesn't taste the same if you sliced it), tearing the leaves off coriander stalks (or Mami would gently protest). Much later, some ingredients became periodically unavailable, but we learned not to complain.

My one regret? Never having learned how to properly make the rempah from scratch from someone who knew how. Opportunities to ask returning relatives or friends to acquire packets of the stuff became fewer; the frequency and severity of storms made travel harder. Some days, I worry I would die and never taste authentic laksa in a humid, noisy kopi tiam again. Home may not be rooted in a location, but food certainly is. Food is identity, food is memory.

Maybe that's the real reason why the family wants me to cook for them whenever I come home.

Food is love.

"What are you running away from?" We'd been at sea for two days at that point, and Carlos had just placed a second cup of black coffee in front of me where we sat in the crew kitchen.

I relished the hint of floral scent, then the chocolate-bitter, earthy taste on my tongue. "Running away *to*, you mean."

He chuckled. I pried my eyes away from his dimples.

"Enjoy that." He nodded at my mug, eyes twinkling. "From our last drop-off in Colombia. I'll be looking for some local liberica when we dock."

"Privileges of a sailor."

"Exactly. Tempting lifestyle, right? We'll just have to work on your seasickness."

I'd rolled my eyes. He'd laughed. My inability to deal with the slightest shift in motion had become a running joke.

The transit dropped other passengers at the port, pausing long enough for me to board. It slid smoothly forward, barely making a sound. Trees whizzed past on either side, scattering morning sunbeams warming the window. The swaying sensation I'd battled over breakfast faded, my body relieved once again to be in motion.

Should I have waited for him? Carlos might have spoiled me on board, but he hadn't warned me about the cruel craving for coffee. My head throbbed.

Nestling between my feet, an enamelled nyonya tiffin remained tightly sealed.

What *was* I running away from? The lingering shadow of a decade-long relationship that should have ended years ago, the memory of Mi on her deathbed. She might have liked to come on this journey with me.

Tears threatened. I breathed them away.

Aunty Lian had refused to let me go without taking a portion of laksa with me. She'd packed the garnishes and the rice noodles in the top tier of the tiffin, keeping the broth separate from the rest, waved away my sea credits. "Hai-ya, you helped make it, no need-lah! Just come back again."

"How can I return this to you?" The tiffin had weighed heavy with the promise of another exquisite meal.

She'd waved a nonchalant hand, laughed. "Whenever you come back-loh. Where you staying?"

In Great-Grandma's time, there had been luxury hotels along the river and the esplanade. These had long been dismantled when the river rose.

"The guesthouse on the hill," I said. There weren't many left.

"Behind St. Mary's? Ah, you're near the library in town." Her brow furrowed, her expression darkened. "May I ask a small favour?"

Of course, I said yes. It must have been important, if she needed a letter hand delivered. I'd promised to do it later.

Closer to the city centre, tall bushes of black pepper and a few ageing palm trees from the old industry dotted the landscape between sheltered vertical farms, built above remnants of roads partly flooded from a recent storm, some of which had been transformed into new paddy fields for growing rice. Beautiful, if in an unexpected, untidy way. I sucked my breath through my teeth. Would Ah-Zho have liked how things have changed? During her time here, she'd been critical about how few alternatives existed for local farmers apart from growing palm trees if they wanted a decent livelihood.

The high rises and raised walkways resembled nothing like the old photographs she included among her pages – though if I squinted, I could spot old structures underneath the waterline; they'd build the new city above the old. On the passageways, young kids held onto their parents' hands, older children in blue and white school uniforms clustered in small groups or wove through crowds on bicycles. Far beneath the light-rail transit, the faded asphalt cracked with rain-filled potholes.

Daily life had been elevated, literally.

The transit pulled into a stop. An old man walked carefully on board, his legs wrapped in an exosuit, right hand on a stabilising walking-stick. He nodded at me but said nothing. I tried on a friendly, if tired, smile. Everything about me must say *foreigner*.

Then, without warning, a bunch of schoolchildren rushed in. The sudden raised pitch of their voices manifested as pain across my brow. Two stops along, just as suddenly, they dashed off the moment the doors slid open.

The old man rose from his seat, smiled at me. He pointed his walking-stick at the sign in front of our cabin. It blinked: *Terminus.*

"Terima kasih," I thanked him, but he'd already made to leave. I stood up, reached for a handrail. The swaying had begun again.

Through the open transit doors, warm air slapped at my face like a damp blanket.

Coffee. I could really use one. Perhaps I should've waited for Carlos.

Too late now.

I shouldered my rucksack and stepped into the city.

Supermarkets barely featured in my childhood.

Every weekend, we would drive about fifteen minutes towards the bridge, where the Sunday Market sprawled across both space and time – vegetable stalls, meat stalls, and vendors selling toys and clothes would begin setting up from Saturday. Once, we'd bought a pet goldfish there too.

If we needed anything else, Mami had her favourite grocery stores scattered throughout town. Often poorly lit, these were stocked from floor to ceiling, stinking of wet cardboard and stale dust. The exception was a small shop by the roundabout opposite St. Mary's Primary School – which my parents' generation considered a modern marvel because it had air-conditioning. Everyone shopped there for imported goods, like the type of butter that Mami wanted for cakes, canned fizzy drinks, fancy biscuits from mysterious countries.

I'd always thought it strange, how the building stood apart from all the other shophouses, which tended to be stacked side-by-side as if they had to hold each other up so as not to fall over. Unlike other premises, where parking had to be shared, this place had a customer carpark of its own – which seemed always full.

Only much later when I made it to western countries did I understand the downsides: if you allowed the whim of a handful of corporation-owned supermarkets to choose what to stock, rather than a varied network of grocers, farmers suffered – food suffered. During my final trips back, a hybrid of these supermarkets and early grocers boomed. They became bigger, shelves grew longer, and a greater variety of foodstuffs sat on them. Some of them were tucked inside malls, so we didn't have to deal with the heat and sweat of doing our shopping out in the open.

All the mechanisms of how food got to our table became less visible, all the mess and muck that it takes to feed a population hidden behind pristine shelves of pre-packaged foods. People didn't know that about 50% of our rice had to be imported. A modern convenience, but we are what we eat, and I fear one day we might forget who we are.

My host at the guesthouse had every confidence I'd find the library. "Over the footbridge across the main road, towards the padang." The field, she'd said, but neglected to mention the multiple paths that led away from the guesthouse premises, several of which wound through a school down the hill. Only when I reached the main road – rendered a shallow river by last night's heavy rain – did I spot the covered footbridge spanning overhead.

The humidity squeezed my lungs; despite having changed into a light dress once I'd settled into my room at the guesthouse, the air stifled. Shouldering my daypack, I gripped the handrail and hauled myself up the bridge. I had to keep my eyes fixed on my feet; the moment I glanced up, the world would sway.

The cover over the footbridge did little to shelter from the sun, heat radiated off the side panels under the railing. I paused in the middle, searching the view northwards. Under the elevated walkways, between rows of shops on stilts built over the original buildings, I finally spotted the old supermarket Ah-Zho mentioned in her memoir, partially under water.

I stole a deep breath. The air smelt of stale rain. A fool's errand – to think I could reconcile this world with the one my great-grandmother lived in.

On the other side of the footbridge, like everything else, the library blended the old with the new. A grass bank set the concrete building back from the roadside, microalgae filled glass tiles of the façade where it'd be most sunny. Inside, an open water garden graced the ground floor, moss dampening the echoes of my footsteps. An escalator had been cordoned off, with a sign *Turned off during floods* but next to it some stairs rose upwards. Gingerly, I climbed these.

At the front desk, a shadowy silhouette sat bent over a counter, long hair braided into a thick black rope. She glanced up at me, smiled. My breath hitched. She could have been a picture-perfect, younger version of Aunty Lian.

Her eyes twinkled – at first. "How may I help you?"

But then she saw the letter in my hand and the smile evaporated.

"I see my mother sent you," she said, voice tightening. "Where are you from?"

"I just came off a cargo ship." I kept my face stoic, expressionless.

A moment's pause, then she extended a hand.

"I'm Zhen."

The warmth of her hand came as a surprise, any friendliness had dissipated from her voice. She opened a drawer and placed the letter upon a pile of identical envelopes, the expression on her face unreadable. I bit down the question on my tongue.

Shelves of books lined the walls behind her, stores of secrets nestling between their pages. Through the window, the skies had clouded over, threatening rain. I thought of Ah-Zho's book fair on the boat.

Zhen looked up, as if surprised to see me still here.

"I'm interested in the library," I said.

Only then, a shadow of a smile returned. She emerged from behind the counter, gestured for me to follow.

"The library spans two whole floors," said Zhen. "Down here, you'll find everything that has ever been written about this city. Also, this – our photography catalogue, including historical images we salvaged from the social media years."

Zhen waved a hand at a small device discretely installed next to some shelves. An image blinked upon a wall: a street busy with cars, pedestrians, and motorcycles along rows of wooden shophouses with shutters, where the top storey jutted out several feet to provide shade for the kaki lima below, a faded world in monochrome.

"The main bazaar before the Second World War, now almost permanently underwater."

I made a mental note to head there – perhaps tomorrow.

She motioned at the projector again. Another image, this time of small wooden boats. "Sampans on the river. You'll still see them, many of them made to be amphibious now."

Zhen's face shone with a quiet intensity; for a fleeting moment, I wanted to get to know her better.

"Sometimes, they showcase craft methods or traditional dance in the studio upstairs. Next week, we'll have specialists demonstrating how pantun is used in bermukun. Come if you like the spoken word."

Behind her, every single book on the shelves beckoned.

An unquenchable desire to see the world – and read all its books.

Finally, I understood.

The skies beyond the window had darkened several shades of grey. In the distance, a flash of lightning.

A thought struck.

"Do you carry memoirs?"

"Over there, in the corner." She pointed to one end of the room. "There's a catalogue if you need to look for something specific. If you need any help – just ask."

I ran my hands over the titles on the shelf and paused where my great-grandmother's name ought to have been. Nothing. The catalogue search, too, yielded a blank.

At the front desk, Zhen stared at the pile of letters from Aunty Lian. When I approached, she shoved the drawer shut.

I waited, unsure what to say.

Zhen sighed. "It's not a secret anyway."

"You don't have to tell me if you don't want to –"

"She wants me to take over her laksa stall."

I hadn't met enough people yet to know whether they chose their own vocations, but Zhen obviously loved her role here, her way of serving the community. I gestured at the shelves. "But what about the library?"

A smile lit up her face, but in her dark eyes, a sadness. "Well, *you* understand."

That tug of war between duty and passion, between tradition and dreams.

My hands reached into my daypack and pulled out Ah-Zho's book.

"I have something that you don't seem to have." My voice trembled, I wasn't sure why.

Zhen's breath caught, eyebrow raised.

"One moment." She cleaned her hands, pulled on a pair of soft, fabric gloves.

Guilt gripped me – here, a precious object that I'd never thought needed preserving.

Carefully, she took the book from me and flipped through a few pages. "Your relative?"

"Great-grandmother."

"This is an amazing acc –"

Something buzzed. Loud, intrusive.

She glanced at a small terminal on the table. "A message from the guesthouse across the road."

"Yes?"

"Someone just asked for you."

Carlos.

My heart thumped, threatening to burst out of my chest. My feet moved towards the door before my thoughts could catch up.

"I'll come back for the book –"

"Wait!" Zhen called but I'd already sprinted halfway down the stairwell, her words dampened by old concrete and fresh rain.

The first few times I'd come back from undertaking my studies overseas during the Antipodean summers, family and friends told me, "You'd forgotten how to be Asian," though I can't fathom how they came to that conclusion. I hadn't changed what I wore nor how I spoke.

But it didn't matter; once I'd left, I ceased to be one of us – one of them. In their minds, any cultural integrity that was my birthright had been corrupted.

A child learned fast; you knew when people thought of you differently. Being othered in a new country – I'd expected that. I hadn't expected to be rejected by my own people, to be accused of having changed.

For ten years, I agonised. Then I decided; if my identity was already fractured, what stops me from fragmenting it further? Then I wouldn't be just either-or. If I opened my world to a kaleidoscope of cultures, I could blend in as much as my linguistic ability and cultural awareness would allow.

Then I would be no-one, and to hell to those want to pin me as A or B, C or D, because I'd be all of the above. I'd be able to read all the world's books – in the languages they had been written.

I heard it before I made it out the doors – rain slapped down, heavy, fast drops churning the grass banks beside the library into splattering mud. I'd left my rain jacket behind in my room at the guesthouse.

Carlos – I hadn't waited for him at the port. Would he wait for me now?

Two steps outside, my clothes soaked through, my hair stuck to my face. The cover over the footbridge offered no respite from the torrent. The squalling wind blew rain through the exposed sides, whistling through gaps in the panels.

Swirl of floodwaters inundated the asphalt below. I paused, mesmerised. In many cities, humans had built roads over rivers, but here, a river had triumphed over a road.

Entropy – *that* was what I'd been trying to run from. That slow disintegration of everything to time, an uncertain journey towards a certain death.

The world turned opaque with rain, rendering the skies dark. I could barely see. I thought I'd left just after midday, had night already fallen?

Carlos had warned me – how near the equator, sundown can come quickly.

The torrent drummed on the cover of the footbridge. I scanned for the path to the guesthouse. The persisting rain, a dense, silver curtain. Why did everything sway? I ventured down the stairs.

My foot slipped. The ground gave way and I stretched for the railing. Fingers brushed wet metal but unable to get a hold.

"Aster!"

I knew that voice. I knew those arms.

Somehow, we made it up the hill. Somehow, we reached the guesthouse, where my host handed us the key to my room.

My body wouldn't stop shaking, despite the warmth of Carlos' arms.

He bundled me into a hot shower, found my clothes, tucked me between clean sheets on a firm bed.

A hand on my forehead, a kiss on my cheek. "No fever. You'll be okay."

"In my great-grandmother's time…" My voice came out as a croak. "They thought the rain made you sick."

"They probably didn't have the science to tell them any different," said Carlos.

Sleep beckoned. I wanted it but I fought it.

"When do you leave?" I asked.

Before I heard his answer, darkness dragged me down.

The sky out the window looked the same pitch black when I finally woke. No telling if I'd been asleep for minutes, hours, or days.

Across the room, in an armchair that must have been there all this time, a dim lamp lit a glowing halo over a silhouette, as if an angel had been patiently waiting for me to stir.

Carlos put down a book he'd been reading, smiled. "Hey, sleepyhead. Hungry?"

Things I Regret:
Never asking my grandparents about their lives
Never learned how to make nyonya kuih from my great aunt
Not having captured my father's childhood stories
Never learned how to make laksa from scratch
Not spent enough time with my mother
Being unable to shake off the past
Not spending enough time making something new
Staying too long in one place
Not staying in one place long enough

Out on the river, the undulating movement of the tide soothed my tired body, a temporary reprieve from the relentless land-sickness. The clouds hadn't entirely lifted, the evening prayer from the floating mosque rode on the timid breeze.

Outfitted with a bioluminescent lamp and solar motor, the amphibious sampan we sat in felt comfortable enough. Several other small boats drifted nearby, their lamps flickering like fireflies in the darkening dusk.

Carlos had exchanged sea credits with a vendor by the river jetty for two bamboo boxes. He balanced one on his knees, removed the lid and handed it to me. The sweet smell of coconut rice married with fragrant rendang spice teased my rumbling belly. Lunch was a very long time ago.

We ate in silence.

I'd seen a photograph in Ah-Zho's book, but also at the library: a tiled esplanade used to span this riverbank, hugging an old road and historic rows of shophouses. Now, a floating walkway set upon telescopic stilts copied its former location, a waterfront with an entire new set of buildings constructed upon the old. Shops, cafés and eateries buzzed with nightlife. Serene and undisturbed, rice-growing rafts floated, tethered along its length. I couldn't tell where river began or where land ended; there could be no definition of a shoreline.

Soft bubbles of golden light glowed underwater; the original shophouses remained a diving attraction.

A mouthful of rendang and rice warmed my tongue, a contrast to the slightly sweet sambal on the crunch of fried ikan bilis. Would someone have eaten this exact dish here on the old esplanade – maybe with true fowl or meat – several decades, even centuries ago?

"You know, generations of lovers walked this riverbank," Carlos suddenly said, putting his now-empty bamboo box aside. We'd return it to the vendor on our way back.

I didn't know quite what to say, so I kept my eyes fixed on a pair of night-divers who flipped themselves backwards into the water from a nearby boat. Beyond them, another sampan like ours drifted, host to another couple. Could I even call us that?

"We go back out to sea first thing day after tomorrow." Carlos gazed out towards the bustle on the waterfront. "It's a short haul, I'll be back in a few days."

No moon lingered from behind the clouds. Dark water rippled gently by the side of our boat.

"What will you do, Aster? Will you stay?"

I turned to face him. The lights from the shore twinkled like constellations in his eyes.

"What are you *really* asking?"

For an answer, Carlos produced a small bundle he'd somehow hidden away in the shadows. He gestured, indicated I should open it.

Books have a certain feel to them, especially hardbound books. Somehow, I could tell its contents even before I slipped off the hand-printed cloth covering. I opened to a first page.

It was blank.

"You were always rustling through your great-grandmother's memoir, I thought you might want…" He gestured at the river and its waterfront, at the glittering cityscape. "…somewhere to write your own words, capture your memories from here, perhaps, and –"

The book held tidy signatures of smooth, good paper. Rare, too.

"This did not come from here," I said, examining the binding.

"No, this came from Italy," he admitted, a bit sheepishly. "They still make the best –"

I flung my arms around him, letting the warmth of his skin soak onto mine, the rough of his stubble catching strands of my hair, overwhelmed by the swell of a feeling I didn't have words for. My shoulders shook.

When I pulled back, he brushed a hand against my cheek, wiping away a stray tear.

"I'll find you when I get back." It wasn't a question.

"I'll be here," I said.

It was a promise.

On the pier before dawn, the white cargo beast pulled away, fully loaded again. A strange feeling, that while I had the hard ground beneath my feet, Carlos would be swayed onboard by the tides of the river, then soon, the sea.

Yet another night where we hadn't slept much. He'd be back soon. To my surprise, my heart fluttered at the thought.

I followed the maze back down to the cluster of coloured containers. Aunty Lian's stall hadn't yet opened when we'd arrived, but now, on my way to the transit, I heard the *whoosh* of her stove, tasted the spice in the air.

"Za! Jiak ba boi?" she called through a waft of white steam.

I drew closer. The prawns hadn't yet been shelled, the coriander still a large pile in a colander, a bowl with eggs sat on the counter.

"Ah, it's you! Did you enjoy the laksa?"

"Amazing." I wasn't lying; my only regret was having to share it with Carlos. I placed the now-clean tiffin on her shelf, nestled it up to a few others just like it. "I gave your letter to Zhen."

Without meeting my gaze, Aunty Lian laid her chopsticks to one side.

"Thank you," she finally said after a pause. "Did she say anything?"

I shook my head.

"She'll never want to do this." She sighed, waved one hand at the stall. "It took me a while – but I understand that now. She's happy there at the library."

When she glanced at me again, her eyes glistened. I kept silent, giving her the space to speak the words she must have struggled to say to her own daughter.

"I have no one to teach my craft to, but I… I can accept that." Her words wavered. "I'm proud of what she does – it's important – but she doesn't know I know that. I just wish she would come and see me…"

Her lips puckered, struggling to contain a sob. Her shoulders shuddered.

I reached for her hand.

"Aunty, I'm not Zhen, but you can teach me – if you want." Somehow, my voice stayed level. "I'm willing to learn."

Wide-eyed, she stared at me.

A lump formed in my throat. *Breathe.* "I want to, for my great-grandmother, who never got the chance."

And for my grandmother, who missed speaking our native tongues. For my mother, who had never seen these shores, her face pale on that hospital bed, her red-rimmed eyes imploring me to come close, the words she wanted to say bottled inside her tiny frail body. I'd leaned over and whispered, "Mi, I know. It's okay. Rest now."

Then I'd held her hand until it went limp. Often, I wondered if I should have let her speak. Now, I'd never find out.

Aunty Lian clasped both of my hands in hers, gripped them tight. Her eyes pleaded with me.

"Never forget, whatever you choose to be, your Mi will be proud of you."

Moving suddenly, Aunty Lian whirled towards the sink and splashed cold water over her face. I waited for her to finish, then did the same.

When she finally spoke, her voice held steady. "I'll start on the next batch of spices tomorrow. If you come late afternoon, I'll show you how. For now…" she gestured at the pile of coriander. I smiled.

In silence, we worked elbow-to-elbow, ghosts of women in my life inhabiting my body. Together, we made food. Because food is identity, memory, community.

Because food is love.

Safe Haven for the
Lost and Found

If I hadn't tripped over the roots of the oak tree, I might have never noticed the signs under the dense undergrowth: that straight line carved into the grassy green, a subtle scar beneath the sharp thorns of a wild blackberry, young leaves coaxed into life by the fresh light of spring.

Tell-tale marks of human interference – left behind, in all likelihood, by a former structure of some kind.

I squinted through trees and thicket. Had I dared rely on my bearings, I'd wager that this was still the same side of the hill that overlooked the city below, a day's slow walk away.

Flipping up my wrist camera, I snapped a few images. The disturbance measured perhaps about four metres across, or thirteen feet in old parlance; though how far back it stretched into the woods, I'd not be able to tell without a lidar drone. Perhaps I might be standing in the middle of someone else's former dwelling – perhaps a threshold into a living space, perhaps a wall. But if Papi's few stories were anything to go by, this might have been the entire width of a small hut or some kind of cabin. Did a storm destroy it? Forced its residents to leave?

The remains must have been dismantled; any viable materials re-used elsewhere. Since the fires, we'd learned to change the way we live.

I straightened, adjusted the straps of my pack and inhaled a lungful of cool forest air, then tried to re-braid the mess that my hair had become, ruining Ruby's loving, careful handiwork from last night. Strands stung my palm; a mild graze. I wiped my bleeding hand across a trouser leg.

Overhead, a low rumble berated the clouds. The sky had darkened much earlier than it should; high noon wasn't that long ago. The temperature had tumbled in the last half an hour. I sniffed; incoming rain. If I could find a clearing large enough, I could set up shelter and wait out the weather.

I forced myself to look away from the unnatural line in the grass, gazing instead into the surrounds. Human feet must have passed here once, stood on this very spot. Pushing my way through the forest, I searched among the leaves for shadows of other human beings but, of course, there were none. Then a sharp gust of wind rattled the branches, a beast careering through the woods. Heart thudding, I paused.

No, I was alone. And if I dared admit it, perhaps even lost.

Story of your life, Iris, Ruby would've joked and not without reason, had she been here, had there been enough signal for me to send a message to her. A sense of direction – literally, and metaphorically – had never been my strong suit. I'd have said to her: *I couldn't possibly be lost if there hadn't been a defined direction, could I?* And she would've laughed in that easy, breezy way I'd so loved every day of our fifteen years together, taking the sting out of the original barb.

I missed her, as I'd known I would. Did she miss me?

Here and now, I nudged forward, trees and brush closing in around me on either side, chiding me for intruding into their sanctuary.

"Sorry," I muttered out loud, knowing that each and every plant could sense my clumsy stumble through their midst.

As if in retribution, the woodland spat me out into a clearing. A path snaked away to my right; the one I should have taken instead of fighting my way through the thicket. Then I saw it: up ahead, just before the path disappeared into the hill, half consumed by greedy creepers – a faded, wooden sign. Commanding my tired legs forward, I reached out, brushed away a string of ivy off its weathered surface.

Safe Haven, it declared, the words neatly spelled out in hand-carved lettering.

Blood pounded in my ears, my breath suddenly shallow.

The mark in the grass should have been a clue.

It wasn't that I doubted Papi's stories. His eyes would mist over, his voice infused with haze, as if the decades between then and now had eroded the sequence of events. Mamie would turn away from the conversation whenever I tried to corroborate their storylines.

But every now and again they spoke of a place on the outskirts of the city – where they'd sought solace until courage found them again.

"Well, hello there," rasped a voice, much too close behind me.

I froze. Then turned around, slowly.

A wraithlike, wizened wisp of a creature stood not far away – skin pale, sporting a woollen hat and a heavy coat that hung straight over their trim frame, in a shade of green that blended with the woods. I blinked, and suddenly the wrinkles I thought I saw on their face smoothed away. Not a witch, not a ghost. Just an ordinary human being, maybe in their late thirties, maybe not unlike me.

The mind played tricks in places like these.

"Hi," I croaked back, my throat dry. For a very self-conscious moment, I wondered how bad I'd looked: a lone, dishevelled traveller covered in blood, dirt and dust.

"Are you hurt? Lost?" they said, the timbre of their voice – soft, warm.

"I'm... fine." I attempted a smile, but it stretched like a scar across my face, mirroring the one over my heart. "Looks like I might have just been found."

"Your lucky day, then," they said, chuckling. One hand raised, they wiped their brow.

A wet drop of rain glanced the tip of my nose.

The stranger tilted their chin at the sky. "Let's get you somewhere warm and dry. And we should clean up that cut of yours."

My pack seemed to weigh down heavier on my shoulders. Being a city dweller, an entire day outdoors had worn on my body. My muscles ached. The promise of shelter – too good to pass up. All those old tales that warned against following strangers in the woods – I ignored.

My new companion ambled along the uphill path, and I followed. We wove our way in the direction pointed by the wooden sign. Here and there, they reached out and touched a branch of a tree, brushed a hand across a cluster of wildflowers, like a wild deer calmly picking its way home.

I didn't have a plan. I'd focused on the logistics, on handing over my duties at the local library, on getting myself out of the city and thoroughly avoided any thought of what it could mean – what I'd do – if I'd found the place. In the beginning, whenever I brought up the desire to search for the Safe Haven, Ruby had been sceptical.

"Do you even know what you're looking for?" she'd asked, though I was certain she already knew the answer I could not give.

Three evenings ago, we sat upon plump yellow cushions on the deck of the Dutch barge we shared, one boat amongst many others in our little commune upon the river. Together, we rode upon her bronchial tides, drifting upon the city's heaving breath. The winter had been a bitter one; some of the river remained partially frozen even now. A small joy then, to stretch out on our deck, to relish the welcome warmth of spring, gifted by the departing sun before the night river rendered it too cold to sit outside.

Ruby leaned back on her elbows, her natural red hair a flaming cascade down her back, the evening breeze teasing the ends of her curls. Nearby, her cup of dandelion brew steamed, never far away from her slender fingers. Jefferson, our tuxedo cat, lounged between us, paws tucked under her body in a fluffy monochrome loaf. I perched cross-legged, nursing my own cup of brew in my hands, my jeans smudging blue stains upon the yellow cushion.

Some days, I couldn't be sure which came first, our love for the river, our love for each other, or for the others in our lives. But what I did know: that love does not possess. That love is a choice, and every day, we choose each other.

Living on the water suited me – far more than when I'd lived in one of the buildings downtown with my parents, shuttered in a cluttered apartment we shared with Papi and Mamie when they'd been alive. Here, the waterborne commune looked after the river, and she looked after us.

Ruby had been the one to approach me when she was a fresh-faced engineering apprentice; I had only just begun my training as a drone technician. The way she laughed so readily, her easy self-assurance, her flamboyant flaming hair – everything I wasn't, didn't have.

Everything I craved.

On our first date, she joked that people might mistake us for sisters because we were exactly the same height.

"Or roommates," I'd said, grinning.

That laugh – that unhindered joy. I'd been addicted to that laugh.

Somehow those years blinked by, and that girl blossomed into the woman lounging next to me on this boat we shared. Some days I imagined she'd grown taller, when I'd shrunk down to a shell of myself. By now, Ruby had taken over managing a section of our local solar grid, teaching the workings to anyone who wanted to learn. I'd been decently skilled enough at a few things, just never content enough to settle. From drone technician to city farmer, from stage musician to a kitchenhand in the community canteen; most recently, I'd taken over the library of shared equipment, but also the history museum alongside.

Some days, gazing into the river, I waited for a gust of wind to break me apart, disperse me into thousands of little pieces, bade the breeze to scatter my fragmented self – like seeds, like confetti, like leaves upon the water.

"Are you resting enough?" the doctor said last week.

I'd never slept much.

"Not just sleep," he counselled. "Mental rest, time to be with yourself. Untether from those who depend on you."

Long ago, after the fires, Papi had returned from the Safe Haven and gone back to work at the robotics factory because that was the life he knew. When the insurance companies went bust and pulled out of the region, one by one, businesses shut down. My grandparents risked their own lives to come here from a warming country, only to lose everything all over again to the fires, then once more to an ailing economy. All of us should be shareholders towards a future we cared about, Mamie said, not like this.

My every stumble, my every failure – a smear upon better futures they'd fought so hard for.

What kind of rest exist for scars like those?

A touch upon my arm. I glanced up at Ruby, kissed the upward curve of her lips.

"You drifted off somewhere all by yourself." She squeezed my hand.

I took in the pained smile on her face and laced my fingers through hers.

"Iris." She said my name, as if it would break a curse. Her arms slipped around my trembling body; an embrace, a home. Her skin carried a scent of lavender, her hair a scatter of peppermint. Or was it rosemary?

"Do what you need to do," said Ruby, pulling back gently. "Take some time away. I'll still be here, on our boat on our river."

She reached out to touch my face, brushed away a tear. Had I been crying? I hadn't noticed.

"When can Hass come?" I asked, swiping the offending wetness off my cheek.

My metamour – Ruby's boyfriend – would move in while I was gone. I'd been the one to suggest it; I hated the thought of her being alone.

"Tomorrow," she said. "But I told him Sunday would be best."

With firm hands on my shoulders, she spun my body around on the cushion, undid the strip of fabric holding my plaited hair, and began re-braiding my dark, unwieldy locks.

"Can't say I won't miss you," her voice, lush in my ear, fingers gliding through my hair, "but you've always wanted to find the place."

I didn't think she saw my smile.

The torrent started suddenly, mercilessly. Rain pounded down and I traipsed behind my new companion through an earthen footpath fast churning into a muddy sludge. Between the rain shower and the unfamiliarity of the trail, I could only blindly follow.

Then, as if by magic, behind a tree – a cabin, a door.

"Come in," my host said.

Once indoors, they pulled off their boots and placed them to one side. I did the same.

The air within smelled of sweet wood and earth, but the sudden warmth took me by surprise – no fire in a hearth, of course, nothing like the old-world cottages in those ancient fairytales we as a civilisation never found the time to properly rewrite. A floor-to-ceiling window made up for one wall by the front door, displaying a view to the outside without censure, grey rain curtaining green.

A stoic, upholstered couch faced the window. A wooden dining table took up the other half of the space, accompanied by chairs that seemed not have been moved for a while – except for one closest to the kitchen. In the far corner, a different door yawned through to another room.

Had the remains of that building I'd encountered once looked like this?

A soft floral, herbal fragrance I couldn't identify drifted to me when my companion shrugged off their coat and hung it on a hook. A silver chain glinted under their collar – a talisman, perhaps. They removed their hat and shook out a surprising mane of long, black hair streaked with silver, dark against the pink-pale of their skin.

"Make yourself at home."

Gratefully, I dropped my pack, hung my coat next to theirs.

"Gets toasty in here, sometimes a little too much." They moved past me and opened the window above the kitchen sink. The patter of rain stole in, accompanied by its slight, acrid scent. "Brew?"

"Please."

"Dandelion?"

"Sure."

I'd tasted coffee only as a child, only whenever Papi made it. One of my grandfather's constant laments: the diminishing availability of coffee since worldwide crops suffered from the onslaught of bad weather.

"The bathroom is through that door."

Until they mentioned it, I hadn't even thought of needing it.

Beyond the door spanned a bedroom, furnished with a lone chest of drawers, a neatly made bed and a folk guitar. A different door led to the bathroom – clean, nondescript. I took a shower, changed my clothes. In the mirror, my reflection could almost pass for my best self, if a little low on sleep.

The moment I'd returned to the main room, my companion placed a cup of brew on the dining table in front of me. "Here."

"Thank you." I pulled out a chair, careful to pick one that had obviously been unused. The brew tasted a little sweet, a little bitter.

"Briar," they said, lowering themselves into the chair that I'd correctly identified as their usual.

"Pardon?"

"My name. I'm Briar. You?"

There was the name my family called me, and then there was the name everyone else used – including those closest to me, like Ruby, Hass, others.

"Iris," I said.

"Forgive me for my brusqueness," said Briar, taking a sip from their mug. "The Safe Haven doesn't get visitors, not these days. I might have even forgotten how to hold a conversation."

"That's my normal state."

They laughed, a resonant, rumbling laugh that rose from the gut. I liked it.

"You're from the city?" asked Briar.

I inhaled the steam from the brew – a little earthy, a little floral – rummaged for words to their true question left unasked: *why are you here?*

"My grandparents took refuge in the Safe Haven during the fires."

Along with hundreds of others.

Briar studied me, waiting for more. What could I say? That I wanted to understand how Papi and Mamie found the energy to recover from the devastation? That maybe if I knew how they drew courage from this place, I could do the same?

"I didn't know anyone still lived here."

"No one lives here." Briar smiled, wrapping their pale, chapped fingers around the white porcelain of their mug.

"You're not no one."

Briar shrugged. "Feels that way sometimes." They waved a hand at the room. "Well, this is one of the original cabins. You made it."

So many questions burned on my lips: how did they end up living here? Why?

But all of it felt too rude, too soon, too intrusive.

Beyond the window, the drizzle escalated into a fervent downpour. My kit nestling by the door seemed to shrink in the shadows. Camping out there tonight on soggy ground would not be pleasant.

"How's the cut on your hand?"

I opened my palm and showed them the stubborn pinkness that remained. There had been a small bottle of disinfectant in their medicine cupboard; I'd taken the liberty.

Briar nodded. "Not too deep then."

The rain on the roof that had been a steady staccato, then a persistent drumbeat now crescendoed into a full-fledged percussion performance. Somehow, the cacophony beyond these walls made the silence easy, companionable, for two people between whom conversation did not flow easily. Together, we stared out at the world for a while, watching the rain cast the outside world into a glistening silver, occasionally gifting us with a green glimpse of forest.

Papi and Mamie's stories never entirely matched up; Papi insisted they'd already committed to a life together; Mamie would say they met at the Safe Haven. Not that it mattered, because we knew what happened in the end: after having fled the fires, they'd found each other here. At some point, they moved back down into the city, Papi went back to the factory, Mamie back to teach at the school – and then they had Dad.

Every time the topic came up in family conversations, Mamie shrank into herself: distant, untouchable, a shadow of her normal warm, smiling self.

One day, when I came home early from school, finding only Mamie at home, I plucked up the courage to ask. She studied me with that clear, steely gaze of hers: eyes that saw through everything, everyone. Then she pulled me close and began to rebraid my hair. "Ma petite fleur, things were complicated then. We lived with a group of friends, people who came over to this country from other places."

That they lived crammed, sometimes several refugees in a room for some time.

Words she didn't say that day: they didn't all survive.

It took me a long time to understand that the aftermath of the fires was something she'd rather forget.

Briar swore loudly, breaking the spell in my head. Carrots, peeled and cut into bite-size scattered over a chopping board. On the stove, a saucepan steamed. Their hand, thrust into cold water running from the kitchen tap.

"All okay?"

"Just a scalding. Always good to be reminded that I'm only human."

On their face, a grin or grimace, I couldn't tell.

"Look," said Briar, drying off their hand on a kitchen towel. "Don't think the rain's going to stop today. How about you stay here for the night, and I'll show you the rest of the Haven tomorrow?"

I stole another glance through the glass window. Could I have said no?

Later, after having fed me a hot dinner and allowing me to earn my keep washing the dishes, Briar returned from the other room, long hair pulled back into a ponytail that swung when they walked. "Take the bed, I can sleep on the couch."

"No!" I protested. I gestured at my pack. "You're being much too kind. I'll be fine, I've got gear."

"The floor wouldn't be comfortable –"

"I'd been prepared to sleep under the stars," I interjected, firmly.

Briar held my gaze for a moment, gave in. Still, they brought out a pile of blankets and pillows.

Left on my own, I watched the black rain shower a forest just as blackened in the midnight dark, and wondered if the world had been as ashen as this – the day Papi and Mamie found their way to the Safe Haven.

I couldn't say if the grey dawn stealing through the window woke me first, or if it had been the song thrush that began its morning declaration on the roof. The temperature had plunged overnight; under the blankets, I cocooned myself in warmth.

The floor underneath my body seemed solid; not gingerbread. No cauldron in the hearth. I might yet live another day.

Did Papi feel like this, when he woke up in one of these cabins for the first time? Did he see what I saw now – timid gold light drifting through the tall glass window, empty table, empty chairs, a cold kitchen? Those must have been anxious hours, frightening days, especially if he'd made it to the Haven before Mamie did.

A tentative buzz to my side made me reach for my watch. I didn't remember removing it before falling asleep.

Network. Enough signal to send and receive messages, not enough for a call.

Swiftly, with a few swipes, I sent a message.

Almost immediately, a reply from Ruby pinged. *Morning, my love. We're okay here. How are you?*

Then a second message followed: a photo of Jefferson, who had curled up under her arm – something the cat normally did in mine. *She misses you.*

Tell her I miss her too.

I recounted where I was. *We'll go to look at the site today.*

Enjoy yourself, she wrote, *you wanted this.*

Even now, uncertainty plagued me. My body, numb. But my heart burst with boundless love for her who knew me better than I knew myself.

By the time Briar emerged into the main room, in a fresh shirt and clean hair wound in a topknot, I'd boiled the kettle, ground down some dandelion roots.

"Brew?" I asked.

"You're up early."

I shrugged. "Never been one to sleep much."

Briar paced over to the window and appraised the world beyond the glass.

"Promising," they said. I thought they'd meant the weather, but they could have meant the day, or a whole of life ahead.

I brought them their cup, and we stood side by side a while, staring out at the dew strewn woods. After yesterday's rain, everything flourished, the trees and bushes had taken on a fresher, deeper sheen of green.

Could I live here? Or would I just feel isolated after a time?

"Hungry?" asked Briar. But they'd already moved towards the kitchen without waiting for my answer.

It felt good to eat.

As soon as we were done, Briar put our plates away. "Come."

We layered on our coats; I laced on my boots.

Outside, cold spring air stung my cheeks. A scent of green rode on the morning breeze, carrying with it a twitter of avian chorus. A clear path led from the front door, so I walked behind Briar, their movements surprisingly swift given their leisurely lope. Not far away, an odd space among the trees suggested a cabin might have stood there too, once upon a time.

The path opened out into a clearing, where a larger, taller wooden building dominated the view. A picture of patience, waiting once again, for when it might be needed.

My feet stopped. I reached down, touched a hand to the cold earth, ran my fingers through the grasses, stirring up the dirt. Yes, I'd made it here. This was *the* Safe Haven: the place that kept hundreds of refugees sheltered when our world went up in flames – where Papi and Mamie began new lives.

Had I expected to be overcome? Elated? I felt none of those things. A quiet, deep-seated peace seeped into my bones – a sense of coming home. Time stood still here with no intention of rushing forward.

"Come meet the chickens," said Briar. "They don't get visitors too often."

Behind the main building, an old-fashioned greenhouse rose in front of the woodland, glass windows catching the morning sun. I hadn't seen one quite like this before; within city limits, we had built mostly underground or vertical farms. Next to the greenhouse, I spot the fruit trees, the perennials, the herbs, the flowers – a food forest. Nearby, artichoke globes reached up towards the heavens, their leaves like frilly green skirts; they'd be ready for harvesting soon.

"The asparagus came early this year," said Briar, gesturing towards the greenhouse. "We'll have plenty of beans, too."

The chickens had a moveable coop with an automatic door, free to wander within an enclosure where last season's crops had been planted. Most of them were already outside, examining the earth with expert eyes, occasionally with critical beaks. Briar's lips moved silently, counting the flock.

"Seven. There ought to be one more – ah."

A brown, fluffy hen strolled nonchalantly down the small ramp.

"Hello, Mrs. Robinson," said Briar. The hen clucked back in greeting, and joined the others, pecking her way into the grass.

I couldn't resist asking, "You have a hen called 'Mrs. Robinson'?"

Briar grinned. "A tradition my grandad started. There's always a Mrs. Robinson, among the hens. This one is technically Mrs. Robinson the Ninth."

The hens chuckled, or it seemed to me.

"Come see the Safe Haven HQ," said Briar. "Or what used to be, anyway."

As was becoming the norm, they didn't wait around for my answer, heading instead towards the main building and placed their palm on a panel to the right of a large door. It slid open, and Briar disappeared inside, leaving me loitering by the doorway.

I turned and squinted into the sun, finally emerging from behind the clouds. Had Mamie spent any time here in the greenhouse? Did Papi work in the gardens? If I'd looked hard enough, would the bark of trees bear their handprints?

Some herbs grew along one wall. I rubbed the leaves between my fingers. Sage, thyme, rosemary, peppermint. The fragrance in Ruby's hair – definitely rosemary. A robin sang an ambitious melody to syncopated chirps of a great tit. The hens clucked among themselves. Mrs. Robinson stood on her own some distance from the others, hesitant. For a moment, I was that hen, that hen was me.

What had been lost had no shape – could it even be found?

I stepped over the threshold into the large, empty hall, aching with silence, a void yearning to be filled once again with life and the living.

There had been plenty of reports, aerial recordings of the fires, horrific recollections of what had been destroyed, of the former city over whose ashes we'd now built anew. The media of the time loved catastrophe and moved its cynical camera away once the fires died down, never capturing the true aftermath. What the world heard less about: how we changed, how we survived, adapted. Stories about ordinary struggles were deemed less important to report than those that shocked or frightened us. How we grieved and continue to grieve.

Windows lined three sides of the hall. Light flooded in, and fell upon nothing.

"People shared meals here," said Briar, their footsteps echoing across the floor.

"You were here?" I asked, incredulous, wondering once again if

I'd misjudged their age.

"How old do you think I am?"

I had no idea, and I said so. Instead of answering, Briar only chuckled, led me through the wide archway along the inner wall, past a dusty stairwell, and into a large kitchen. Fresh cobwebs glistened in the morning light. Briar opened the drawers: cutlery, crockery, cooking utensils, all still here – once touched by many hands, fed many mouths.

I placed a hand on the cold stovetop. There would have been murmurs of laughter here, of sumptuous meals being prepared, the banging of crockery being washed, the chatter of stories being told. In a cupboard, we found large glass jars, clean and empty.

"Might be good for preserving the summer's bounty," I said.

"You know how to do that?" Briar asked, surprised. "Think we can start with the beans and the asparagus?"

I gazed into their eyes. I'd not noticed how blue they were until now.

"Sure." I wasn't.

"Pickling, preserves – something I'd never really learned," Briar continued. "On the upside, we have heaps of excellent compost."

I grinned. Then Briar reached behind a cupboard, found a broom and began cleaning up, apologising out loud to the spiders.

"You can look upstairs if you want. I won't be a moment."

My feet moved before my mind had the wherewithal to protest. My shoes thumped on the wooden stairs, stirring dust with every step. Every movement I made seemed too loud.

The layout of the second story mirrored the floor below. The space directly above the kitchen accommodated a bathroom and a small office – tidy, untouched. In a corner, a cabinet bore a sign in red capitals: *First Aid*. Two desks sat perpendicular to the door, empty except for papers in the middle upon one, held down by a small tool chest. A shelf of idle drones lined one wall under a cork board. Faces stared out of pinned photographs, smiling, including an image of a very young Briar, hair already long, with a caption scrawled in a child's handwriting: "Briar, (he/they)".

Footsteps on the stairs. I turned around.

"Photo, top right – that's my great-granddad who founded this place," said Briar, manifesting by my side. A sepia image of a man, youthful despite the shock of white hair.

"His smile is just like yours," I remarked.

"Everyone thought so."

Before I could make more useless observations, Briar stepped back out into the hallway. I examined the drones, some of which needed obvious repair. Perhaps I could fix up a couple for the greenhouse, or even for a controlled burn – defence in case of another forest fire.

Briar's footprints tracked in the dust towards the main room. Low-wall partitions hung from the ceiling, carving up the space the footprint of the main hall below. Pale, morning light shone in through windows that could use a clean, segmented into inequilateral triangles and irregular trapeziums, landing on walls and floors where they could.

I listened for the voices that had found solace here. Silence spoke.

"This used to be the overflow room," said Briar.

"Overflow?"

"There was a time when all the cabins were taken up."

Once more, I tried to hold his gaze. "Were you here then, during the fires?"

That would make him much, much older. And yet, we looked like we could have been born within the same season.

"Still guessing?" he said, chuckling.

Perplexed, I simply smiled.

We stepped back outside through a back door, into the rising warmth of the day.

Several cabins dotted the landscape down the hill.

"What shape are they in?"

"I check on them every few weeks." Briar's steps paused, but he didn't look at me. "If you want to stay, we can clean one up for you."

Over by the greenhouse, something moved. The chicken coop had rolled itself into a shady corner. Mrs. Robinson and the hens seem entirely unfazed.

I hadn't thought this far.

"Yes, I'll stay." I heard myself say. "Just a few days, perhaps."

A playful punch to my shoulder caught me by surprise, nearly knocking me to the ground.

Briar grinned at my bewilderment. "Thought you might."

My sweetness,

First of all – I'll just get this out of the way – I miss you. I miss our daily rituals. I miss us. So it was entirely wonderful to get a long e-letter from you, quite the treat rather than our short, sharp exchanges.

Hass has settled in well, and Jefferson has learned to tolerate Popcorn. Thankfully, for a young dog, he's quite chilled. The boat's adjusting to the warming temperature, the river seems to be enjoying the spring.

I'm glad to hear you've got someone nice to spend time with. You wished for me not to be alone, but I might not have said – I wished the same for you. I know, I know, your threshold for being on your own far exceeds mine.

Tell me how things go, and don't hold back on my account. I'm okay.

Fascinating to hear about the greenhouse. Will you plant something there? Of course, I'd love to come visit – yes. We'll figure out when.

Speaking of which, I dropped by your parents' two days ago. They are fine and asked if I had more news. I think they'd been keen to come too, at some point. Funny how they had never been curious about the Safe Haven before.

Love,

Ruby.

I hadn't noticed the fire pit the first time we walked to the main building from Briar's cabin. Hard to believe how. I'd have thought it'd be impossible to miss the grey pockmark upon green grass, a ring of stones encircling a dark patch of ash, as if the past that had burned away could be contained.

No one lit open fires any more – or any fire, for that matter – not after what happened. It had been strange to read about fireplaces in fairy tales; as a child, I had to ask Papi what they were.

Briar set thin twigs over the fire pit first, then slender branches, layering them by their thickness. I stood to one side and watched, captivated. When a wisp of smoke curled up, he blew air into the base, until suddenly a reddish glow grew from within, and from it flames licked outwards – hungry, orange tongues. Only then did he set down a larger log by the pile.

How fast a spark could grow to a flame, to a fire that could consume a log of wood, to engulf an entire city. I shuddered, but its mesmerising dance drew me close. The warmth – delicious. Something about fire spoke to the soul, something primal. Fear and fascination mingled in my gut.

"You'll have to teach me how to do that," I told Briar. It can't be a good thing, to have completely forgotten how to manage a fire the old-fashioned way.

"Not something I do often." He shrugged. "But today feels like a special occasion."

Earlier, he'd brought out a metal stand from somewhere and placed it over the fire; a cast iron pot now hung over the flames, not unlike a witch's cauldron.

He tossed vegetables we'd picked from the greenhouse into the open pot.

"Should last us a few days." It took me a moment to realise he meant the stew.

We had spent the afternoon cleaning out one of the cabins – one which had called out to me – on the far side of the greenhouse, not far from the permaculture patch, right beside a peach tree in full bloom. While I swept out the cobwebs and wiped down surfaces, Briar made sure the heating worked, tested the filtered rainwater for safety. Then we'd retrieved some furniture from a storage room tucked behind the main building, cleaned those down, reassembled them. By day's end, I had a bed frame, a mattress, a kitchen table and four chairs – though I'd only ever need one. Perhaps two, if Ruby decided to visit.

It could almost feel like home.

At sundown, we checked on the chickens.

"Won't want them accidentally roasted," Briar said, wielding a long, wooden pole with what looked like a bird perch at the end. One of the city farms I'd worked in housed a few hens, but they'd been free to roost wherever they liked.

"What's that for?" I pointed to the pole.

"Last resort encouragement," said Briar. "In case they end up in a tree."

But in the end, all the hens had already made their way to the coop, and the pole went mercifully unused.

Here and now, Briar studied the fire, eyes to the shadowed earth; I gazed up at the darkening sky. The temperature had plummeted the moment the sun disappeared behind the hill; overhead the clouds gave way to the stars. Mamie would have loved the unhindered view.

"There has never been a time when civilisation did not read its fate in the stars, ma fleur," she used to say, on many nights when we'd stood outside together, huddling under blankets. Years later, I tried to tell her that the future doesn't work that way – that there are many futures, not a single destiny.

Above us Orion stretched out, ready to fire into oblivion, Sirius nipping at his heels. The Great Bear roamed, nonchalant, steady in its stride. Lower on the horizon, Castor and Pollux followed each other across the sky – together forever, never apart.

I wanted to capture an image for Ruby, but no camera I had could do justice to the majesty of the night sky out here, away from city lights.

"I see you send messages sometimes," Briar suddenly said. "You left a loved one behind?"

"Ruby and I share a barge, but…" I fumbled for the right words. "It's not exclusively us."

"I see."

Briar propped open the lid on the stew, stirred its contents with a long, languid motion. Steam billowed with promise of a good meal. "Bit watery still."

He leaned over, and the pendant from his necklace slipped out from under his shirt – a tree of life, encircled in silver. The bridge between heaven and earth, between death and rebirth.

The stew bubbled, a waft of thyme and earthy vegetables simmering in a rich broth teased our appetites. My mouth watered, hunger clawed at my insides.

Briar sat back down onto his chosen tree stump. "It's been a long while since I'd been with someone."

Where was he going with this?

"While you, you and your lovers on your barge –"

I stifled a giggle. "We don't *all* live there."

For some reason, that made Briar laugh out loud. "I had this image of you all squeezed onto a small boat."

Now I laughed too. "Relationships take the shapes they need to take, we don't all end up in –"

"But I like the way you think of it."

"Oh?" I said, still trying to contain my chortling.

"How love isn't a commodity to be consumed, not a resource to be –" Briar paused, chewing over the words, "extracted, expected from someone."

"Love without possession," I said. "Not without its challenges, of course."

"Makes so much sense." Briar stood up, glanced into the pot, and stirred its fragrant contents. "I'm going to call it. Shall we?"

I passed him the bowls, and he ladled out generous helpings of stew, while I fumbled in the dark for spoons we'd left somewhere.

How had our ancestors worked out that certain vegetables go well together when cooked for long hours in a pot? Trial and error? I slurped the slightly watery stew, savouring the flavour. Today I might ingest these carrots, this celery, these potatoes, but one day the earth shall have my dust and bones.

"When my great-grandparents laid the foundations of this place," Briar said between mouthfuls, "they wanted to create a space where people could get acquainted with nature again – a place for rest. When the fires came, my family was already here, ready to accommodate."

"Your parents remember the fire?" I laid my bowl down next to my feet; it had emptied rather quickly.

"They were kids, too young. They'd grown up here, eventually decided to move to the city."

"But you came back."

Flames licked at the base of the pot. Shadows danced across Briar's face. "Someone had to make sure the Haven remained functional and safe – in case we need it again."

"That's a lot of work for one person."

The look he gave me then – undecipherable. Grief? Regret? Hope? Perhaps all of the above.

Eventually, he shrugged. "I'm not suited for that kind of life. But I like it here. This place has soul."

Neither of us moved, until Briar got up, tossed on another log, and poked a long stick into the fire to prop it up. The flames leapt.

"Fire loves air, can't breathe without it."

I exhaled. "Just like us."

"Yes, just like us."

"So it's me, the Haven, the plants and the chickens." Once more, Briar held my gaze. "And you too, now, if you think you might stay."

I searched the flickering flames reflected in those blue eyes, for all the words he hadn't dared speak, for all the fears I hadn't dared voice.

The fire crackled, embers glowed.

To him, I smiled. "I suppose Mrs. Robinson and I might have to learn to get along."

Somewhere in the trees, a nightingale trilled.

We sat in silence, listening to the breeze rustling through the leaves, and scoured the night sky for our destinies in the stars.

End Notes

Some years ago, I had the luck and privilege to meet Professor Dan Hill; one of the stories he told caught my attention – the idea of the "One Minute City" and "Street Moves" – which encouraged local communities to become architects of their own streets. I was enthralled by the idea that citizens could be empowered to design their own neighbourhood to suit the needs of their community – without the typical top-down interference from the design profession. Streets can become that increasingly rare third place to allow communities to thrive and strengthen the social fabric at a most local level.

The outcome of that one conversation can be witnessed in "The Perpetual Metamorphosis of Primrose Close", first published in *Parsec Issue #11* and longlisted for the 2024 BSFA Award, and "The City Walks Through Me", a story commissioned by Air and Nothingness Press (first published 2023) on the theme of the dérive, a practice of drifting through an urban landscape to induce surrealist experiences between oneself and the social environment.

Libraries, too, are valuable third places; the closest social infrastructure we might have today in terms of a shared commons. "La bibliotheque d'objets quotidiens" was the closing story of the *The Librarian* (Air and Nothingness Press, 2022), an anthology showcasing a Dr. Who-esque character – a librarian who travels across the multiverse with their sidekick Satchel, paying late fines on behalf of patrons, lending the right books to the right people at the right place and time. In this story, I extended the concept of 'library' beyond books, to acknowledge other forms of libraries, in particular, shared tool libraries, the 'library of things' movement, but also to give a nod to valuable, open maker resources such as

Appropedia.

Knowledge lives on in libraries, but also through heritage and lore; what happens when these are affected by climate change? In "Coriander", first published in *Bright Green Futures* (2025), I wanted to imagine a past-future relationship through the written word and the cultural significance of food through generations. In "Soul Noodles", (*The Bright Mirror*, 2023), I'd been inspired by some horrific photographs of recent floods in my hometown – so much worse compared to my own childhood experiences – and through it, imagine how a city may change in response. I also explored a different social model around urban food production, and the challenge of the reproducing a lost ingredient for a culturally important recipe. "Shadow Among the Leaves" is a story set a town in the heart of Borneo, where I addressed the environmental grief of upriver logging and the symbolism of post-colonial heritage; it was first published *Solarpunk Magazine Issue #10* (2023).

"Anatomy of Emotion – The Carving of Chance – Seize the Moon" was written in response to a call to celebrate the centenary of Yevgeny Zamyatin's *We*, and was first published in *The Utopia of Us* (2024). In the original novel, very little time had been given to the people beyond the Green Wall whom D-503 met in Record 27. With this story I followed the thread of how a troubled character might fare in that outside world centuries after the city fell. It became an opportunity to examine rituals and culture – allowing 'old' science and indigenous practices to co-exist side by side with touches of high-tech, where some engineering knowledge had been retained, some deliberately 'forgotten'.

The inspiration for "Night Fowls", first published in *Solarpunk Creatures* (2024), came from stories of the Whitsun weekend clash between the Mods and the Rockers in 1964 on Brighton's beaches, just one of a series of fights that exploded in seaside towns across the south coast of England that year. When I began writing "Night Fowls", I was trying to process whether our ingrained storytelling mechanisms – especially the requirement for conflict – inevitably leads us to narratives in which people who are unlike us can be reduced to obstacles we must overcome, or different people we must keep out of spaces we deem to be ours. Core to this story, however, is the question of our place among nature: what right do we have, to consider ourselves the most exceptional species in comparison to all others?

To adapt to our changing climate and overcome challenges, we are going to need everything across the gamut of human knowledge, skills and technology. Too often, I've witnessed people taking sides in believing that their evidence is the only version of truth – whether it's empiricism or folk knowledge – to the extent that we would reject each other's perspectives without listening to each other, because we are blinded by prejudice or tribalism. In "The Scent of Green" (*Fighting for the Future*, 2023), I borrowed from my past experiences in grassroots activism to examine the challenges of knowledge-sharing between communities that were autonomous, self-reliant but fragmented. An earlier version of "Dandelion Brew" first appeared in *DreamForge Magazine Anvil Issue #6* (2021) and was nominated for the inaugural Utopia Award. This story was my way of exploring the uneasy relationship between technology and lore, and to play out a tiny slice of this conflict and examine how we might find common ground. These themes are also echoed in "Where the Garden Grows", a story first published in *Solarmarx* (2025), that was inspired by a trip I'd taken to Portugal – where it was possible to identify a former fire line by rows of juvenile eucalyptus.

"Emily's Farewell Coat", first published in *Vivid Worlds* (2025), explores a collaborative social model as an antidote to one of the most polluting industries in the world. At the time of writing, the globalised fashion industry production comprises 10% of total global carbon emissions, is the second-largest consumer industry of water – and 85% of textiles end up in landfill each year. (Source: earth.org). It also provided me an excuse to imagine what a positive, ethical AI-human collaboration could look like.

Finally, in "Safe Haven for the Lost and Found", I aimed to examine the notion of rest as we deal with environmental grief and generational scars even after we've transcended to a better world.

Some sections of the preface to this collection has been published prior in *DreamForgeAnvil #11* as "Write the Future You Want to Live In" (2023) and from a number of blogposts.

My eternal thanks to wonderful editors and publishers who have believed in my work:, Francesca Barbini, Somto Ihezue, Susan Kaye Quinn, Teika Marija-Smits, Scot & Jane Noel, Todd Sanders, Donna Scott, Sarena Ullibari, Francesco Verso, Phoebe Wagner, and Ian Whates.

I owe my craft to Michael Todd Gallowglas, Mary Robinette Kowal, Howard Tayler, Dave Farland, and to my critique groups, partners and friends: Ceci Black, J Meade Carey, Spectrum Writers London, the Chalk Scribblers, and ORQD. Special thanks to Paweł Ngei, Martyna Lysakiewicz, Renan Bernado, Command Jugendstil and Tales from the EV Studio, Jo Hall, Professor Thorunn Helgason, Mimi Bird, Yen Ooi, Juan Pablo Zamora and Roberto Zamora for inspiration, authenticity reads and specialist advice.

About the Author

Ana Sun (pronounced "Soon") writes from the edge of an ancient town in the south-east of England. She spent her childhood in Malaysian Borneo and grew up living on islands. Her Solarpunk short fiction has been shortlisted for the inaugural Utopia Award, nominated for the BSFA longlist and selected for *Best of British Science Fiction*. In an alternate universe, she might have been a musician, an anthropologist – or a botanist obsessed with edible flowers. More at: https://singingtotigers.com/.

ALSO FROM NEWCON PRESS

Cities Are Forests Waiting to Happen – Cécile Cristofari

Decades after a catastrophic collapse caused by climate disasters and pandemics, an urban explorer discovers that a rogue artificial intelligence is threatening the communication-via-whale-song that her world depends on. She travels to the former metropolis of Toronto (now a semi-rural settlement surviving under the ivy-covered ruins of skyscrapers), determined to find and destroy it.

Blood in the Bricks – edited by Neil Williamson

Sinister tales of the city, redolent with ritual and drenched in dread. Housing schemes and suburbs, gilded business districts and gated communities, industrial wastelands and crumbling tower blocks... Who knows what our old bricks were made of or what lies beneath our brightly lit pavements? Who knows what goes on behind locked doors?

The Other Frankenstein – Melissa F. Olson

Elizabeth Frankenstein's life had been carefully planned, until that future was stolen from her. Elizabeth and Heck Saville's parallel, intersecting stories encompass murder, loss, trauma and ultimately empowerment, in this stunning feminist saga that uses the classic story of *Frankenstein* as a springboard and weaves a potent tale of horror, love, and revenge.

The Essence – Dave Hutchinson

Michael's troubles start with the breakdown he suffers following the death of his wife. He learns there's a phenomenon – a force, a spirit, a flaw in Reality – known as *the Essence*. A small group of people have been attempting to study it for centuries but are none the wiser. Now, some very powerful people believe Michael may hold the key and they will stop at nothing to claim it.

Make-Believe and Artifice – Rose Biggin

Debut collection from an author who has long been delighting readers 'in the know' with beautifully crafted stories. A mix of otherworldly fantasy and cunning mysteries from the past decade. "Effervescent, artful and joyfully mischievous, *Make Believe and Artifice* dances with the reader at every page. Rose Biggin is a fabulous writer." *– E.J. Swift*

www.ingramcontent.com/pod-product-compliance
Lightning Source LLC
Chambersburg PA
CBHW031214260626
47169CB00007B/2055